AWAKE

EDWARD J. MCFADDEN III

SEVERED PRESS
HOBART TASMANIA

AWAKE

CHAPTER ONE

Years of experience investigating anomalies kept Don from emptying his Glock 19 into the monstrosity huddled next to the beat-up recliner in the corner of the living room. A middle-aged woman with short, jet-black hair sat in the opposite corner with a rifle pointed at the thing. Don assumed she was Mrs. Marie Redro, the homeowner who had called the police.

"Where did that creature come from, Mrs....?"

"That *creature* is my husband, Phil," she said, and Don stepped forward to help her. She turned the weapon on him. "Step back. And put your gun away. Now!"

Don froze, and dropped his Glock into its shoulder holster. He wore his usual blue suit, its once sharp lines faded and stretched. His red tie had a small spot of chili on it, and above that a yellow dot of mustard. One chilidog, two stains.

"I only agreed to let you in because you sounded different than the rest." She jerked the gun barrel toward the door. "I called those asshats for help and they show up in a tank. All they wanna do is shoot him. That's not the help I need."

Mrs. Redro had called the police two hours prior at 12:51AM local time, and law enforcement had laid siege to the house, creating a standoff. The delay gave Don enough time to travel to the suburbs of Miami and be on scene before the natives did something really stupid.

"What happened here, Mrs....?"

"You can call me Marie."

"Okay, Marie."

Emergency lights streamed through the windows, and the house creaked and moaned as the thing Marie called her husband shifted back and forth, pounding the walls. Engorged blood vessels pressed against tightened skin, creating a spider-work of black lines across the creature's pink and purple face. Orbitals that looked like a Botox treatment gone wrong encircled eyes with huge pupils and shrunken red irises that stared at the floor in a

1

sleepy daze. Saliva leaked from swollen lips as it ground its teeth and snarled, but kept its distance.

Marie said, "Why did they send you?" She considered him, obviously unimpressed. "You piss-off your boss or something?"

"I work for the government, and *this,*" he said, gesturing toward her husband, "is my job."

"This kind of thing happen often?" Marie said. She shook her head. "Don't tell me. I'm never going to be able to sleep again as it is."

The creature who had been Phil started forward, but pulled back when Marie screamed. He squeezed his eyes shut, and shuddered like he was having a violent dream. His skin writhed as muscle and tissue swelled.

"What happened here?" Marie shook her head, tears welling in her eyes. "This will be off the record. Tell me so I can help you."

"We were just sitting, watching the TV. Phil had just finished dinner, and..." She paused, her eyes shifting to Don, then to the floor.

"Just between us," he said.

Phil wailed, clawing at his face.

"Oh, hush, you fool," Marie yelled.

Phil sprang back like he'd been smacked and retreated into his corner.

"He had a few beers, then took some ride."

Don knew what ride was. "I've heard of that psychoactive crap. A new designer drug, a stimulant, and what's in it depends on who you get it from.

"That it?" Don asked, pointing at a gold pillbox with black skull and crossbones on the lid.

She nodded.

"Please, go on."

"That's it. There is no more. We were watching TV. I heard him snore, looked over at him, and he was changing. Blowing up like a tick." Tears streamed down her cheeks, and she sniffed between words. Phil pounded the walls harder, and the sheetrock cracked, letting loose a cloud of dust.

Marie shot him a glare, and he stopped pounding. He tore at the remnants of his shirt instead.

Marie continued. "When I got the gun, he went ballistic. I ain't gonna let them kill my Phil." Desperation filled the woman's eyes, fear and pain cutting across her face.

"Did you take anything?"

"No, I don't do that shit. It can kill you."

"Seems like it's done more than that. You heard him snoring? Like he was asleep?" Don asked.

"Yes."

"And he was fine prior? Nothing else you can think of? Any other drugs?"

Her eyes shifted to the floor again, then she said, "Not that I know of."

Phil growled and moved towards them.

"Stop that! This man is trying to help," Marie said. Phil understood her because he stopped and focused his red eyes on Don. "You look terrible!" she said. "Go sit on the sofa."

The thing did as it was told.

Don was running out of options. In five minutes, the SWAT team would join them, and Phil Redro would be riddled with bullets. So the time for sugarcoating had passed.

"I have to take him in, Marie."

The thing that had once been Phil Redro clawed at the walls and moaned.

"Nope. That wasn't our deal." She swung the gun in Don's direction again. The weight of it pulled her arm down, and she almost dropped the weapon, only pulling it level at the last instant.

"You fire that thing and I won't be able to hold them back. Then it's over for him." The tip of the gun barrel dipped slightly. "We can knock him out with a tranquilizer and bring him to the hospital." Don sold bullshit for a living. It was one of the unpleasant tasks that came with giving people bad news. He saw no way Phil would live unless he figured out what had caused his transformation and there was an antidote to bring him back. Both would take time, and might not be possible. Don's five-man support team waited outside with a portable quarantine unit and by sun up, Phil would most likely be on ice, his ride over for good.

3

"No. Let's just give it some time and see if it wears off. The ride will end. It always does," she said.

"And you're always there to bring him back. Nurse him to health."

"I try," she said.

"He listens to you. If you told him to go with us, do you think he would?"

"Not happening. And he doesn't always do what I say. When I tried to get close, he went for me," Marie said. She was relaxing a little, and had lowered the rifle so it pointed at his kneecaps.

"Who did he get the ride from?" Don asked, assuming that to be his line of investigation going forward.

Marie's face twisted. "That loser Teapot on 45th Avenue. He stands on the bridge that goes over the Blue Lagoon, right in front of the cops. They don't do nothin."

"How long has he been copping from him?"

"Shoot... those two fools go way back."

"Any reason Teapot might want to hurt Phil?"

"None that I know of. Phil always paid cash, so I can't imagine what the problem would've been."

Don could imagine many possible problems. Phil's last batch of ride might not have taken him anywhere, or perhaps it took him some place he didn't want to go. Or maybe he was shorted a pill, or Teapot didn't give him back the proper change. With drug deals, there were an infinite number of things that could go wrong.

"Do you know where Teapot lives?"

Marie jerked back, and her lemon lips returned. "Why would I know where that dirtbag lives?" She looked over at her husband and frowned. Drool dripped across his swollen chin, and his face undulated like tiny worms were burrowing beneath his skin.

Don glanced at his watch, and Marie noticed. "What now?" she asked.

He didn't want to answer her because she wasn't going to like what he had to say. The two of them stared at each other, hoping something would give, and when the bullhorn outside started issuing ultimatums, Marie vaulted from her chair. "You said you'd help keep the cops away."

Don closed the distance between them, trying not to look at Marie's gun. "Help me work through this."

Marie scowled, lifting the gun as Don moved for the weapon.

Phil sprang, jaws snapping, arms reaching out to tackle Don, who dodged, letting Phil crash into the entertainment center. The old pressboard unit teetered, the heavy tube TV toppling the cabinet and its years of accumulated crap down onto Phil.

Don went for Marie but was met with the point of a gun. Marie sucked her teeth and gave Don a look that would have wilted fresh lettuce. She trained the rifle on his head.

Don dropped to the floor and pulled his gun.

He swung the Glock forward, only to have the Phil-thing clamp its bloody hand around his wrist. He got tossed across the room, the gun flying from his grasp as he hit the glass doors enclosing the fireplace, shattering them. Blood trickled from a cut on his cheek, and suddenly Don was very aware of the open wound, no matter its size.

Bleeding in front of monsters could be a very bad thing.

He backed against the wall and looked for his gun, which lay in the rubble of the entertainment center. His belt buckle was a small throwing knife, but that was the only remaining weapon. Footsteps echoed on the porch outside, and the bullhorn issued one last warning. They would break down the door with a battering ram in sixty seconds.

"Go," Marie said, as she pointed the rifle toward the door.

Don's mind swam, and for an instant, he thought he might leave. Who said he had to put his ass on the line every time?

The cops would blow Phil apart, and before he and his crew could get control of the situation, countless officers and emergency workers would be exposed to an anomaly they knew nothing about.

Don dove for Marie, trying to draw Phil in.

Phil caught Don in the head with an elbow as he flew passed, and Don crashed into the pile of entertainment center rubble. His Glock lay right next to him, and he grabbed it.

"Enough!" It was Marie. Phil snarled at her, and she pivoted her rifle towards him, and then back at Don, and back to Phil again. Tears streamed down her face, leaving dark mascara trails.

When Phil went for Don again, she shot him.

The rifle blast caught Phil in the arm and spun him around. He went down then, taking bookshelves with him. The police were pounding on the door with their ram, and in seconds, they would be through. Don scurried across the room to where Phil lay, and when he arrived, he stopped short, his mouth hanging open.

Phil's eyes were clearing, the blood draining away like dirt down a sewer. He looked bewildered, and when he saw Don, he said, "Who are you?"

The door broke open, and Don's men came in before the local SWAT team. "You okay, Boss?"

Don didn't have time for that. He positioned himself between Phil and the police, shielding him. "Hold your fire." The cops were in full body armor, their identities hidden behind tinted face shields. They poured through the door showing no signs of halting. "I will shoot the man who fires his weapon."

One by one, the officers lowered their guns when they saw a middle-aged man in torn clothes staring up at them, his eyes glassy, eyebrows furrowed. Phil's natural color was returning, his face smooth. The gunshot leaked blood down his arm, but he didn't appear to notice. Dark bags hung under his eyes, and thin white lines ran across his face where the blood vessels had pushed against tightened skin.

"Why are you all here?" Phil asked.

"You don't remember anything?" Don said. His men were clearing the room, and the locals retreated.

"No. I dozed off, then... you woke me?" He hadn't seen Marie yet. She lay on the couch. She'd fainted. As if reading his mind, Phil asked, "Where's Marie?"

"Here," she said.

When Phil saw her, his features softened.

"You're awake," she said, and went to him.

CHAPTER TWO

Maureen Hughs hated sunrise launches. She liked to sleep in when she was on vacation, but it wasn't to be on this trip. Tim booked the tour with a local company, and to save money, they'd flown through the night, and would paddle into the Everglades at sunrise. She'd slept most of the flight.

Tim's head hung into the plane's thin aisle, eyes pasted shut, a large drool stain on his tiny pillow. His blond hair fell across his face, which looked stressed. Her heart swelled, and then she remembered the night he had hit her.

She tried to forget, but that night floated like a bad dream on the surface of her subconscious, causing waves and tides in every decision she made. Innocence had fled, and while that idea might be corny, it was the truth. She would have never thought Tim capable of hurting her, but he had, and all the gifts, apologies, and dinners in the universe wouldn't put Humpty Dumpty back together again. Not that she was afraid of him. It was the reverse. His brief outburst made him overcompensate, and he was now a shell of his former self. The trips to remote, dangerous places proved this. He hated the outdoors, but knew she loved being with nature and the thrill of adventure.

The plane's tires shrieked as they meet runway pavement, and with a rattle and pull, they were on the ground. Daybreak was still a few hours off, and the lights of Miami sparkled in the distance to the west. A long line of aircraft waited, and as their plane taxied to the jetway, no planes took off.

"You ready?" Tim asked, rubbing sleep from his eyes.

The plane jerked to a stop, and everyone went for their overhead bags. Maureen and Tim waited until those around them finished and then pulled down their backpacks. Since they had no checked luggage, they breezed through the airport and were the first to arrive at the tour van. It was easy to find due to the jungle mural covering the entire vehicle. There was no one at the van to greet them, so they dropped their packs and waited.

***

"Oy," yelled a man as he approached. He looked Cuban. "I'm Dante. I will be your guide for the first part of the trip. You are Mr. and Mrs. Hughs?" Maureen and Tim nodded. "It's my job to get you to the launch an hour before dawn. We have until then to get anything you may need."

Tim looked to Maureen, who said, "We're good."

Dante opened his mouth to say something, then shut it without speaking.

Two more people arrived. Their names were Conrad and Lilly. Conrad was a well-built African-American man of roughly thirty years with keen hazel eyes and a cropped beard. Lilly was what her name portended; she was slender, delicate, white, and blonde. They came together, but Maureen didn't think they were a couple. She was good at reading people, and it took little to see they didn't know each other well. Everyone exchanged names, handshakes, and hellos.

"We have six others joining us." Dante stacked packs onto the luggage rack as everyone loaded into the van. "But they'll meet us at the launch site."

Lilly and Conrad whispered with Dante up front as he drove. Tim played with his cell, unconcerned. Sometimes she wanted to shove that phone up his ass and pull it out his mouth. Conrad asked about something called ride, and gave Dante money.

"Got to make a quick stop," Dante announced, as he looked in the rearview mirror at Maureen.

"Where?" Maureen asked. She knew why they were stopping; it wasn't that hard to figure out. On adventure trips, people expected to find themselves and get answers to the bigger questions in their lives. She'd felt that way when she trekked across Joshua Tree, and paddled through the Grand Canyon. Why people needed those experiences heightened with drugs, she didn't know, but perhaps it had something to do with the desensitization of the human race. She'd seen enough nurses turn into zombies to know that eventually everyone builds a cocoon around themselves.

"Chubby Rain," Dante said. "It's a club my boy here wants to check out real fast. Then we'll head to the launch."

Maureen said nothing. Tim didn't look up from his phone, and she wanted to punch him and never stop. Dark commercial buildings and storefronts gave way to houses, and then to restaurants, clubs, and strip malls as they got closer to the shore.

Chubby Rain looked like a dive. Crowds of people poured from the club and loaded into their cars. Dante spun the wheel, turned the van around so they were right in front of the exit, and pulled to the curb. "Wait here a minute." As he got out, he turned and said, "Uh, Conrad, let me go check this out, but we're looking like a no go." Dante threaded through the cars fighting to get past the van.

He walked against the tide as the crowd fought to leave the parking lot, and then circled back to a man leaning on a red Toyota Celica with a black hood. The man was short and balding, and he smiled at Dante, and clapped him on the shoulder. The men didn't appear to notice the surrounding chaos, and they talked and laughed. It was a complex ritual that Maureen couldn't even track. They hit each other on the back, shook hands, and touched each other in many other ways, and she knew they were exchanging money and drugs, but she couldn't see it.

A gunshot cracked in the distance, and Tim looked up, noticing for the first time he was in a nightclub parking lot waiting for his driver. Maureen's stare spat lava, but Tim was a rock of denial and managed not to look at her.

There was another gunshot, and Lilly screamed. Dante went down and started crawling back to the van.

The short, balding man jumped into his Celica and tore past them. Dante got up, people streaming all around him. Sirens roared as police cruisers entered the lot. Most of the cars continued to flee, and people scattered onto the surrounding streets. Dante was hurt, but he was making his way back to the van, limping, and trying not to draw attention to himself. Police cars tore past, and Dante slowed, turning away.

"Come on," Conrad said, willing Dante forward. If they sat where they were much longer, the exit would be blocked by the cops and they'd be detained.

Dante walked toward the car, trying to blend into the chaos. More police cars tore past, and Dante fell. Conrad was out of the van and at his side in seconds, helping him to his feet, and urging him forward. A dark bloodstain grew on his Dante's right leg.

"What the hell?" Tim said. "Did that guy he was talking to shoot him?"

Lilly said, "It didn't look like it."

"No," Maureen said. "The guy didn't have a gun. It must have been that second shot we heard. Stray bullet."

Dante and Conrad were almost back to the van. More police cars ripped passed, and there weren't many people left in the lot. Things were settling down, and it would only take a few more seconds before the police noticed the van in all its jungle-colored glory. The side door slid open. Conrad threw Dante inside and jumped into the driver's seat.

"You think it's a good idea to leave now?" Maureen asked. "Dante's been shot. We should report that and get him to a hospital."

At this, Dante stirred, and his face grew panicked. "No... please, no. I can't go to the hospital or the police. They'll send me back to Cuba. Please. The bullet just grazed my leg."

"What would we tell the police? We have no idea what happened," Lilly said. "And he doesn't want us to."

"We'll miss the launch and get Dante deported. And for what?" Conrad said.

Maureen looked at Tim, who shrugged. Then she turned to Dante. "You sure you're okay? Bleeding to death is worse than going back to Cuba."

"Says you," Dante said through clinched teeth. "I'll be fine."

Silence fell. Conrad started the van and inched out onto the road, and away from Chubby Rain. Dante whimpered a little, blood still seeping from his wound. Maureen wasn't comfortable with this, but she'd been outvoted, and as usual, Tim didn't even take a position, let alone support her. She was used to this. As a nurse, Maureen did things that would appear revolting to the average person, and those experiences strengthened her. More than once, she'd taken control of an emergency or an operating room, but things on the streets were different.

"Let me at least mend your leg," Maureen said.

"With what?" Lilly asked.

"This," Tim said, pulling a first aid kit from the rear door panel. It had bandages, tape, gauze, and a bottle of aspirin.

"Here, take some of these." She handed Dante four pills, and he swallowed them. Lilly climbed into the back of the van with Tim, and Dante laid his wounded led on Maureen's lap. She ripped his pant leg open and examined the wound.

"Looks like the bullet took out a small chunk. I'll—"

"Which way?" Conrad said.

Dante forced out directions through clinched teeth and turned to Maureen. "Thank you for doing this. You a doctor or something?"

"Or something," she said. "I'll clean the wound and bandage it, but I suggest getting meds so an infection doesn't take hold. I don't have any alcohol to clean the wound and—"

"Check the glove box," Dante said.

Holding the steering wheel with one hand, Conrad reached across the passenger seat, popped open the glove compartment, and found Dante's silver flask. It had a brass eagle on one side, and before Conrad handed it to Maureen, he took a quick pull, and winched. "Vodka."

"Perfect," Maureen said as she went about cleaning the cut. To Dante's credit, he only squeaked as the alcohol drenched the wound, and she wrapped it in bandages.

Civilization faded as they drove further southwest. Large open areas filled with palmetto trees and unfinished housing developments gave way to waterways that led to the inner Glades. It was surprising how fast the city had fallen away. Insects hummed and buzzed, frogs sang, and night birds squawked. The bright lights of South Beach were gone, and Miami seemed very far away. Dead pine trees poked through the palmetto, and in the moonlight, Homestead looked deserted.

They tried to stop at two gas station convenience stores only to find them closed, despite the hours listed on the doors insisting they were open. The eastern sky grew purple, and the light of day fought back the darkness. If they had no more delays, they would hit the launch right on time. Dante said he felt fine and promised to get stitches. Lilly stared out the window, and Tim still played with his cell phone. Maureen punched him on the shoulder. He didn't look up. She grabbed the phone and shut it down.

"Hey," he said. His voice was submissive. No emotion.

"We're disconnected. Period. I don't want to hear any bitching. Pull on your big boy pants," Maureen said. She would push him this trip. She'd been a kayaker since childhood, and she could paddle better than she walked. Tim had paddled with her one time in the ocean, and he'd been tussled so hard he never went again. She couldn't wait to see his face when they kayaked past gators.

Dante instructed Conrad to turn down a dirt road, and in moments, they were traveling through a thick forest of pine trees. "Maureen and Tim have already switched off their phones, and I suggest you two do the same," Dante said. "Hawk don't like any outside interruptions interfering with his tour. 'Specially cell phones."

"Done," Conrad said.

Lilly hesitated. She was young, and her face wrinkled as she rubbed her phone between her hands. Everyone stared at her, waiting for compliance. Lilly shut off her phone and let it drop to the seat beside her.

"And before I forget," Dante said, reaching into his jacket. Then he glanced at Maureen and Tim, and didn't continue.

With their digital connections severed, the group fell silent. Crocodiles rumbled as the darkness slowly drained to the gray of early morning. A sour-sweet breeze snaked through the van's open windows, and the sounds of the world waking carried over the growl of the van's engine. A key instrument was missing from the band that plays civilization's music. No planes. This close to several major airports, there was always a plane streaking through the sky, yet Maureen heard no jet engines.

"Here we are," Dante said, and with his words went all thoughts of planes, civilization, and her future.

CHAPTER THREE

The danger was gone for the moment, and cops stood around drinking coffee. Don rolled his shoulders, stretching his back as concern rose in him like a tide, invading all his empty spaces, his mind looking five steps ahead. Three related calls had come in while he was dealing with Phil and Marie, and the situation had picked up speed.

Two of the calls were isolated incidents similar in nature to Phil Redro. For now, he'd decided to move no one, and confine victims in their homes until he knew more. The third call was from a club owner who claimed to have a monster mash going on in his nightclub. Law enforcement on scene were being held back at Don's command. The locals were pissed, but Don was impervious to the complaining of people who deemed themselves important, because no matter how high the local bigwigs complained, he couldn't be called off.

He was part of a team buried so deep within the Department of Defense the president's office would have a hard time finding their budget allocation. Support came from all branches of the military, and even Don didn't know who ultimately controlled his unit. He assumed it was the president, or someone close to him, because not many people had major threat authority.

Across the spectral currents of the United States—and when the higher-ups deemed it important, other countries—Don sailed on a sea of oddities whose only similarity was that the United States Government considered it important to investigate and catalog them. Like most governmental tasks, the finish line often remained hidden, and the mission unclear.

A man in a blue jumpsuit matched Don's stride as they left the house and headed for the support van. Don recognized the kid. He had ready teams all around the country, but personnel shifted often, so he could go years without meeting a recruit. Don stopped next to the van and addressed his man. "Shut down the airports. Make up an excuse and issue it through the FAA. Block the main roads heading north with some accidents. I need time to determine how bad this is." The man nodded and disappeared into the van.

Don rode shotgun, with one of his men driving, and the other four in the rear partially shutting down Miami. Phil Redro had been checked out medically on scene and nothing major jumped out. He was somewhat back to normal, but had no memory of the two and a half hours he'd been transformed. The question no one had asked, but everyone knew needed to be asked, was what will happen when he falls asleep? Don could put him to sleep. That remained an option, but for now, Phil was overdosing on caffeine.

The club, Chubby Rain, was on south beach, off the main drag a few blocks. The city stirred, and they passed delivery trucks and other early morning workers as they started their day. They went over the bridge and headed for A1A. Soon large mansions replaced the businesses, apartments, and office buildings. Nothing stirred in the bloated community except security guards who patrolled the rich areas twenty-four hours a day. It was amazing how the high-dollar neighborhoods encroached right up to the strip. Lights from tall hotels and condominiums rose above the palm trees in the distance. His man made a right, and had to stop when a tour van covered in jungle decals inched out onto the road in front of them. Don's driver cursed as he made a fast left, and they entered a parking lot filled with people, cars, and police.

As he exited the van, one of his men said, "Four more calls have come in."

"Make sure all cases are confined. Speak with the local watch commanders personally."

It didn't take long to find the officer in charge. Captain Lou Campo held court outside Chubby Rain, the purple facade of the building giving him a star-ish quality. The captain noticed Don, stopped lecturing, and made his way through the crowd. He looked putout as he approached—they always did. The locals never liked having rank pulled on them, and the feelings usually got worse when they meet Don in person.

"I'm Captain Campo. You the guy holding up this mess?"

Okay, if this is how you want it to go, Don said to himself. Out loud, he said nothing. He stared at him, a slight grin goading the man.

"You going to say something?" the top cop asked.

The man was under significant strain, so Don decided to forgo his usual manipulation tactics. "What have you got?"

"First, why have I been held back? I've got a situation here, and I need to act."

So much for doing things the easy way. Don stepped forward and got in the man's face. "You'll act when I tell you to act, and not before." No response, but the man didn't back down. Don liked him already. "Now, what do we have here?"

The captain stepped back, and shook his head, and in doing so shed his arrogance. "Hell if I know. The club owner said a patron passed out in the bathroom, then came running out attacking people. And he had, um... changed. They evacuated the building, but a few people were trapped inside."

"What are they doing in there?" Don asked.

"There's about ten of them in there now, huddled in a corner of the dance floor. They look like... oh shit, just go see for yourself or you won't believe it."

Don chuckled. "Okay, how are you watching them?"

"From the main office above the dance floor. I've got two men in there now. I've been keeping in contact via radio. We can get up there easy enough."

"I take it most of the people who were inside have left? So there's no point in detaining the crowd hovering around?"

The captain looked sheepish. "They busted out of every exit when the fire alarm sounded, and most of them were gone before we arrived."

"Have your men disperse this crowd. Send everyone home except the club owner." Campo issued orders and waited. Don turned on his heel, motioned for his men and Campo to follow him, and entered Chubby Rain.

That name. Where had he heard it? A memory way in the back of his brain told him it was from a movie, but he couldn't place it. He'd seen so many films with Desiree. That's all they did together outside of bed. Don had been young and inexperienced, speeding toward the edge of a cliff he couldn't see. She had been a young officer, with nothing but business on her mind. They'd met in the line of duty over the years. She always picked movies that made him think. Made him question what he stood for and why. Chubby Rain wasn't one of those.

The locals hadn't cut the power and dance music with exaggerated bass still pounded through the place. Decorative lighting created the illusion of purple rain running down the walls. Was Purple Rain the movie? *No.*

They went up a narrow staircase that lead to a door and entered. The room was small, and one entire side was a large window that looked out on the club. Two plain-clothes officers crouched under the windowsill, peering over its lip. Purple light danced on the walls, and the music pounded. The room smelled of smoke and beer and sweat.

Don didn't bother hiding as he peered out the window. The dance floor was deserted, the bar empty... then he saw them.

Don had investigated many strange anomalies during his years of service. He'd seen bodies decompose in seconds, a man who could make plants grow, a two-year-old who spoke with Abraham Lincoln, and many other things most people would judge to be impossible, but still his jaw dropped a little.

The mutated people huddled together in a corner, just like Campo had said. They resembled Phil, and were nodding and moving their heads as if communicating through their sleepy haze.

"How long have they been like that?"

One cop kneeling before the window said, "For the last half hour. Since they got the last guy."

"The last guy?"

"One customer got trapped behind the bar, and when the others found him, they attacked."

"That's new. The other victim I've seen was somewhat timid."

"Yeah, until they get together."

Something still didn't make sense. Though he didn't know much, Don knew the transformation took place when the victim fell asleep. The last man hadn't taken a nap after he'd been attacked and infected. "Did you see it happen?" he said.

The other officer said, "No, we watched the security video."

"Show me."

The cop went to a desk against the far wall. He sat, played with a mouse, and the large computer screen lit up. Don stood over his shoulder. The footage was grainy and a bit fuzzy, but it was easy to see. The officer cued up the file, and Don looked on in amazement as the first victim came out of the bathroom.

"Doesn't look like he's attacking anything," Don said.

"Wait," the cop said. The victim walked erratically out onto the dance floor, and bumped into several dancers, knocking a thin blonde woman to the floor. A mountain of a man punched the victim, and he went down, only to bounce right back up.

A melee ensued, and it was hard to see what happened. "Pause it. Where did those two new ones come from?"

The cop ignored Don, and didn't pause the video. "Keep watching."

For another fifteen seconds the fight raged on, then the strobe lights of the fire alarm filled the room. The purple lights went out, and the emergency lights came on. "Their computer system turned the decorative lighting and music back on as soon as the alarm shut down. The bass seems to soothe them a little," the cop said.

Don's phone buzzed, and the officer paused the image as he answered it.

"What?"

One of Don's men said, "Sixteen more calls in the last few minutes, and the locals are running out of people."

"Any early trends?"

"Of the victims we've been able to identify so far, almost thirty percent are connected to the drug trade in some way. Users and low-level salespeople, mostly. Arrest reports and citations mention ride."

"Okay. I'll be out in a minute. Prepare to call in the Big Dogs." He clicked off, and the cop restarted the video.

Two normal people were cornered. The walkers went for one of them, and the other ran behind the long bar for cover. The remaining person didn't have a chance. They grabbed the young man, who looked to be Hispanic and about twenty-five years old. They held him while the others bite and ripped at him as though he were a rib roast.

A sleepwalker head-butted the young man so hard he fell to the floor, unconscious. "Watch close now," said the cop, and Don leaned forward.

The walker stepped away, watching as the man lay on the floor, his eyes closed. Over the next few seconds, the man transformed. It was hard to see the finer details due to the video's resolution, but when the man got up he looked like Phil had, and he joined the group with no protests. They had forgotten about the guy behind the bar, and huddled into the corner like a lost flock of birds with no wings.

"That what happened to the other guy?" Don asked.

"Yeah," the cop said. "He made a run for it and they caught him. They look like they're in a mindless haze and uncoordinated, but when they want to move fast, they can."

"It appears they have basic cognition as well. That one knew he was knocking the guy out and probably why," Don said. His watch read 5:09AM. Sunrise in less than an hour. "Keep them locked in here and don't disturb them." The captain said nothing, and the cop returned to his spot behind the window.

Don left Chubby Rain, and called command. Major threat authority meant he could bring high-end resources to bear on any problem he deemed to be a significant danger to national security. He'd quarantined a college campus, and now he was going to quarantine a huge chunk of a state. At least his area of demarcation was surrounded on three sides by water.

He exited into the predawn dusk as a monotone male voice answered. "Yes?"

"2719 dash, 3385 dash, 0289," Don said. It was his universal ID number.

"Please hold."

"Don?" asked a female voice.

"It's me. We've got a major problem down here. I need everything south of Alligator Ally locked down. Full quarantine. I need all local radio and TV to broadcast our standard stay in your homes message. Confined curfew. All businesses closed. Current emergency workers on duty are to stay on post until further notice. Have the message say a deadly chemical was released into the air and staying inside will guarantee safety. Say the threat should pass in 24 hours."

"This will go worldwide within minutes. You sure you want to lie?"

"We have to. If we say what it really is, we'll have all kinds of morons out on the streets monster hunting like they're playing some stupid video game. We can always feign ignorance later."

"You're 100% sure? They will wake the president on this one." The woman's voice sounded conciliatory.

Don laughed. "I'm afraid he's going to be awake for a while." He clicked off and took a deep breath. If he was wrong, he'd be in the deepest shit of his life, but he wasn't wrong. All he needed to do was think of Chubby Rain.

Captain Campo approached, the expression on his face so grim Don almost felt for the guy. "What now?" he asked.

"We're quarantining the entire area so we can keep this contained."

"So I assume a cyclone isn't on its way? And the multi-car pileup on 95 wasn't an accident?"

Don said nothing.

Pale light crept across the sky as Miami woke up, and the reality of Don's orders took hold. "You ever hear of a guy named Teapot? Local ride dealer?"

Campo's eyebrows rose. "No. But if he does business here, one of my men should know of him."

"Get his home address. I need to go see him."

Campo nodded and left to go give more orders.

Don wandered over to the van and jumped in back. Computer monitors, a gun rack, and other equipment filled the interior. All five of his men worked feverously at terminals, bringing a cage down over southern Florida. The Navy and Coast Guard would control the sea and ports. The Air Force would control the skies. Troops would be brought in to create a barricade to the north, and eventually, the Army, National Guard, and Marines would occupy the streets. An operation of this size was well beyond anything Don had been involved in before, and there were bound to be mistakes. He hoped none of the people who escaped quarantine… and there would be a few… were infected.

What he needed was a sample of the pathogen. The ride pills he'd recovered from the Redco house were being analyzed, but he was skeptical of the drug being the cause. In his experience, when something looked too good to be true, it usually was.

A knock echoed through the van and Don swung open a rear door. Campo stood there.

"I've got Teapot's address," he said.

The sun peeked its head over the rim of the world.

It was 5:21AM.

CHAPTER FOUR

The Everglades are a mosaic of marshes, weed-filled lakes, cypress stands, hardwood hammocks, bay heads, and endless fields of sawgrass. Willow heads like the one Maureen and company had just paddled through are filled with water during the wet season, and the mangrove trees pierced the surface of the still water like giant dried spiders. The Glades are a massive drain, and the depth of the water fluctuates as the seasons change. Besides Mother Nature, the natural ebb and flow has been dramatically altered by man. One thousand seventy-four miles of canals, seven hundred and twenty miles of levees, eighteen major pumping stations, and two hundred and fifty manmade water control channels made the Everglades of 2015 a computer-controlled ecosystem almost as artificial as Disney World, two hundred miles to the north.

A dragonfly sat on the tip of Tim's paddle as he rested, and a faint breeze redolent of rotting peat brushed it away. He looked to the sky, pushed his hat off his head, and wet his face with water from the stream. He looked miserable, and Maureen smiled. Then she frowned. What did she hope to find out here? How would this trip change their situation? No matter what happened out here, they would still have to go home. Back to their house, and with that would come all the bad memories. She was scared, and she hated the feeling.

"Wow," Tim said, and he stopped paddling, and waited for her.

Crocodiles were everywhere, and insects and birds competed to see which could make more noise. Maureen recalled an article which claimed forty-five species of mosquitoes inhabit the Glades, and she was sure she'd been bitten by all of them already. That same article said during the dry season the water disappeared, and in many places, one could walk on the hard-packed peat between the spreading crowns of the trees. Then the insects became bearable, and the crocs retreated to their holes.

The stream narrowed, and a thick patch of undergrowth with wide green leaves rose just above the water, and tall stems topped with purple flowers blocked their way. The expedition had cut through them, breaking many stems and pounding the flowers and leaves with their awkward paddle strokes. A green carpet with white water lilies stretched into the trees as they came free of the stream into a pond choked with sawgrass.

They were about halfway across the pond when the sky darkened, and cold rain lashed them. Maureen paddled hard, and arrived first at the closest hardwood hammock, where she waited under the cover of a pond apple tree for the isolated storm to pass. The tree was short and swollen, its trunk tapering abruptly, and disappearing into a spray of contorted limbs above. Crowds of air plants and ferns grew on many of the tree branches, providing excellent cover. Maureen reached up and picked a yellowish piece of fruit. She knew from experience it wasn't a true apple, but it was edible. She stowed it, and adjusted her foot pegs as she waited.

One by one, her fellow travelers arrived. Raul first, and then several others Maureen had barely met. Tim limped in second to last, not counting Hawk. Only an older woman named Sheryl took longer. Hawk threw his head back and tried to catch rain in his mouth as he stroked backward to stay behind Sheryl. The rain came in torrents, and no one spoke as they huddled beneath the tree. Even the animals took shelter, but as fast as the storm had appeared, it tapered to drizzle.

Conrad pushed off first. He looked uncomfortable in his kayak, and over corrected to every tilt and roll of the boat. Bungeed to the deck before him was a collapsible cooler and a spare paddle, and behind a pack and tent. Most of the kayaks were similarly outfitted. Lilly followed him out into the flow of the stream, her smile so wide Maureen couldn't help but wonder if she was on another kind of ride. The others left, and Maureen tried to remember their names as they paddled away.

Raul went next, followed by his wife, Wendy, and then went Saura and Ping. She hadn't spoken to any of them, other than to say hello when they'd been introduced. They were already a foursome, as they were similar in age, married, and based on the smiles on their faces, Maureen deduced life hadn't knocked any of them on their ass yet. Then came the swinging singles, Sheryl and

Geoff. Sheryl was pushing seventy, but still looked sixty, and Geoff was younger, but not by much. Both had lost their spouses recently, and were hoping an adventure would provide them with a way to carry on. They both spilled their stories to her while they were waiting for Hawk to arrive at the launch site, and they both seemed to relax once they counted her as a friend. Nurses attract older people like honey attracts ants.

A mist-like drizzle was still coming down. Maureen and Tim waited until the others were gone, then pushed away from the hardwood hammock, leaving Hawk, who had informed everyone that he was always in last position so he didn't lose anybody. A huge rainbow crossed the stream as sunlight broke through the cloud cover, and the storm moved on and broke apart. When it reached Cape Sabel, it would be nothing but a few clouds.

"These very waters we now paddle came all the way from Orlando via the Kissimmee River," Hawk said. Maureen had heard him tell the others the same thing several times. Their guide was a paradox of features: he had a bandanna decorated with peace signs wrapped around his head, but he wore a confederate flag T-shirt. He was clean-shaven like a banker, but his arms were tattooed with images of dragons, superheroes, and historical figures like Martin Luther King and Ronald Reagan. Hawk said the arm tats told the story of his life. He sported an old six-shooter in a shoulder holster, and there was a rifle strapped to his front deck.

They paddled through the thick sawgrass as best they could. There was a grumble to Maureen's right that sounded like a growl and duck quack blended. Grass snapped and cracked as something worked its way toward them. A gator dropped from its perch atop a mound of weeds into the shallow canal the paddlers had created, and she went cold. It was a big boy, ten plus feet. It turned to look at her, then bent its head to look at Tim.

"Be still," Hawk said. "Get out your camera."

"My camera." Maureen's voice was shrill.

"Yeah. He probably won't attack," Hawk said.

Maureen's head swiveled and Hawk lifted his rifle. "Shoot it," she said.

"Can't shoot crocs or I'd have the rangers on my ass. How could they possibility catch me, you might ask?" Hawk pointed the rifle in the air and fired. The croc dove back into the water and disappeared. "They use animal tag information, guide data, cameras, conservation reports, autopsies, and an array of sensors and other monitoring devices which are all around the Glades and track everything from bird migration to human intervention. Savvy?"

The water got deeper, and the grass gave way to swamp punctuated with hardwood hammocks ranging in size from a few feet around, to half a mile wide. Ponds packed with grass and stands of splash pine separated some of the bigger islands, but there were large sections that were a labyrinth of tiny hammocks packed with mangrove trees and dense weeds. This was where Maureen would have some fun with Hawk.

For a few minutes, the entire party was together on the lake, and Hawk took the opportunity to give a speech about the snowy egret, and explain how it looked like a heavy metal version of an American egret. "They used to fly around thick as gnats, and now you have to search for them to see one," he said.

Maureen enjoyed when the guide shared information about local wildlife. Seeing native animals was a big part of why she loved the outdoors. She also felt the urge to ask questions because that had been so ingrained in her while in school that she still needed to prove she was paying attention. It didn't take much to see Hawk wasn't a question kind of guy, so she kept to herself. She had considered heading out into the swampy wilderness alone with only a guide map, but Tim had drawn the line there, and he'd been right. She'd already be lost. Hawk gave exact directions, and he instructed the lead party to stop if they were unsure which way to go.

"We're going to head into that patch of mangrove there. There are a hundred ways through, so don't sweat it, and feel free to take the path less traveled. It all dumps out into a big lake to the east. Wait there for me," said Hawk. "Oh, and keep an eye out for the wildlife we spoke about. And don't get out of your boats. For any reason." No one said anything. "Go then," he said, and sat back.

The fab-four darted forward, leaving Conrad and Lilly trailing behind. Sheryl and Geoff paddled together, and that left Tim, Maureen, and Hawk.

"How come you're always last, Hughs?" Hawk said.

Maureen and Tim both turned. "Sorry?" Maureen said, lifting an eyebrow.

"Why are you always last?"

Maureen chuckled, and pushed off into the trees.

"Man, you got your hands full there, huh?" Hawk said.

Tim didn't answer.

Maureen paddled through the mangroves, and around small hardwood hammocks. Frogs, snakes, turtles, raccoons, small crocs, egrets, herons, pelicans, and many other birds she couldn't identify fought for supremacy across the lush landscape. A light breeze brought the scent of rot and low tide. Insects filled the air, but Maureen and Tim had applied bug spray, and that helped. She didn't like putting the chemicals on her skin, or breathing the fumes, but the birds and insects carried thousands of diseases. While extolling the virtues of bug spray, Hawk had told them that sixty-six percent of all black vultures in South Florida tested positive for encephalitis, and the forty-five species of mosquitoes had tested at seventy-one percent. As a nurse, she understood how scary those numbers were.

Maureen rested her paddle on the kayak's gunnel, and rubbed her eyes as Tim caught up. They'd just passed through the maze of hardwood stands, and she'd managed to get behind Hawk. After his twenty-minute speech about he how he had to be the last person in the chain, Maureen had no choice but to teach the man a lesson. She figured people didn't do that to Hawk often.

She'd backtracked several times, causing Hawk to guess which way they'd gone at least once, and they'd slipped behind him.

Now she was second-guessing her decision to mess with Hawk. She took her job and the safety of others while in her care just as seriously as he did, if not more so. Yes, he'd broken her shoes a little, but nothing more than lighthearted banter.

She let her hands dangle in the refreshing water, and took a deep breath. Was her passive-aggressive behavior toward Tim leaking onto Hawk?

Hawk waited at the edge of the lake, and as they grew close, he shook his head. Tim glided by Maureen, and she fell into last position. She let Tim get way ahead, and then she stroked hard.

"Why'd you do that?" Hawk asked. She could tell he was pissed. "I'm responsible for you when you're out here whether you like it or not." Maureen darted past him out toward the center of lake. "You hear me? At all? Anything getting through?"

"Easy, canary," Tim said.

Maureen's paddle froze mid-stroke. Had Tim just called Hawk a canary?

There was an awkward silence, and then Hawk laughed. "Okay, hotshot. We'll see what you look like in three days, when the sawgrass is done slicing you up, and your back is broken from sleeping on the ground, and every muscle in your yuppie body aches with the pain of your entire life," he said.

"Wow. That was good," Conrad said. "How long you been saying that?"

"Twenty years," Hawk said.

A screeching sound made Maureen jump. The supply barge that Hawk towed rubbed against a dead tree branch sticking from the water. In addition to the personal gear stowed on the kayaks, Hawk towed an aluminum boat filled with food, drink, and other supplies that would allow them to live in the wild for three nights and four days. The noise had died down a little, and again, Maureen was struck with the notion that she heard no planes, and couldn't remember the last time she'd heard one.

"Are we out of the Miami airport's flight path?" she asked.

"A bit. What are you worrying on now?" Hawk said. He pulled up next to her and looked genuinely interested.

Tim maneuvered his boat between them, and asked, "Can we stop there for lunch? We've been paddling almost five hours, and my stomach is rumbling."

"No, my young little ass. I know it looks like a beach, but that's where the gators sun themselves. Not a good place to break out food. We'll stop there," Hawk said. He pointed toward an island that was so big they could only see half of it. Its southern tip disappeared around a bend into a spray of grass.

They eased the kayaks onto the shore, and lifted themselves out, stretching muscles and cracking joints. Maureen checked her watch and was surprised to see it was already 10:47AM.

The sun was baking off the moisture, and she practically swam through the thick, moist air. A path led into the trees, and Hawk said there was a nice spot to rest in the center of the island. "You can explore a bit while I get the grub ready," he said, pulling the tarp off the supply boat.

Maureen and Tim headed down the path, watching for snakes and spiders. Cypress trees dotted the edge of the island, but as they went deeper the cypress gave way to oak, saw palmetto, and gumbo-limbo trees. The shade felt nice, and there were fewer insects. They were alone, the soothing sounds of the forest putting their minds at ease. The fab-four had gone ahead of them on the path, but they were nowhere to be seen.

A scream pierced the stillness. Maureen looked to Tim, who shrugged. Maureen thought it was a woman, maybe Sheryl, and without discussion, they both lurched back into motion, running back down the path the way they'd come.

They got about halfway back to the kayaks when they found the finger. The bloody digit lay in the center of the path, tendons and muscle hanging out one end like stuffing from a decapitated teddy bear. Drops of blood trailed down the path. Maureen stopped short, and Tim almost ran into her. She was used to gore, Tim wasn't. He dry heaved, spittle leaking from his mouth, eyes bulging from his head. "What the hell?" he said.

There was yelling and screaming off in the trees, and Maureen sighed. "What the hell indeed."

CHAPTER FIVE

Don rode shotgun again as they made their way across town to drop-in on Teapot, but he was under no illusions. Teapot sold to the end user, which meant he resided on the bottom of what Don hoped was a short pyramid. The city was quiet, but there were people out and about—gas stations, convenience stores, and the like just getting the news that they were to lock their doors and stay inside.

He tried not to think about what was happening across the United States at that moment. Thousands were being deployed, many of whom would live in tents for the duration of the operation. The quarantine stretched through the Everglades and down to the keys, and both areas would be hard to patrol.

It reminded Don of his first mission as a Navy SEAL. He'd been sitting around drinking beer with some mates, off duty, when the call came. His unit deployed in three hours, with no briefing, and no operation-specific training. He'd lived in a tent on the edge of a lake in a country he didn't know the name of for six months. Each day, he'd be ordered to free dive in the lake and report anything suspicious, but he wasn't told what they were looking for. He and his unit were briefed when they left and ordered to erase the mission from their collective memory. Don learned later that Agent Massie had been at that lake, but they wouldn't meet until years later.

They passed rows upon rows of houses as they cut through West Miami. Motive. Don was an investigator, so the cogs and gears of his brain were powered by motives. As in there must be one. What possible gain would someone hope to get by destroying a city? Perhaps the world. Terrorists? Enemies of the west? Extremists? A wacky dude like in the Bond movies who'd been rejected on South Beach? None of it made any sense.

"The city's emergency communication system is now down. All nine-one-one calls are getting dead air," yelled one of Don's men from the rear of the van.

"That's not good. People panic when there's no voice on the other end of the line." A fat raindrop plopped onto the windshield. Don frowned. He and water had a complex history.

As a young boy, his father had cured his fear of the water by throwing him into the Atlantic Ocean. The undertow had sucked him under and rolled him like a stone, and it had taken his father and two others to fish him out. It was one of those memories etched in his mind, and one his close SEAL friends never let him live down. A moment of honesty while sitting in the shit, followed by a lifetime of good-hearted abuse. Then there was the virus that could live in water that got the better of him. Facing his fears had led him to the Navy, but lately, he was a SEAL out of water.

Black nimbus clouds darkened the sky, moving fast east to west, and in the distance, thunder cracked. Southern Florida's weather is unpredictable, and clear skies can turn into black cloud nightmares in minutes. The rain came in hard, turning the windshield into a blur. Wipers worked overtime to clear the water, and it was still hard to see the road. The area they drove through had seen better days; large plots and big houses that were now either abandoned, or broken up into apartments. It was a reminder of how fast things could change, and how falling rarely felt like flying.

"A good washing never hurt anything," the driver said, his voice rising above the sound of the pouring rain pelting the van's roof.

"Unless the pathogen is now in the water system," Don said.

The driver said nothing. They passed silent houses, and saw nobody on the streets. The van pulled to the curb in front of an old mansion with dilapidated grounds. A crumbling stone wall with rusted steel ramparts surrounded the place.

One of Don's men stuck his head into the front cab. "He's in apartment six."

"How many others inside?" asked Don.

"Unknown, but there's only eight apartments in the place, so collateral damage should be minimal."

Don got out and waited for his men. "You and Driving Ms. Daisy here stay behind with the van. I'll go in with the others."

The street was deserted and unnervingly quiet. He drew his Glock, pressed the trigger safety, and nodded for his men to lead the way as they jumped from the van, their MP5 machine pistols at the ready and loaded with 9mm parabellums.

The old iron gate at the end of the driveway looked like it hadn't been closed in years, and the four agents slipped through, holding to the brick wall, and staying out of sight. The rain was still coming down, but barely. Don was soaked, tired, hungry, and depressed at the thought of what was to come.

When they reached the house, Don sent one of his men around back and tested the communication mic on his ear. "Rouge one, are you in position?"

"Affirmative."

He checked in with the men in the van while he waited for the lock on the front door to be picked. No need. It was unlocked, and they entered the house like wraths.

The foyer was dim, dirty, and reeked of mold and decay. One-dash-four was written on the wall in marker next to the stairs, with an arrow pointing upward. They passed through the foyer into what would have once been the living room, but was now a warren of hallways leading to different apartments. The opposite side was one door. Probably the biggest apartment. Nothing was numbered, but Don was pretty sure where Teapot lived. He pointed to the single door, and stood back while one of his agents knocked the door down, and rushed in, swinging his gun side to side as he passed inside.

They all froze as they entered the apartment, weapons held level.

Teapot was a big man. Bald, massively overweight. He sat on the couch in his living room, his face pale and drawn. In the corner was a female victim. It had long straw-like blonde hair, with eyes so big she looked like a fish. She growled at Don, but otherwise didn't appear threatening.

"Hey," Don said.

Teapot looked at him, but said nothing.

"How long has she been like that?"

Don inched further into the room, and his men fanned out around him. Nothing looked out of place. Teapot had returned his gaze to the wall, eyes focused on something Don couldn't see. He appeared to be in shock and was afraid to accept what crouched terrified in the corner. Teapot's girlfriend, or wife, or mother, had mutated into something he couldn't process.

"How long has she been like that?" Don asked again.

When Teapot didn't answer, Don turned, sighted his weapon on the walker's leg, and fired. The boom of the Glock discharging filled the room, and the transformed woman screamed in pain. Teapot sprang forward, lunging at Don. He was intercepted by Don's men and gave up the fight when he saw his woman.

Don's shot had grazed her leg, and buried itself in the wall behind her, just as he'd intended. She was more afraid than hurt, but she was also awake. Her natural color was returning, and her skin had released its tense grip as the disease retreated like a spider when put under a light. Don nodded to his man, and he let Teapot go to the woman. They embraced. Don gave them five seconds.

"She your girl?"

Teapot nodded.

"When was the last time she took ride?"

"She didn't."

Don looked at Teapot like he was a cockroach. "She didn't take ride?"

"Sherri don't do that shit," Teapot said. "I do. She gets it for me from a rich dude who wants to… " He looked at his girl.

Maybe it wasn't a bad batch of ride, yet the drug chain had led him right to another victim. Unless Sherri was lying to her man. "You 100% sure you didn't take ride?" Don asked the woman. "It's important."

"Never," she said, eyes clear. Unfortunately, Don believed her. She was infected, didn't take ride, but her boyfriend did.

"Tend to her injury and give her a caffeine pill," Don said, and two of his men went to work bandaging Sherri's superficial wound.

There was an explosion outside, and Don went to the window. He gasped as balls of flame and smoke rose above the brick wall in the area where the van was parked. When his men didn't come through the open gate toward the house, his heart sank. He tried to contact them, but got only dead air.

Rouge One was still in position at the rear entrance, and Don ordered him to investigate the blast and report back. If the van was gone, he was screwed. He would have to pull out. Their chopper waited at Kendall-Tamiami airport, but the airfield and local military installations would be locked down tighter than a frog's ass, and it would take time to convince them he should be let in, and longer still to get into the air. That all assumed there wasn't a host of sleepwalkers controlling the airport.

The faint sound of metal tapping on metal came from the second floor. Don put a finger to his lips, and everyone went silent. Someone was hammering on the plumping. Teapot and his girl jumped when the rhythm was answered by a louder, more deliberate tapping from one of the first-floor apartments.

Don put his hand to his ear. "Go ahead, One."

The agent sounded worried and out of breath. "The van has been burnt out, and it looks like our men were in there. There's a chain going around the van holding the doors shut. They were burnt alive."

"Any signs of who… or what did it?"

"There's a crowd of victims down the street, thirty or more, huddled together, watching me." There was a pause and a scuffling sound. Then, "They're coming up the street fast, and I'm trying to close the gates, but they're broken."

"Forget it, Rogue One. Retreat to me at once."

"Copy that." The comm channel went dead.

Don looked at his two men, then at Teapot and Sherri. "You have any guns? Anything you can protect yourself with?" Teapot nodded and disappeared into his bedroom, then returned with a shotgun.

The front door of the house slammed, and they heard more tapping on the pipes. Don's third man appeared in the open doorway, his eyes wide, panting hard. "They're coming. Several are entering the house behind me," he said. The agent entered and closed the door behind him. The two others placed the couch in front of the door.

Don pulled out his sat-phone, dialed up his contact, and recited his number. "I'm in need of support. Grab the coordinates from my phone."

"You're going to have to wait. The shit has hit the fan. You're on your own for now."

Don clicked off and looked at his men. He didn't need to say anything. They slipped into combat mode, positioning themselves and Teapot around the apartment at all possible entrances. Don ordered them to shoot for the legs and arms, but Teapot's shotgun wouldn't be that selective. The tapping pipes reached a fever pitch, then went silent. Everything was still, not a single creak.

The room imploded.

They came through the ceiling, the thin sheetrock partition walls, the windows, and the door. All at once, together in what appeared to be an action controlled by one mind. The walkers paused then, holding their heads in pain, as if the great exertion and commotion had hurt them. Don used their hesitation. He squeezed off eleven shots and woke eleven people. That cut the horde in half, though more were crowding together in the hallway outside the apartment.

The newly woken people were dazed, and in shock. They sat, or lay prone on the floor, clawing at the wounds that had woken them. One of Don's men was yelling, attempting to get them together so he could protect as many as possible, but it was like trying to herd cats. Sheetrock dust filled the air, and Sherri was screaming. Teapot positioned himself in front of her, his shotgun held before him. There was a loud wail, and one of Don's men got ripped from his feet and thrown across the room. His MP5 fired, and left a ribbon of holes in the wall, and across two walkers. The gun tumbled from his hand and skittered across the floor, coming to rest in front of a sleepwalker.

The walker picked it up, and studied it closely, turning the barrel toward his face. The weapon discharged, and blew the walker's head from its shoulders in a hail of bullets, leaving a lump of flesh, brain, and blood on the wall as the body fell. The fallen agent shook his head, and started to get up, but was pounded across the face with a length of pipe, cracking his temporal bone and driving the shattered fragments through his brain. The sleepwalker stood over the agent's lifeless body. When it bent over to start taking bites of the man, Don lost it.

His Glock barked four more times, emptying the magazine. The clip dropped from the gun, and he snapped another one home before the four walkers hit the floor. "We need to get out of here!" Don yelled.

Teapot pointed toward the bedroom, and Don nodded for him to go for it. As soon as he moved, two of the walkers dove for Teapot as he pushed Sherri before him. The fat man stopped short and let loose with four shots at point-blank range. None of those four victims would ever wake.

Don's remaining two men were firing into the crowd of sleepwalkers as they pushed into the apartment in a sleepy haze. But they were coming through the walls, and from above, and soon his men were drowning in a sea of bodies, the rattle of the machineguns fading beneath the pile of walkers. Don followed Teapot and Sherri into the bedroom.

Don's last two men had joined the ranks of the sleeping dead. They came after him, all recognition gone, any trace of humanity hidden. They fired, and bullets tore through the door as Don slammed it shut, locked it, and dove for cover. The MP5s stopped discharging.

Teapot tossed a desk chair through what was left of his bedroom window, and pumped another shell into the shotgun's chamber. He fired. Pumped again. Fired. The path cleared, he helped Sherri out the window, and followed. Don heard screaming, the shotgun boom, and then silence. Seconds passed while Don waited, breathing heavy. The walkers pounded on the cracking door. Two others were creeping toward him from above.

Teapot, Sherri, and their new friends were coming through the window. Teapot fired at Don, who only had to avoid one shot before the gun clicked empty. The sleepwalker that had been Teapot continued to pull the trigger, the dull clicking sound as the hammer struck nothing oddly clear amidst the turmoil.

Then they were on him.

Don emptied his weapon, but there were too many. The walkers covered him like ants on a candy bar, ripping off his clothing, pulling at this hair, taking his weapon and phone. As Don struggled, he saw a young girl, standing well away from the melee, her brown hair drenched with sweat and matted to her face. Her eyes burned, and her lips were pulled back in a wicked grin.

CHAPTER SIX

A heron with a patch of yellow feathers atop its head screeched like an alarm, insects large and small buzzed, the wind rattled a million leaves, but the pounding of Maureen's heart was louder than them all. She steadied herself as she came to terms with the fact that things had just gotten real. Vacation was ruined, and instinct told her that was just the dressing on the turd sandwich. Tim looked like he was about to go down, his eye sockets and cheeks white against his sunburned face. Maureen stared at the severed finger, hesitant to go near it. The fingernail was painted pink, with a small rhinestone glued near the cuticle. The island went still, and the trees whispered and sighed as a gust of wind pushed down the path. She looked to Tim for guidance, knowing she'd find none.

"Hey," Raul yelled, as he came up behind them. "Did you hear a scream? What are you…?" He stopped short when he saw the finger. Wendy arrived, stood behind her husband, and said nothing. Saura and Ping followed.

Raul looked up the path, his eyes following the thin trail of blood. The others were dazed. Raul had processed what he'd seen, drawn conclusions, and developed a plan of action. He wanted to follow the trail of blood, like her.

"Like, should we pick it up?" Saura asked, as she twisted her hair around a finger. She was a slight woman, with a big presence. "If we leave it here, it will get eaten."

"She's got a point," Tim said.

Maureen snickered. He supports the attractive young Asian woman who he hasn't even met, but not his wife.

Raul was staring at everyone like they were nuts. "We need to go after the rest of the person or they'll be too many body parts to pick up, Tila Tequila." He didn't wait for approval, or agreement. He left the crowd, and headed back toward to the kayaks, following the drips of blood. Wendy fell in line behind him like a child, and Ping, Saura, and Maureen trailed behind. Tim stood over the finger, then bent down to pick it up, but couldn't.

"For Christ sake, use a leaf," Maureen yelled, and Tim's face lit up like he'd been thrown a life preserver. He ripped a large green leaf off a tropical plant and rolled the finger in it.

As they jogged down the path, Maureen's mind ran through the possible scenarios they might face ahead. It could have been a wild animal, a croc or bobcat that attacked either Lilly or Sheryl. A snake or turtle could have bitten the finger off, and Sheryl or Lilly ran back toward where they thought they'd find help. The problem with these scenarios was that she'd seen no animal prints around the finger, no signs of a struggle at all.

Hawk had been in business for years, and his likeness matched the one on the tour website. She couldn't see Geoff biting off anyone's finger, so that left Conrad. All the others had been deeper in on the island than her and Tim. Another gust of wind scattered the insects, and the path opened up. Through the cypress the bright colors of their kayaks stood out against the dark brown peat. There was yelling ahead, and Maureen ran faster.

Saura screamed, a thin wail that would have broken glass had there been any within thirty miles. Maureen's first thought was the woman was being a drama queen, but she was wrong.

Maureen and Tim cleared the cypress trees, and the path ended on a peat shore. Sawgrass ran off to the right, and a patch of cypress trees to the left. What remained of Hawk was pinned to a cypress tree with the broken shards of his classic wooden paddle. Both arms were gone, one leg had been hacked off at the knee, and half his head was missing. Deep red blood covered the remains, and the way the body was nailed to the tree made it clear this hadn't been done by a wild animal, at least not one indigenous to southern Florida.

Trauma shock ran through the crowd, and everyone but Maureen froze. When others stepped back, she stepped forward. She examined Hawk's remains. His pistol was gone, and she looked toward his kayak and saw that the rifle was still strapped to the deck. She called to the group. "Tim, come help me get him down. Raul, go find Lilly and the rest. They can't be far." She paused, then added, "And take the rifle."

Raul looked at her, at the thin path that trailed into the tall grass, then at the rifle, and nodded his head. "You got it, Katniss."

"Hello. Looking for me?"

Everyone jumped. Conrad strolled from the cypress, seemingly oblivious to the crisis unfolding around him. He looked tired, but was otherwise unharmed. There was no blood on his clothes, and he carried his pack over one shoulder like he didn't have a care in the world. When he saw Hawk's remains he froze, his eyes glazing over. Conrad vomited, undigested eggs and bacon from his breakfast sandwich reentering the world with a flourish. He leaned against a tree and wretched again, his body shaking. Every few seconds, he looked at Hawk, then jerked away his gaze like two people fought within him.

Maureen and Tim finished cutting Hawk down, and laid him on the soft peat. That done, Maureen went to Conrad. He whimpered like a child, his body racked with pain. He mumbled and yelled like something unseen was attacking him, and then she remembered the ride. She guessed he hadn't planned for his ride to include their guide getting ripped apart. That stirred Maureen's memory; where were Hawk's two arms and half a leg? They weren't on the shore or around the body.

Thin white lines crisscrossed Conrad's face like scars, stretching across his cheeks and forehead. They stood out against his black skin, which was beaded with sweat. Ping produced a canteen, and Conrad drank deeply, water spilling down the front of his shirt. He appeared not to notice what was happening around him. Maureen figured the scar-like white lines were from the sawgrass, which scraped, poked, and cut anyone who was brave enough to wade through it.

"Where have you been, Idris Elba?" Raul asked. A crowd had formed around Conrad, and Raul's voice was laced with more than a little suspicion.

"I wandered off along the shoreline there. Took a break under a huge tree and fell asleep. I woke up and came back here," Conrad said, his eyes straying to Hawk's mutilated body.

"Did you see Lilly or Sheryl?" Saura asked.

"Or Geoff?" Ping added, as he gagged and cleared his throat.

"No." Conrad seemed to realize they might accuse him of something, and his eyes widened. "What's happened here?"

"Don't know," Maureen said. She knew Conrad better than everyone except Lilly, but Maureen hardly knew him. They'd only met that morning at the airport, but she knew enough to know that Conrad was no fool. "Tim and I followed the path in the island's core. Raul, Ping, Wendy, and Saura were also in the interior. We heard screams and headed back here."

"Along the way, we found this," Tim said, as he unrolled the leaf and displayed the finger with pink nail polish.

"That's Lilly's," Conrad said, as he bolted upright, and reached out to take the finger as though it was the last piece of Lilly on Earth.

Tim drew back it back, out of Conrad's reach, and rolled it in its leaf wrapper. It grew silent, and Maureen took in a long breath of fresh air, and bit her lip. She found it amazing, and somewhat ominous, that the Glades could go from a total cacophony of natural sound, to silence in a moment. It was nature's alarm, and in the silence that alarm rang in Maureen's head like a siren.

Raul and Wendy seemed to notice the quiet also, and they looked around, searching the forest for any signs of their missing companions. "We need to do something with Hawk," Raul said.

"And find Lilly, Sheryl, and Geoff," Maureen said.

"Maureen, you're a nurse, right? What do we do with Hawk? Can't bury him. The water table is so high you can't dig here but a foot before you hit water. Can't build a can, there aren't any rocks. We could burn him, but somehow that doesn't seem right. So what?" Ping asked as he sucked phlegm from his throat.

As a nurse, Maureen was expected to be an authority on everything. There was nothing a nurse didn't know, and no boundaries to her vast store of useful knowledge. Truth was nurses, in general, were smart, well thought out, persistent problem solvers who used their skills constantly and thus keep them finely tuned. In this case, she was unsure.

"We'll call for help," Ping said, sucking mucus. He fired up his phone, and this sent everyone digging for their tech like they'd just been released from prison. Those who had battery power had no signal, and when they found Hawk's emergency GPS radio, they discovered it didn't work.

"We have to do something about the body, or the animals will solve our problem for us," Maureen said. She was reluctant to foist upon them what she had realized some time ago; everyone's vacation was over. She bit her lip, and felt the scar on her neck throb. "I think we need to wrap him as best we can with wet blankets to keep the body as cool as possible. Then we need to paddle him out."

"What about Lilly?" Conrad said.

"And Sheryl and Geoff?" Ping said. He cleared his throat like a foraging pig.

No one responded. Flies, gnats, mosquitos, dragonflies, and beetles clogged the air. The Glades appeared untroubled, unhurried, and in a state of constant calm. The affairs of men, and their petty problems, meant nothing amidst the tall sawgrass and cattails. In the distance, a limpkin wailed, wild, strange, and eternally sorrowful. Above, a steel gray snail kite labored into the wind, head down, searching for apple snails. Its bill and legs glowed orange in the afternoon sun and its rump and under-feathers were white as snow. Maureen remembered reading that snail kites had been on the endangered species list since its creation.

Raul said, "Should we split up? Half look for the women, and the other half goes for help and brings Hawk's body?"

Maureen never thought splitting up was a wise decision. There was strength in numbers, and whatever—or whoever—had killed Hawk was still on the loose. "The living are more important than the dead. We should all look for Sheryl, Geoff, and Lilly." Maureen said it without thinking, and immediately thought she'd shared too much.

"I have an idea," Wendy said. They all paused and looked at her, waiting. "We break the backrest out of his kayak, stuff what's left of him into it, and seal the cockpit with rope and branches. Then we put it as high as we can in a tree."

Things didn't always have to be complicated. In fact, the best plans never were. Maureen's mouth dropped. Recovering, she said, "Good idea. Wrap the body in wet blankets and put it in a plastic cocoon. Then we can come back and get him after we find the others."

"Like, how the heck are we going to mark our spot? Anyone have any idea where we are?" Saura didn't sound panicked, but she wasn't calm. She twisted her hair around her index finger so tightly its tip had turned purple.

"There's a map with his things," Wendy said.

Maureen smiled. Wendy was coming around, and she needed her. No further discussion appeared necessary, and they went about preparing Hawk's body for its kayak casket. Raul created a sling to pull the boat high into a cypress tree where it could be held between two thick branches and secured with rope. Maureen wrapped and wet the body, and what was left of Hawk fit easily into his plastic coffin. Wendy and Ping climbed the tree to guide the plastic sarcophagus, and everyone else pulled on the guide ropes, lifting the deceased into the air with ease. They went through Hawk's stuff and found the map. At Maureen's urging, Tim slung the rifle on his shoulder, and handed Hawk's hunting knife to his wife.

Maureen and Tim got ready to move out, but it looked like some of the others were settling in. They hadn't discussed a plan. Did they need to? She went to Raul, who was pulling a beer from his cooler. The body gone, and out of mind, he was resuming his party.

"What's the best way for us all to look? Pairs of two? Here is our home base?" She was asking. Asking the same way she did when she "asked" a doctor or patient when she felt they'd crossed a line.

He opened his beer, took a long pull, and then looked at her with a smile she didn't like very much. "What's your rush, Nurse Jackie?" When she didn't respond, he said, "Yeah. That sounds smart." Then he giggled. "Hey, man, what's in that shit you gave me?" Raul lurched past her toward Conrad.

Maureen's neck scar burned as she clamped down on her lip. She wasn't their mother, or their nurse, or anything to these people at all. She could control her own actions, and to some extent, Tim's, but if the others didn't want to search, how could she make them?

Conrad was getting ready to head into the cypress trees, and Tim was comparing notes with him. Raul stood next to Conrad, talking at him, but Conrad ignored him, and continued to pack up his things, conferring with Tim as he did so. Maureen went to Saura and Ping, who were also resting. Saura appeared dazed, and Ping looked put out, like a designated driver chauffeuring around a carload of drunks.

Maureen caught his eye, and mouthed "ride," and the thin Asian man nodded and made his frog sound. A thought bounced around her head, and she tried to brush it away, but couldn't. Maybe the ride was causing people to become unbalanced. Perhaps that's what happened to Hawk?

"Are you guys going to search?" she asked Ping.

"In a bit after we rest," he said.

Maureen nodded and went to join Tim, who was still speaking with Conrad. Raul had wandered off, and she wrote him off as useless until his ride was over. "We're going to follow the path along the shoreline and work our way around the island. Conrad is going across the island," Tim said.

"Wish you hadn't given them that stuff, Conrad," Maureen said.

Conrad looked up from what he was doing. "I gave it to them before—"

"Yeah, well it's knocking the crap out of Raul and Saura."

"Everyone's ride is different. Body chemistry and all that," Conrad said, as he hefted his pack. "We'll see you here later?"

"Yeah, we'll be back by dark, or sooner if we find them," Maureen said.

Conrad stalked into the trees.

In the Glades, sawgrass creates and defines the ground on which it grows. The Everglades have been called a giant river obscured by grass, and as Maureen and Tim skirted the edge of the sawgrass field, it became clear how invasive the plant is. They followed the path around a bend, and their kayaks and companions were lost from view. Grass filled the shallow water that encroached almost up to the trees where the peat path meandered and curved around the water's edge.

They came to a section where the vegetation was pounded down badly. Every few feet there was a drip of blood, and it was clear something had been dragged that way. Neither of them wore high boots, so following the path was impossible because of the water, the grass, and what lay within.

A scream rose above the sounds of the Glades, and it was close. Maureen ran down the path, leaving Tim behind.

CHAPTER SEVEN

"When the boys hit the brew! When the boys hit the brew! When the boys hit the brew!"

At first, Don thought he was dreaming, the loud music tearing through the room like a gust of wind. The walkers were fleeing, and as fast as he'd been trapped under a mountain of flesh, he was free.

"When the boys hit the brew! When the boys hit the brew!"

He didn't recognize the song, but it was some kind of death metal, because the tune was a jarring cacophony of guitar and drums that would have shaken the windows and rattled the walls had there been windows and walls left to rattle. Don sat up.

A man wearing a gasmask, and dressed in jeans, a flannel shirt, and orange gloves stood over him. At his wrists and ankles were bands of silver duct tape that sealed his improvised biohazard suite. Behind the large glass lenses of the gasmask, eyes the size of quarters stood out against the man's dark brown skin. He blinked as sweat dripped in his eyes. His shirt's armpits were soaked through, and he held a hockey stick before him, a speaker taped to its end. A wire ran from the speaker into the man's pocket, where Don surmised he kept an iPod or some such.

The sheetrock dust settled, and the energy in the room eased as his adrenaline levels fell. The tips of his fingers tingled, and he scanned the room expecting to see walkers coming at him. Don took deep breaths, trying to calm himself. He'd been in dangerous situations many times, but that was only the second time he'd come that close to death.

The first time was something Don didn't like to think about. He'd built a wall around that portion of his life, and though it was healthy to remember the past so you didn't repeat it, Don was comfortable excising that portion of his life. But that was never possible. The scars ran too deep, and the good memories of halting his fall made him what his was. If he hadn't gone through everything he had, he might never have met Agent Massie, or realized his full potential. He'd pulled out of the dive then, and he would now.

The horde was gone, and the man shut down the music. "They don't like loud noises. That's why I was surprised at how they came at you," the man said, as he reached down to help Don up. The image of the sleepwalkers holding their heads in pain after they broke through Teapot's walls came back to him. "I don't have any guns, so I thought this might work." He proudly held up his hockey stick with the speaker attached to its end.

Don rose and patted himself down. He'd lost everything. His ID, weapons, sat phone, watch, belt and knife, shoes, jacket and tie. He wore his underwear, torn pants, socks, and a shredded white T-shirt. The good news was he felt no cuts. Music man had shown up just as things were about to get nasty.

"Thanks for the help," Don said, and he put out his hand.

"No worries. I'm Lester," he said, taking Don's hand.

Don laughed, and Lester stared at him through half-closed eyes. He brought up the sound gun, and Don laughed some more. The realization that he was currently in the deepest shit of his life had left Don relieved. He'd been reborn and stripped of everything he held dear. He had no weapons, no ID, no way to communicate with command, and had lost his entire crew.

In the end, training took over, and Don moved forward in a daze, his body knowing what to do. It didn't matter how Don felt, or what he thought was right. He went forward because that was all he knew how to do.

"You see us come in?" Don asked.

Lester nodded as sweat dripped in his eyes.

"You see what happened to my men? My van?"

He nodded again, then said, "You were a cop? Or higher up?"

The use of the past tense aggravated Don, but he pushed it down. "I'm the federal agent that shut the city down, and I need to find out what is causing people to… " He shrugged. "I guess what I'm asking is, what do you have going on today? Your country could use your help." That was Don's final card, the one he rarely played.

Lester laughed. "Yeah. Problem is my country hasn't been there for me." There was a long awkward silence. "You were a SEAL?" Lester asked.

"Yeah, how did—?"

Lester pointed to Don's tattoo, which was clearly visible through his torn T-shirt.

The hooting and yelping outside was getting loud, and Don felt a crowd might be forming. He cracked his neck and calmed himself. This guy had to want to help. The way he was dressed, and the way he talked, made Don think he might be enjoying his real life video game and may have no interest in getting out. He was living the dream, and for Don, this was further proof that the human race as he understood it had been doomed long before judgment day in southern Florida.

"Look. I want to hear your story. I do. But if we don't get out of here now, I might not be able to," Don said.

"Bull. I got this," he said, as he held up his speaker-stick.

"Look. These things are smart. They'll figure out how to cover their ears. Then what, genius?"

Lester's entire body sagged. He said, "There's a way out in the basement. A tunnel that goes to the old garage. The maintenance people had to use it so the people who lived here didn't have to see them walking across the property."

Don searched the apartment, but all the guns were gone, and he saw nothing that could be used as a weapon. He was in the bedroom, putting on some of Teapot's sweatpants and shoes, when he saw the elaborate bedpost that tapered off to a point with finely carved finials. He snapped one off and held it in his hand. It felt good, and it could be used in close combat until he got something better. He finished his ensemble with a purple jacket with rhinestones down the sleeves. Mrs. Teapot's wardrobe was much closer to Don's size.

Though Lester looked ridiculous, he'd executed a basic emergency biohazard suite. At this point, Don didn't see the point in him duplicating it. If the stuff was airborne, he was already infected.

They left Teapot's place, and crossed the foyer to Lester's apartment. He had a backpack, and they filled it with some canned food and two large bottles of water. They took all the cheesy knives from Lester's knife-block, and Don duct taped one to the end of his pointed club.

A low buzzing sound filled the room, and Don opened the refrigerator. No light. He flicked the switch on the wall. No light. The power was out.

"We need a couple guns and some ammo," Don said.

"And some pure caffeine powder, or caffeine pills. Coffee at least. Got me?" Lester said. He was watching Don as if he were a sick animal.

Don felt fine, but he knew that meant nothing. Lester didn't need to know that, though. "I'm fine. Not a scratch on me."

"Thanks to me," Lester said.

"And that's why I will get you out of here if you help me." Behind the thick glass lenses of his gasmask, Lester's eyebrow lifted. "Did you know Teapot? What he did?"

"Drugs. Everyone in the house was a customer except me."

"You know where he..." Then he remembered what Teapot had said. "You know who Sherri got the stuff from?" Even though it appeared ride wasn't the cause, the logical continuation of the investigation still looked to be the drug chain. Don recalled what his man had said about thirty percent of the victims they'd identified being connected to the drug business, and he put that together with the fact that he'd just been attacked by a horde walkers in a house filled with ride users. Maybe only some of the ride was tainted, and people could be carriers without symptoms and unknowingly spread the virus. He hated making decisions based on incomplete facts, but the drug chain was his only lead. That scared him a little. He was used to having his sat phone, and being able to get the answer to any question within minutes, and move personnel and equipment around at will. If he wanted to be useful now, he'd have to go back to his old school investigation techniques while trying to survive and stay uninfected.

"Rick Dempsey is the main ride dealer 'round these parts. Everyone knows that."

"Except the cops, apparently."

"Oh, they know. But he's a rich guy with powerful friends. Got me? Even the feds tried to nab him once, and he walked," Lester said.

"Why do you know so much about it?"

"Sherri is my sister. This used to be our granddad's house."

"I'm sorry, Lester. But you saw me bring those others awake. Maybe we'll be able to save her." That made Don think of those people he'd helped. They'd either fled during the attack, or had returned to their sleepwalker state.

"Maybe."

"You know where this Dempsey guy lives?"

"Yeah, he's over in Chicken Key on Biscayne Bay. I went over there with Sherri a few times. You need to shit gold and piss Cristal to live over there," Lester said.

"Not anymore. How far away we talking?"

"Across town."

That was a problem. They had no vehicle and driving one was going to become increasingly difficult as the city continued to fall apart. There'd be cars and other things blocking roads, victims shooting at cars, and probably much worse.

"We need a motorcycle," Don said. "A dirt bike would be best. That way we can take the road less traveled."

"Jerry's got one. Might have some guns too if nobody's broken into his place yet."

"Your friend?"

"Yeah. He's deployed in Iraq."

"Where is his place?"

"Not far. A mile or so toward the coast."

As they talked, they left the apartment and went down a long set of stairs, which ended in an old root cellar. A large black door stood closed in front of them. Beyond was a decent-sized room and Lester locked the door behind them. Don held a flashlight, and that helped them avoid the massive spider webs that covered the walls and ceiling. There was a desk, some chairs, and an ancient rusting file cabinet. Everything was covered with a thick coating of dust.

Don went to the file cabinet and pulled on the top drawer. It was locked. He rammed the tip of his stick into the gap above the handle and pried it open. After a few minutes, the front bent outward, and Don was able to break the lock mechanism.

The draw was filled with money. Maybe ten grand in small bills. Don chuckled. What good was money now? The currency looked old, and had some kind of fungus growing on it. The rest of the cabinet was filled with paperwork.

They continued on through the tunnel, and out into the garage, where they realized taking the passageway had been an unnecessary precaution. They saw no walkers, but they heard them in the distance—barks, howls, and screams of pain and terror, but they appeared to be staying out of sight.

The rain clouds were gone, and the sun beat down on them as they left the garage, sticking to the brick wall until they exited through the front gate. Don didn't spend long examining the van because he knew that would draw attention, but there were some things he had to do. Like get his men's tags. The front windows and windshield were blown out, so Don didn't think that was going to be a difficult task.

Except when he got to the van, he discovered his men's remains weren't there. Nothing in the front, or the rear. This made Don nauseous, but also brought a little hope. Maybe they got out and were roaming the city with a pack of walkers? The blood on the front seats and hood made that a hard sell.

"Come on," Don said. "We're going to cut through yards. We'll stick to the street patterns as best we can. I'll try to avoid high fences, and other impediments." He wanted to be sure they didn't get caught in a confined space.

They cut across the first lawn that didn't have a wall or a fence and went southeast. Lester said there was a bodega that might have caffeine pills on the way. They slipped through a high hedge and came out on a thin private driveway that divided one piece of property into two homesteads. As they walked by the front of the first house, two children stood in an upper window. Don stopped and waved, and the kids waved back.

People were listening. They were staying inside and digging in. Don was thinking that maybe he could still win this thing when a huge dog bolted around the house and headed straight for them. Don and Lester froze, and when the dog arrived, the giant beast simply sniffed them and wagged his tail. Don had yet to see an animal affected by the disease. That was another important thing his people back in the research labs needed to know.

The dog wouldn't leave them, and as they cut across yards, through gates, and around houses, it padded after, its tongue hanging loose. The area had gone from former rich, to the cheaper properties of the people who had served them. The mid-day sun baked off all the moisture, and Don wondered if the heat might be why the sleepwalkers were staying out of sight. He judged it was a little after noon. There was still almost eight hours of daylight left.

They hopped a tall wooden fence to get to the bodega, and that's when they lost the dog. He couldn't climb the fence, and getting him over would've taken time and energy. The bodega was trashed, but the walkers who'd wrecked it hadn't been looking for NoSleep pills. There were two boxes, which was forty pills. They also found three dusty cans of Jolt on the floor, under the beverage rack.

They went out the back entrance and worked their way diagonally through several yards. They came into a backyard filled with palmetto trees, and thick waves of green vines with grape-like purple flowers. The perfume-like scent of the wisteria filled the air.

A young male sleepwalker sat in the shade with his back against a large tree, knees pulled up to his chest. He rocked back and forth, and smacked his gums. Dark blood vessels pulsed against dark skin, and his eyes burned like cinders. He was no more than ten, his dark hair matted with sweat.

Don went to him. He vaulted to his feet, and retreated into the corner of the fenced-in yard, nowhere to go.

"That's weird," Lester said through his gas mask.

"No, it's not. You just haven't seen one alone. They're not so aggressive when they are only one or two."

Lester picked up his pace, and so did Don. The boy looked terrified, covering his face with his arms, and hissing and whining. Lester stepped forward and smacked the boy smartly across the face. The walker screamed and fell back. Don felt a twinge of guilt, but then remembered the sound-gun hadn't woken the others, so there was no reason to believe it would work now.

A gunshot rang out, and Don and Lester dropped into a crouch. The shot sounded a few blocks over, but they both paused for a few seconds, watching the surrounding trees and listening hard.

"Mister?" It was the timid voice of the boy Lester had just woken.

He wore tattered blue jeans, and black sneakers. His face glistened with sweat, blood vessels shrinking, skin loosening. His right cheek showed the red swelling of where Lester had slapped him. He didn't seem to notice it, smiling like he understood he'd just escaped a horrible situation.

"What's your name?" Don asked.

The kid looked up at Lester, smiled, turned to Don, and said, "Tobi."

CHAPTER EIGHT

Maureen and Tim found Geoff in a thick patch of sawgrass. They had run along the water's edge, investigating the scream they'd heard, when they came upon the blood-soaked chunk of flesh floating in shallow water. Cattails stood all around what was left of the body, and Geoff's tattered red flannel shirt was the only sign of identification. All his limbs were gone, as was his head. Tattered muscles, shattered bones, and gristle saturated in blood seeped from the torso. The water around the remains flowed red, and tiny pieces of skin and fat floated on the water like dried leaves.

Tim wretched, but his breakfast had already been tossed, so he only dry heaved, and sounded like a horse getting a rectal exam. He bent over, hands on his knees, as his skin faded a few shades of white. Spittle dripped from his mouth, and he breathed in and out hard, trying to settle his stomach.

Seeing people reduced to rump roast or chop meat was common for Maureen. Her hospital caught many accident victims, and it never ceased to amaze her how much damage two tons of metal, plastic, and rubber could achieve when colliding with things at high speeds. But she wasn't in a hospital, and whatever happened to Geoff wasn't an accident.

A chilling, all-encompassing angst gripped her. Death is around every corner, watching, waiting, and hoping for a slip-up. She believed most people only realize this when alone, while sitting before the void like patient lemmings thinking about how everything they have, everything they've done, could be gone in an instant. It is only then that one realizes how fragile the world is. How fragile humans are. She'd learned this in the ER, and sometimes it was a challenge to beat back the darkness.

She bit her lip. The darkness. She looked over at Tim and he transformed from the man she'd loved into the asshole she now despised. That night he'd come home wasted, as he'd done regularly before the incident. She asked where he'd been, which launched them into their regular fight, with all its repetitive issues, always rehashed, but never resolved. She'd seen the fire of his anger growing and took pleasure in stoking it. The blow came without warning, a harsh slap that sent her reeling, a thin trail of blood leaking from her lip. He looked at her in horror and cried like a baby. She hadn't shed a tear.

The screech of a heron brought her back to the present.

Unlike with Hawk, and Lilly's finger, here there were signs of a struggle. All along the water's edge the cattails had been flattened, and a blood trail led into the forest, which was easy to see due to the broken tree branches and stomped plants. There were many prints on the shoreline in the soft peat, but it was impossible to tell what type of prints they were, though they were large enough to be human.

They found none of Geoff's body parts. Maureen tried to convince herself this was evidence that there was a giant gator gorging itself. Bobcats and panthers leave very distinct footprints, and she'd seen no cat prints. What scared her was she couldn't sell herself the idea they were croc prints. Gators tails and underbellies often dragged when they walked, and she expected to see marks in the peat indicating this, but hadn't. Also, crocs couldn't nail someone to a tree with a broken paddle. The only species in the southern Florida bigger than the gators and cats was humans. Yet that thought was unthinkable. In the group's panic and eagerness to find Lilly and Sheryl, they'd pushed the manner in which Hawk was killed from their minds.

"What now?" Tim said as he cracked his knuckles.

Maureen racked the bolt on the rifle and loaded a bullet. She looked down the path the way they'd come, and nothing moved but the swaying grass and cattails, and the rustling of leaves. Clouds streaked by overhead, and Maureen suddenly felt like she was running out of time. "We follow that trail of blood and find out what did this."

"I think it's run for our lives time."

"That says it all," Maureen said.

"You think we can do something for Lilly and Sheryl? They're gone, Maureen. Deal with it," Tim said. With the increased danger, his balls had grown three sizes.

Maureen paused, composing a statement that would end any hope they could again be a real couple, but instead went with the worst copout available. "Whatever. We have to check it out."

Silence fell between them. A turkey vulture swooped in and landed on a cypress tree along the shore. It watched them with its gleaming eyes, as if calculating how long it would take to pick their bones.

The Everglades are a tapestry of halftones. There are no bold strokes of color, or a deep esthetic resonance, but in the quiet of the Glades, away from the world of people, Maureen felt empowered. The symmetry of nature, the confident way the animals went about their lives, and the seamless way they fit into their environment made her envious, and she drew strength from the ecosystem.

Tim looked away when Maureen smiled at him. Her neck muscles tightened as she remembered that night two years ago, and all the anger came rushing back. This drove home that she was in the middle of nowhere, with no communication, no clear path of escape, and something was running around eating people. So logically she should alienate her husband, the one person who might be able to help her.

"I'm sorry," she said. She didn't mean it, but she didn't think he knew that.

Tim's eyes softened, and whatever guilt he may have felt he hid from her.

Maureen followed the drips of blood, and the cypress gave way to oak, royal palm, and wild banyan. Saw palmetto, the spiked-leafed weed of southern Florida, clogged the ground beneath the tree canopy, and vines cut through the treetops providing almost complete shade. Beneath the tree cover the air was cool, but at the water's edge in the full sun one could cook an egg on a stone. A pelican cawed as it looped overhead, changing direction erratically. Birds fought and screeched, but those sounds faded as they went deeper into the island's interior.

Maureen stopped short and put her hand up to silence Tim before he could speak. There were whispers on the breeze, and the faint echo of crying. She heard a chain being pulled through a steel ring, the sharp tapping of the rounded metal links hitting the steel loop causing a sharp pain to run down her spine. She clamped down on her lip. The rhythm of the tapping slowed, then stopped.

They had entered a thick stand of dead oak trees, and the saw palmetto's spiked leaves rose five feet tall, making it difficult to see. Maureen took several hesitant steps, and the rattling of the steel chain rose again, filling the dead forest with the sound of metal on metal.

"Shit," Maureen said, and froze. "Don't take another step, Tim!" She recalled several years back when she had been in the badlands with friends, and they'd come across a rattlesnake. There were diamondbacks in the Glades, and that sound was one saying, "Get the hell away from me or I'll kill your ass!"

Tim cracked his knuckles, and said, "It could be anywhere in here."

"We'll backtrack and cut through a little further down," Maureen said, surprised he'd figured it out.

"That'll get us through this spot, but these damn things are probably everywhere in here. I've got flip flops on for shit-sake."

Maureen wore wetsuit booties, and had instructed Tim to do the same. He hadn't listened, and she snickered at his stupidity. Then she scolded herself. She didn't like what she was becoming. More and more she recognized how toxic she'd become toward Tim. She'd played a part in the deterioration of their marriage, continually torturing Tim, and letting her anger and resentment rule her life. Maybe it was time to let the past go, but she couldn't get by him striking her. Physical violence is never acceptable.

"Go back and wait for me on the shore," she said. He had a point, as much as she hated to recognize it. If a diamondback went for her, its bite would go through her booties.

Tim looked at the rifle Maureen held, then said, "No. We should stay together. Wait here for a minute."

"Where are you going?"

Tim didn't answer, but he was only gone a few seconds, and returned with several stones. He tossed them. First to his right, then moving left in an arc. The rock he threw directly in front of them elicited the now familiar rattle, and in this way, they adjusted their course, and avoided the beast.

Though it pained her somewhat, Maureen said, "Good idea with the rocks, boy scout."

Tim chuckled and smiled at her.

They were forced to detour two more times before they broke free of the palmetto and entered a healthier section of forest. Here the ground was dirt, and several varieties of trees filled the area. The ground was mostly clear, but it was so hard packed; seeing a print of any kind was impossible. Maureen deemed that they had reached the center of the island, and she wondered if Conrad had come this way.

"Which way?" Tim asked. While there was no clear crossroad, clearly they were at one, and as usual, Tim deferred to her.

"Wait here. Don't walk around and mess stuff up," she said, as she began searching the area.

"Mess stuff up?"

"Yeah, like stepping on something like this and obscuring it," said Maureen. She bent over a bone fragment streaked with blood. It was impossible to tell what type of bone it was, but Maureen judged it hadn't been there long. "This way," she said.

They walked on, an occasional ray of sunlight breaking through the tree canopy like a spotlight. They weren't close to water so the insects had backed off. No birds chirped, and they saw no smaller game, like gecko lizards, squirrels, rabbits, or muskrats. It was as if a freight train had just passed, and everything still hid from its wake.

There was a growling ahead, and then what sounded like a strangled yelp. Maureen crouched, and shouldered the rifle, looking down its sight into the tangle of trees before her. At first, she saw nothing. Gnats tickled her nose and she sneezed. Something ran between the trees and disappeared into a small thicket. There were no native creatures that stood that tall.

"Stay with me," Maureen said, and she started forward, half-crouched, moving from tree to tree, playing army like she had with her brother as a young girl. They moved toward the thicket, slipping around saw palmetto and climbing over a fallen tree. The silence deepened, and it wasn't until Tim took her by the shoulders and shook her did Maureen realize she was screaming.

A pile of arms and legs with Geoff's head resting atop it lay before her. This time, she threw up bile filled with specs of egg and sausage. She staggered back, and Tim caught her as she fell. Realizing she was in his arms, Maureen jerked violently, and twisted from his grasp. She got to her feet and brought up the gun.

"Who's there? Come out now!" She moved the rifle from side to side, looking for a target. When one didn't appear, she lowered the weapon. "This is nuts."

All clothes had been torn away, and the body parts looked like crabs had been gnawing on them for days. Geoff's head was smashed, and missing an eye. Maureen did a fast count and realized two limbs were missing, a leg and an arm. While they were gnawed badly, all the hands and feet appeared to be intact. No missing fingers.

There was blood everywhere, which made it hard to determine which way the missing body parts had been taken. Maureen heard growling, and then a gunshot rang out. It missed wildly, and cut through the bushes to their left. Another shot, then another, and neither came even remotely close.

"That could be Hawk's gun," Tim said.

Maureen remembered their dead guide's pistol was missing from its shoulder holster. "Great," she said as she stared down the rifle barrel, aiming at the thicket.

"It was six-shooter, so there should only be three shots left," Tim said. He was behind her now, looking over her shoulder.

They waited.

With a suddenness that made Tim gasp, the world went silent. Every bug, bird, lizard, and frog fell still. Even the wind died away, leaving a stagnant stillness. The smell of dirt and decay saturated the air.

The earth vibrated. Maureen turned to Tim who stared back at her with vacant eyes. The ground shook harder, and a low murmur, like the coming of a great swarm of bees, rose to a fever pitch. A whisper of wind returned, quickly growing in strength, and twisting and rattling the trees. The sound rose like a wave and became a deafening roar. Wind tore through the forest. Leaves were ripped from branches, and clouds of dirt billowed over them as a gale shredded the island.

Two helicopters glided by overhead, the roar of their rotors flattening everything, and ripping thin limbs from trees. The copters were flying low, but Maureen didn't think they'd see her beneath the trees. She looked around for a clearing, but before she could react, the helicopters were gone. The woods settled, and one by one, the sounds of nature returned.

It was 1:39PM.

CHAPTER NINE

Don gave Tobi some water and a few pretzels, and the kid looked much better. He was a ray of sunshine through dark clouds, his innocence refreshing. There were the telltale white lines on his brown face where blood vessels had swollen, and dark patches beneath his eyes, but other than that, he looked alright. If the child was aware of the disease inside him, he didn't let on. The red mark where Lester had slapped him was fading, and Don wondered if it would be as easy to wake him the next time he fell asleep.

They were back within the shade of the large tree where they'd found the boy. Even though the disease had retreated, the sunlight and heat still bothered him, but didn't appear to hurt him in any way. Don took off his jacket, and exposed his arms to the sun's rays, and felt nothing.

In the distance, they heard a dog barking hard, and the faint *whomp whomp* of a helicopter approaching. Don looked at Lester.

"Leave it be," Lester said.

"It's on the way. And we can't bring Tobi with us without real weapons." Don searched the area around him, the feeling that he'd been in one place too long making him nervous. "You'll have to hide here with him while I check it out. Give me the address. I'll go get the bike and weapons, and come get you. We've still got plenty of daylight left. I'll move faster alone, and it's safer for Tobi." The boy watched them with a bemused look on his face, as if he instinctively knew that nothing they were discussing mattered at all.

"I'm not staying in one spot, got me? You said that's how'd they'd get us," Lester said. His shirt was drenched as he sweat buckets.

Don was surprised Lester had listened. "You woke him, so he is your responsibility. Step up your game. I will be back to get you both," Don said.

"So, trust you. That's all you got? That don't work. Got me?"

Don said nothing.

"You want me to stay in one spot, while you run off? How about I go and you stay with Tobi?"

"Come on, Lester. Really? You think you can do this faster and more efficiently than an ex-SEAL federal agent?"

Lester's eyes shifted to his feet. "How long should I wait?"

It was a fair question. He was only halfway to Lester's friend's house, so he'd need at least another half hour, and that assumed everything went perfect. Then he needed to break in, find the guns, and get the dirt bike going. All that would take another half hour. An hour in total. Don decided to double it. "Give me two hours. If I'm not back, hunker down somewhere and help him as long as you can."

Lester nodded.

Without another word, Don strode across the yard, and exited out the front gate. He made a hard right, and wedged himself between two fences that separated the backyard he'd just been in, and the one to its north. The fences were only two feet apart. It was one of those lost spaces where neutral territory had somehow been established. He was able to travel two blocks in that way, only being exposed when he crossed a road. The barking was getting louder, and he heard the mumbles of walkers. The commotion was coming from his left, and he cut across a lawn and hid behind two large bushes in front of a six-foot stockade fence. He inched along the fence, looking for a knothole.

Two Seahawk helicopters thundered overhead, cruising low. They were Navy, getting advanced intelligence in the early hours of a major crisis. If this had happened years ago that might have been him up there, one of the lucky ones patrolling from the outside looking in. Unfortunately, promotion had its privileges.

As soon as copters appeared overhead, they were gone, the sound of their rotors receding. When he found a good-sized knothole, he knelt, looking around first to make sure nothing was sneaking up on him, and then put his eye to the hole.

The dog was trapped on a raised deck partially covered by a large awning. Two stainless steel bowls sat on the deck by the back door. The dog had gone for some food, and the walkers had trapped him under the awning. They were howling, and jumping forward, then pulling back. The dog barked and growled. Foam and saliva dripped from its mouth. It was their dog, no doubt about it.

Don sighed. Should he risk himself to help the animal? His training said no. His mind said no. His body said no. But they were all overruled by his heart, and Don just didn't see the downside to having a big loyal animal at your side when you went to war. Damn the potential logistics. He'd worry about that when the time came.

He continued following the fence. When he came to its end, a white PVC fence picked up where the stockade left off. No gap in between. He quickly retraced his steps, and stopped at the point where the fence came closest to the deck stairs. He crouched as low as he could, coiling like a spring. He hurled his club over the fence, and leapt upward with all the strength he had.

His hands caught the top of the stockade fence, and he pulled himself up. One of the fence tops snapped off, and he fell. His pants leg caught on the broken picket, and he hung upside-down, pinned to the fence as he struggled to free himself. His pants ripped, and he landed on the thick turf.

One of the walkers jumped from the cover of the deck into the hot sunlight, and cringed with pain, but kept coming. It rushed forward with a snarl, teeth bared, black lines crisscrossing its face.

Don grabbed his club and pounded the walker's head, and it went down, writhing on the ground as the disease retreated.

All the barking and wailing had stopped, and every creature on the deck was now looking down at him and the walker he'd just woken. He got up, and ran up the steps, screaming as loud as he could and hitting the railing with his club. The walkers were stunned, and thankfully, the dog was a smart one.

The animal bolted forward, through the stunned walkers, and past Don down the steps. Don jerked to a stop, and followed the animal. They ran down a brick walkway toward the gate that led to the front yard. The walkers didn't appear to be coming after them.

They hid behind the same two bushes Don had prior, panting and catching their breath. Don poured some water into the dog's mouth from a plastic bottle he kept in his jacket pocket. When the dog was done drinking, Don finished the bottle and dropped it to the ground.

He knelt, and took the dog's head in his hands. "I'm going to call you Tank. You like that, Tank?" The dog lifted a paw, and its tongue wagged free. "I can't see how we'll be able to stay together. But what the hell." He rose, and peeked through the shrubs, trying to get his bearings. He should be on Crist Street. The number on the house directly in front of them was nineteen. He had to get to fifty-seven.

They stayed on the same side of the street, creeping as close to the houses as possible. They were forced to cut through a backyard when the road curved, and they came out too far up the street, and had to backtrack to Jerry's house. There was no sign of walkers. A few generators buzzed in the distance, but he heard no cars.

Tank padded beside Don as he mounted the steps to Jerry's place, and peered through the thin glass windows beside the door. He didn't see anyone, but he did see a dull red pulse in the reflection of a poster hanging on the foyer wall. An alarm. If he simply broke the glass and unlocked the door, an alarm would sound. And it would be loud.

The question was, did it really matter? Based on what he'd seen, he didn't think walkers would go out in the full heat of the afternoon sun to chase a loud noise unless they had to. But he couldn't be sure. When the creatures were in large groups they appeared fearless. He'd be in the house ten minutes, and he didn't have time to try and disarm the alarm, which he didn't think he could do. Any alarm worth its installation price has some battery backup, and would work for hours after a power loss.

Don broke the window next to the door with his club, then threw it in the bushes. No way there wasn't a better weapon in a soldier's house. As he reached around and undid the deadbolt, the alarm sounded. It was a thin, warbling squawk that didn't sound right at all, like it wasn't getting enough juice. Don and Tank entered the house, and Don locked the door behind him. Most people kept their guns near and dear to their heart, and what good was a gun if it was in the basement if you needed it quickly? It was Don's experience that most people kept their guns in their bedroom closet, or in a dresser drawer.

They bounded up the steps, taking them two at a time. At the top, he ran down the hall, opening doors and looking for Jerry's room. When he found it, he searched the closet, the dresser, under the bed, but he found no guns.

There was a private bathroom off the master suite, and he looked in the medicine cabinet. He found some aspirin, and a small bottle of pure caffeine powder. Soldiers got the stuff so they could put it in food, or drink. It was actually dangerous, and Don had heard stories about kids overdosing on the stuff.

He went to the toilet, flipped open the lid, and urinated. The sound of pee hitting the water was relaxing, made him feel normal for an instant. Normal was something he wasn't used to. Life hits you when you least expect it. That had been a major part of SEAL training. You never knew what was outside your front door, or where the sidewalk might take you. Don's mother had read The Hobbit to him when he was a young boy, and that message had never dissipated. You had to take moments of peace where you could find them, or else they might never come. Planning a trip or taking a bubble bath usually weren't in the cards, so relaxation had become more of a state-of-mind than a reality. That was Don's normal.

He flushed, zipped up, and went to find better clothing. The soldier didn't disappoint. Don changed into camo fatigues, boots, and he grabbed a heavy Army jacket.

Tank sat and watched Don dress, his cool grey eyes never leaving him. It was amazing the connection people could make with canines. Don had encountered many service dogs over the years, and every one had been different, but they all had been efficient, thoughtful, and obedient. Tank looked like a mix between a Great Dane and black Labrador. His ears were overlarge, and he had boney hips. The dog swiveled its head and looked over his shoulder, as if to say, "Shouldn't we be getting out of here?"

Don patted Tank on the head, and headed back into the hall. He searched the other upstairs rooms. The guns were under a single bed in one of the spare bedrooms. Jerry had a pump-action shotgun, and an old M16. Don lifted the old combat weapon, and racked its slide. He was thrilled until he saw that both weapons had trigger locks, and good ones. He ran his hand down the smooth length of the M16's barrel, and caressed the stock. It looked to be in perfect working order. Jerry was deployed in Iraq, and was most likely using his newly issued M4 carbine. There was a box of ammo for each, and two large combat knives with notched backs.

He inspected both trigger locks, looking for their weakest points. As he did so, Tank started to whimper and run up and down the hall. Don called to the dog, and when he came, he did his best to silence the animal. Nothing moved in the house. He went to the window, and there were no walkers outside.

"Sit here and stay calm." Don sat on the bed. The alarm still rang faintly, but it sounded like it would die at any moment. He was losing daylight. He didn't really want to think about that, but he had to soon. Being out and about when darkness came would be problematic.

Don figured if he got a hacksaw he might be able to cut the trigger guards, and pry out the locks. He raced down the steps, jumping two at a time, Tank on his heels.

The basement door was in the kitchen. They went down slowly. It was dark, and though there was some light streaming through the basement windows, it was hard to see. Don went to the workbench and grabbed a flashlight. He clicked it on, and scanned the tools that hung on pegboard behind the bench. A hacksaw with a new blade hung from a metal bracket.

Don clamped the M16 into a large vise mounted on the workbench as carefully as he could. He didn't want to bend or break anything that would make the gun unusable. Once he was assured the gun was steady, he started sawing at the thinnest part of the trigger guard. Ten minutes later, his arm was ready to fall off, the hacksaw blade was nothing but a butter knife, and he'd barely scratched the M16's trigger guard.

Tank sat, and watched with his calm gray eyes, his tongue hanging out.

Don removed the M16 from the vice and locked down the shotgun. He fastened a new blade to the hacksaw, and started sawing. Twenty minutes later, the final two blades were burnt to useless metal, but he was half way through. He took down a hammer, and the largest chisel on the board. He positioned the chisel in the cut he'd made, and started hammering.

The shotgun's trigger guard snapped after six swings of the hammer, and Don used needle nose pliers to pull the lock free. He made a sling from a piece of rope so the gun could hang from his shoulder as he rode, but still be accessible. When he was done, he loaded half the shells into the gun, and pumped one into the chamber. Then he strapped the M16 over his shoulder, and patted Tank on the head. He'd have to worry about the other gun later. There was an old watch on the workbench with no band, and it read 2:27PM. He pocketed the watch, and ran back up the stairs. He was running out of daylight, and he still needed to go back and pick up Lester and the kid.

The dirt bike was in the garage just like Lester had said it would be. He opened the garage door, put on his backpack, and made sure the M16 and shotgun were secure. The bike started on the second kick, and Don lifted the kickstand. He put it in gear, twisted the throttle, and the bike bolted from the garage into the mid-day heat, Tank hot on his tail.

CHAPTER TEN

Maureen stood dazed for several seconds, the *whomp whomp* of the helicopter fading as the sounds of the Glades rose. The midday sun poked through the tree canopy, and somewhere an egret cawed and a chorus of herons sang. Tim dropped to one knee, wiped his face with his arm, and then shook his head. Maureen was always the strong one, but recent events were beyond even her metal stomach and sturdy mind. She brought up the rifle and scanned the forest. Nothing moved. Whoever they'd been following was scared off by the copters.

They searched for any sign that would help Maureen decide what they should do next. Chasing whoever killed Geoff seemed like top priority back when she and Tim stood on the edge of the woods. Somehow she'd felt braver, more in control, with the steadiness of the Everglades supporting her. That courage had fled when she'd found Geoff's head and the pile of legs and arms.

There was no rational explanation for what was happening. No matter how hard she tried, Maureen couldn't come up with a scenario that explained everything that happened. Her initial instincts suggested animals as the attackers, but it was now clear they were dealing with a human. Perhaps a hermit who'd been living in the swamp for years. Or maybe the person was a fugitive from justice. These ideas made perfect sense until she factored in the head and pile of limbs.

Maureen opened her mouth to speak, then closed it again and bit her lip. Tim didn't look good, and she wasn't sure he could handle what she had to tell him. She needed what little was left of the man, and telling him they were most likely being hunted by some sicko cannibal wouldn't improve his mental state.

"Let's head back the way we came," she said. "Finish going around of the island and join the others." Tim wagged his head and cracked his knuckles. "Then we can figure out how to get out of here."

Tim's mood shifted. "I'm glad you came around." He looked like it was Christmas morning, and he was sitting in front of a mountain of gifts.

Maureen marveled at his self-delusionary skills, and wondered again what they ever saw in each other. Tim was the type of person who let others lead the way and let others take the risks and blaze the trail. She created the path, led others down it, and protected them. The problem was, the more she led Tim by the nose, the clearer it became that there were rough seas ahead for them.

As they backtracked, they came across the pile of limbs, and Maureen was unsure what to do. She knew leaving the arms and legs was akin to providing the animals a feast. Maureen was still a nurse, and she respected the human body, and the sanctity of one's self. The idea of crocs and birds feasting on Hawk and Geoff's body parts made her itch in all the wrong places, and her scar sting, but what could she do? Bring them with her? The ground was hard, and they had no tools to dig. There was no rope or anything to string the limbs into a tree the way they had Hawk's body.

Reading her angst, Tim said, "Honey, you can't be everything. You can't solve every problem."

She snickered. Honey? Then she caught herself again. He was trying to be kind, and she was being a bitch. Also, he had a point. Their lives were in danger and worrying about people who were already dead made little sense. Yet, something gnawed at her. "Is there no way to protect them so they don't get eaten?"

Tim shrugged.

So it was that they left the head and limbs as they'd found them. Maureen didn't like it, but the day was wearing on and she wanted to be off the island by nightfall. What would happen when darkness fell, she didn't want to consider.

As they backtracked, the forest sang with life. Birds squeaked and chuffed in a cacophony of notes that sounded like fingernails being drawn across glass. Green and yellow frogs hid within the banded wildpine that grew on many of the lower tree branches, the airplants brown-striped spiked leaves crawling upward like tentacles. A gray fox darted into a thicket of brambles, and several squirrels fought for supremacy in the trees. Beetles buzzed Maureen as they tore through the trees, and as she brushed them aside, she almost missed the bone fragment.

It was a tiny splinter the size of a pin laying atop an oak leaf streaked with blood. How they'd missed it the first time she didn't know, and then it occurred to her that it might not have been there. They hadn't seen which direction the killer went, so there was no way to know if the fragment was there prior, or if it had been recently dropped. Maureen picked up the leaf and examined it. She'd seen enough broken bones to know the fragment was a splinter caused by the snapping of a bone. She dropped the leaf, and looked back the way they'd come, uncertain. If the killer had come this way, perhaps they should take a different path. They could cut straight across the island.

Tim cracked his knuckles and said, "We most likely missed that on the way in. And think of all the other dangers in the forest; cats, spiders, snakes, scorpions, and all kinds of other creepy crawlies that can sting and bite us much easier than some nutball with bad aim can shoot us."

Maureen considered this. She had the rifle, and could defend herself at need, so she nodded, and started walking again. They reached the patch of dead oak trees, but this time, there was no rattling of a diamondback. Instead, as if it had heard Tim's plea, an adult panther watched them from behind spiked-shaped green leaves, its keen black eyes appraising them. Maureen froze, and Tim bumped into her.

"What the…?" The panther licked its lips, and came forward, slipping beneath the leaves. The cat's black hair filled gaps in the undergrowth, but it moved so fast it was hard to keep track of where it was.

Maureen brought the rifle to her shoulder, pointed it skyward, and fired. She considered what the gunshot might bring, and realized she just sent up a flare and alerted everyone on the island, but she'd seen no other choice.

The cat spun around, and darted back the way it had come, its sleek black body shooting through the foliage. Maureen pulled a bullet from her jeans pocket, inserted it into the firing chamber, and slammed the bolt home. She continued on slower, warily watching every patch of saw palmetto, and every thicket with increased scrutiny.

As they broke free of the forest, Maureen remembered Geoff's body. His torso still lay in the cattails, blood leeching into the clean water, and all the same thoughts and problems that had arisen with respect to the body parts resurfaced. There was really nothing she could do, and pulling it from the water would be no help.

"We can't just leave him like that," Maureen said.

Tim frowned. Nothing moved along the shoreline, and there were no signs of other people. If Saura and Ping or Raul and Wendy had come this way, they'd left no signs of their passing. "We have to leave him. You know that. Maybe we can come back and get him later."

Maureen couldn't even look at him. "Yeah, no croc will munch him. I'm sure they'll leave him be. You're right, though. We'll have to leave him."

With that decided, they started off down the trail again. It seemed like a long time since they'd heard the scream and left the water's edge, but it had only been a little more than an hour. Maureen figured the rest of their party was still lounging around camp, enjoying the ride. She would have to take control when she got back. Raul seemed strong and competent, but he was on a ride, and she couldn't count on him. She couldn't count on any of them. Perhaps when she told them what she'd seen they'd come around, but she doubted it.

Maureen's legs hurt, and she was starving. She looked back at Tim and he trudged along like he had two hundred pounds on his back. The stress and fear had worked their bodies harder than any paddle or hike ever could. Tim up-chucked most of his breakfast, so he was running on fumes from last night's dinner on the plane. She took off her pack, but didn't stop walking. She pulled out an energy bar and shrugged the pack back onto her shoulder. She tore the bar in half and pressed one half into Tim's hand. They ate in silence as they traversed branches, roots, sawgrass, and mangroves.

As they came around a sharp curve in the shoreline, they noticed a great bay stretching into the distance. Dotted with hardwood hammocks and mangrove trees, most of the bay was choked with grass, and would most likely run dry during the arid season. Flocks of birds, and squadrons of insects filled the air, and a light breeze pushed everything toward the island.

"We're about halfway around, I'd figure," Tim said, as he consulted his compass.

They trudged on, the air along the shore hot and sticky. Maureen was soaked through, and her booties chaffed her feet. She took a pull of water from her canteen, and clipped it on her belt. Tim hadn't brought water, and he had to ask for sips of hers. She heard him behind her, barely lifting his feet as he stumbled along, not appreciating anything around him. Everywhere there was life in its purest, most simple form. To her, the animals looked like they had it good.

The path ended, and they were forced to climb through a thick patch of mangrove trees. Tim carried his flip-flops because he was afraid of losing them, and every few minutes, she heard the knock of his leg hitting a tree or a restrained cry as he hit his head or bumped his elbow.

"There!" Tim said, like he'd been floating on a boiling sea, and had just seen land.

The bright colors of the kayaks stood out through the mangroves. Tim walked with the light footedness of a young child skipping through the gates at Disney World. Maureen was relieved, like a part of her had never expected to make it back.

"Hello," Saura said. She sat on a blanket along the shore, wearing only her bikini, and sunning herself as if on a beach.

"Hi," Maureen said, restraining a laugh. Obviously, the woman didn't know a croc could spring out of the water and drag her in like she was a steak. Or that scorpions and an array of spiders were everywhere on the island. She was a nurse, but she wasn't the girl's mother. When Maureen noticed Tim gawking at the young woman, her humor fled, and she punched him hard on the shoulder.

"Shit! WTF!" Tim said.

"Grow the... " She reined herself in. Looking at a pretty woman isn't a crime, and to be expected. Maureen and Tim hadn't touched each other in months, and she'd caught herself gawking at

Raul. She tried to play it off. "You okay, boy scout?" She rubbed his shoulder.

Tim's eyebrows rose, and he smiled, eyeballing Maureen as if verifying she was joking. She smiled back. Turns out drama class prepares you for life better than any other high school subject.

Acting had been her dream when she was younger, and she still fantasized about being the next Nurse Jackie, and she smiled thinking of Raul calling her that. She'd done a community play a few years back and received nice compliments. Often she wondered what would have happened if she'd stuck with it, but Dad's speech on money broke that spell. She still dreamt that one day she'd give it a serious try.

"You guys hungry?" Ping said. He sat on a kayak, gazing out across the water like there was something there that Maureen and Tim couldn't see.

"A little," Tim said, as he rushed past Maureen.

Ping had broken out Hawk's supplies, and was cooking burgers on a small barbeque. Gray smoke blew across camp, and the smell of roasting meat tormented Maureen's senses. She was going to scold Ping, but for what? She accepted a burger, and tore into it like she hadn't eaten in weeks.

Between bites, Maureen asked, "Where are Raul and Wendy?"

"Like, out looking," Saura said.

"Any sign of Conrad?" Tim said.

"Not since you guys left," Ping said, sucking mucus.

"And what are you guys up to?" Maureen asked. They both looked extremely happy, as if they didn't have a care in the world. No doubt the ride.

"Raul said to hold down the fort," Saura said. "We figured we should enjoy ourselves as we did it."

"Yeah, well..." started Maureen, but she was interrupted by yelling as people came from the forest.

"Yo ho ho and no bottle of rum. Yo ho ho and no bottle of rum." It was Conrad, followed by Raul and Wendy, and they were singing as they walked. They came to a halt when they entered camp and stopped singing. Wendy and Raul giggled.

Maureen rolled her eyes. "You find anything?"

Conrad looked at her as if she had just ended his party, and reality had once again crept into his head. "No. Nothing. I heard gunshots, and growling. Found some blood, and two bones, but no sign of Lilly."

"No Sheryl or Geoff either, Mother Teresa," Raul said, then he giggled.

"Yeah, I know where most of Geoff is," Maureen said, and that silenced everyone.

"Like, what do you mean most of him?" Saura said, twisting her hair.

Maureen told her story from first to last, pausing briefly to let Tim tell of the discovery of the head and limbs. When she was done, she'd ruined their ride. Ping cleared his throat and hawked every few seconds. Wendy couldn't take her eyes off Raul as she waited for a reaction. He stood in a trance, eyes down, silent.

Conrad sat on the ground, all energy drained from his body. He looked to the sky, then at the kayaks, then back up at the sky. He was lost, and Maureen understood why. Lilly was most likely dead, and that thought, late in coming to her, kindled a new fear that worked its way through her like a worm. Then she sat down where she'd stood, the damp ground wetting the butt of her jeans.

The late afternoon sun sent errant rays of light through the tree canopy onto the peat shore. The sun felt good and brought new energy and perseverance. Maureen rose, went to the center of camp so everyone could hear her, and said, "I'm taking my chances and getting off this island now. Who's coming with?"

Camp erupted.

CHAPTER ELEVEN

The dirt bike screamed as Don tore down the driveway onto the street with Tank in tow. The dog ran in long, looping strides, and Don quickly left him behind. He'd follow. The motorcycle was making a lot of noise, but he was going so fast he didn't see how any walkers could impede him. So far, he hadn't seen any of them using weapons, or laying any significant attack plans.

Though the noise of the bike didn't attract the attention of any walkers, it appeared to be alerting citizens who hid in their houses. Don had looked for a helmet to cover his head, make it look as though he wasn't breathing the outside air, but he couldn't find one. So it was that his short hair blew in the breeze, and he hoped he didn't inspire anybody to venture outdoors and follow him. The birds, cats, lizards, and other animals simply went about their business as though nothing was happening.

People appeared in their front windows, hiding behind curtains and peering out into the street. Kids waved, a couple of dogs barked, but he was approached by no one, and in five minutes, he was turning onto the street where he'd left Lester and Tobi. As he passed a thick hedgerow, he thought maybe it wasn't a good idea to just tear-ass up the driveway to where his friends waited. Better to shut the cycle down and walk it the rest of the way, and at least make a half-hearted attempt at stealth.

He killed the dirt bike's motor and coasted to a stop next to the line of hibiscus shrubs, their pungent floral scent making him sneeze. His ears were ringing from the intense noise, and his hand shook from gripping the throttle. He was hungry, thirsty, and tired. His last drink of water seemed like days ago. He flicked the kickstand out and left the bike standing in the bushes. Then he skirted the front of the house, slipped through the gate, and headed for the shade tree where he'd left Lester and Tobi.

There was nobody there. No sign of them, or where they'd gone. He pulled his watch free. It read 2:49PM. He'd been gone more than two hours. Even if Lester gave him extra time, clearly he hadn't waited long enough.

"Sure would be nice to have a cellphone," Don muttered to himself. Landlines and most cell towers went out with the power, and whatever lines were available got a recorded message about quarantine or static. His sat phone would work, but it was long gone.

A part of Don was happy Lester and the kid were gone. He couldn't keep taking in strays, and still conduct a fast, successful investigation. When night came, things were going to get much worse, and tomorrow wouldn't be much better. He couldn't be worrying about them and still perform at the highest level. But Don couldn't lie to himself. Some people were good at it, self-justification and borderline delusion acting as a cocoon that many folks hide themselves in. Don wasn't one of these people, and he knew Tobi and Lester had no chance without him.

The backyard was enclosed by a five-foot fence. He went through the front gate, made his way across the front yard, and looked up and down the street, searching for any sign. There was nothing.

Then he heard it. That damn song.

"When the boys hit the brew. When the boys hit the brew. When the boys hit the brew." It was coming from the house across the street.

Tank rounded the corner, and bound up the street, ears back, tongue hanging from his mouth. Don greeted him, and the two of them stared at the house the music emanated from. The death metal pounded through the house's walls, and seemed to be getting louder.

Lester burst out the front door. The hockey stick was cracked, and the speaker on its end hung like a broken wing. Lester ran right at them. He no longer wore his gas mask, his full face revealed for the first time. He looked older than Don had imagined. His gray hair was matted to his brown face, and dark black bags hung beneath his eyes. Tobi wasn't with him.

He switched off the music. "I... I hoped you'd come back. We were waiting for you. Looking out that big picture window there," Lester said as he panted. He turned and pointed to the house he'd just come from.

"Where's Tobi?"

Lester looked at the ground and said nothing.

"Where is Tobi?" Don asked, a bit sterner than before.

"I don't know," he said. "I was watching for you, and he fell asleep, despite the caffeine pill. He was exhausted. I think I was just attacked by his parents. Got me?"

"Then what?"

"He ran from me when his parents showed up."

"Mannnnnn." Don threw up his hands and started pacing. Tank sat and watched Lester with cold gray eyes. "I give you an easy task. Don't ask you to do shit, and you mess it up. All you had to do was babysit a little kid." Don stopped, and the eruption appeared over. Then a secondary surge pushed out more lava. "That why you lived in the drug house? You some kind of loser?"

Lester jerked back like he'd been punched, his face twisting with anger, sorrow, and fear. "Yeah, I am. I've lost everything. You're a great detective."

Every muscle in Don's body tensed, his stomach grew hot, and he began to sweat. This man saved his life and had provided him the lead for the very clothes on his back. "Lester, I'm an ass. I am."

"This is an out-of-control situation. No one's perfect. Not even you."

That reality struck home for the first time in Don's life. Despite the fact that he'd been a military brat, and then went on to the academy, he'd never focused on how little control he had. Now that he had none, he began to think about the choices he'd made.

The decision to forgo a family, a home, a place to belong, had been made so long ago Don didn't remember consciously making it. This is what he did. It was what he'd always done. Except, that wasn't true. He'd become jaded. His power, though it hadn't corrupted him, had molded him, and he became dependent and soft. Worst of all, he was alone.

He'd gotten lost once at a huge carnival in Europe when he was a young boy. His father insisted that he didn't stray, so of course, Don had spent the entire afternoon doing just that. He'd never forgotten the feeling of terror and utter loneliness as crowds of strangers streamed around him, paying him no mind. It had been the longest two hours of his young life.

"I can't see looking for him," Don said. "We've got to move on."

"He's probably with his parents. They'd both transformed. He told me so. And when those two walkers showed up, they knew him. If they weren't his parents, they were adults who knew him well."

That was a crazy, yet insanely soothing thought. Therefore, Don did believe it possible. "Let's go. The bike is down the block a little." They started off down the street. Lester appeared downcast. He hung his head and didn't look at Don.

"Here," Don said, handing Lester the M16. "Still has the trigger lock on."

Lester nodded and took the weapon. "I can pick that given a little time. Jerry lost his keys all the time."

"Where's your mask?" Don asked, as they threaded their way through the bushes to where the bike waited.

"When I lost Tobi, I freaked and ripped it off. Couldn't believe I'd done it. I deserved it, I guess."

"Don't worry. I doubt very much it's airborne. I think we're dealing with a contact killer, but I'm no scientist," Don said. They walked a bit further, and Don grumbled, "What the…?"

The dirt bike was gone. Don felt his pockets, and confirmed that he still had the bike's key. Whoever… or whatever took it, couldn't have gone far. Don's mind started revising plans and making new calculations. His stomach went cold. Everything he'd tried so far had met with more than expected problems. He'd wasted three hours getting supplies and the bike, an effort that was in jeopardy of being wasted.

Tank barked. Don went to him and saw the tracks from the motorcycle's knobby tires. They followed the tracks through the hibiscus, and came out on a patch of grass. The street was to Don's left, and a fenced-in alleyway cut between houses to his right. This piece of neutral territory was six feet across. Weeds ran along the fences, and a thin path of dirt cut down the alley's center. A manhole cover marked the center of the path, and Don surmised that power and communication lines ran under the service alley along with waste pipes and the water supply.

The motorcycle's tire tracks ran down the dirt path. Don didn't like the long confined space. It reeked of a trap. So far the walkers had been mostly mindless, but he'd also seen them act with thought and purpose. What real choice did he have? Going around and picking up the trail at the other end would expose him even more, and he needed the motorcycle. Then he remembered the oldest trick in the book.

Don picked up a broken piece of concrete the size of a golf ball. He ordered Tank to sit and stay. Then he hurled the stone as far as he could, making sure it hit the fence. It nailed a section of white PVC, cracking it. Nothing happened at first, but after a few seconds, a section of stockade fence further along the alley slide out of place.

Don lifted the shotgun and turned to Lester. He'd removed the speaker from the broken hockey stick and now held it in his hand. "You ready?" Don knew where they were and had the advantage.

Lester nodded and turned on the music. They started down the alley, staying in the weeds and hugging the fence. When they were halfway, Don realized he'd been wrong, a section of fence hadn't been removed. He turned quickly, acid burning a hole in his stomach. The end of the alley was clogged with people wearing gas masks. They stood in a line holding knives, clubs, and a couple had guns. A crowd was gathering at the other end. They were trapped. He'd been tricked into thinking he knew where they were, where they'd come at him, only they had circled back.

Somewhere, the dirt bike sparked up, and then receded into the distance. The men were inching into the alley. The air stank of gas and smoke, as some of the walkers carried torches. Tank was barking, and the loud heavy metal music wasn't having its normal effect. As Don looked closer, it became clear why.

These weren't sleepwalkers at all.

This was exactly what Don had feared. The younger generation lived their lives hoping for the zombie apocalypse, and many retail companies, military surplus stores, and religious zealots only threw fuel on the fire started by video games, the internet, and the panic-driven media. These people had no idea what they were doing, and Don cringed at the thought that they might even be having fun.

The lead guy yelled for Don to drop his gun. They were getting closer, and guns were being sighted, and arrows notched to bows. There were people coming from the other direction as well. Don fired two shots in quick succession, blowing a huge hole through the PVC fence to his right.

Tank was the first one through, followed by Lester, then Don. All three of them ran blindly through a border of bushes, out onto a thin patio, and then fell headlong into an in-ground pool.

Don came up sputtering and coughing. Lester was already climbing up the steps out of the pool, and Tank was swimming as only dogs can, legs pumping, head nodding above the water. Don scrambled toward the nearest side and was impeded by the shotgun slung over his shoulder. That caused a moment of panic as he looked frantically toward Lester. The pack was still on his back, but was dripping wet, and he still held the M16. Hopefully, the ammo wasn't drenched.

Don pulled himself from the pool, and ran after Lester and Tank. A shot rang out, and a bullet whizzed by his head, and planted itself in the side of the stucco-covered house in front of the pool. There were muffled screams as the men chasing them tried to communicate through their gasmasks. Another shot rang out, and Don was hit, and went down on the patio that surrounded the pool. He rolled over and leveled his gun on his pursuers. He knew it probably wouldn't fire, but he had no other options. Don didn't want to shoot these confused assholes, but he was fighting for his life, and one of them shot him.

The gun did fire, and the first man through the bushes got blown from his feet. He pumped the slide, waiting to shoot again. A moment passed. Then two. Don jumped up and headed for the house. Lester stared through the backdoor window, waiting for him. The door was opened a crack. He had forty feet to go.

"Duck!" Lester yelled through the crack, and Don dove randomly to his left, and went into a roll. A bullet hissed by, and Don came out of his roll facing his pursuers.

He pulled the trigger, and the gun didn't fire. Don racked the slide, ejecting the wet cartridge. Another bullet hissed by. Don's closest pursuer was firing on the run, with what looked like a rifle.

That was difficult even for an experienced marksman, and he guessed the only firing range these chumps had been on was Xbox.

He fired twice, and both times the powder caught, and expanded. The double boom, and the felling of two of their crew, paused the rest of the rouges. Don got up and ran to the house. His leg hurt like he'd been stabbed, but he felt lucky. When he reached the house, Lester let him inside, and they barricaded the doors and lower windows as best they could.

Don collapsed against the wall and pulled his fatigues down. The bullet had passed through his upper leg, and missed bone. Lester arrived with a damp towel and cleaned the wound.

"Damn," Lester said when he saw Don's bare legs, which were a spider web of scars. "You look like a ragdoll."

Don chuckled as he tore off a piece of drapery that hung beside him, and tied off his bleeding leg. He'd been shot and stabbed a few times before, and he'd been lucky this time. "Yup. Almost all of it for king and country. That long one there is from a particular perp. The ass had fallen, but in his panic, he continued to fire his machinegun. The eight shots almost severed my leg, but if he hadn't fallen, I'd be dead. This gunshot is nothing by comparison."

But now he had an open wound.

There was an explosion in the distance, and the ground rumbled, and the windows shook. Don and Lester looked at each other. "What do you think that was?"

"No idea. Get that pack off and get the ammo out. Make sure it's dry."

Lester realized what Don had minutes ago, and fear tugged at his face. He opened the backpack, and looked up at Don. "Looks fine. The inside of the bag is dry."

They all collapsed in the living room, stealing glances out the front window. It was quiet outside. Don let his head fall in his hands. He wasn't used to losing, and he didn't like the feeling.

He was still dripping wet, and he was watching a puddle form when he heard the M16's trigger lock hit the floor. He looked up to see Lester breaking down the weapon.

"That was fast."

"I've picked that lock many times."

"And you know how to field strip an M16?"

"Jerry taught me. We used to time each other and see who was faster." Lester got up and disappeared into the kitchen. When he returned, he had a dishrag, and resumed his work cleaning and drying the weapon. Don laid his shotgun next to Lester, and he and Tank went through all the rooms in the house. Other than a cat hiding beneath an upstairs bed, there was nobody there.

When Don got back, Lester handed him the M16. "Locked and loaded. This stuff should be good to go as well." He'd dried the bag, and had it on his back. The shotgun was slung over his shoulder. "Check this out," Lester said, as he went to a side window. A Nissan Pathfinder sat in the driveway. "And look." Lester pointed at a key box.

Don looked at the keys, then out the window at the Pathfinder. He'd tried the subtle game. I hadn't worked. If cops wanted to join him at Rick Dempsey's place, great. Otherwise, it was time for him to move on.

Night was coming.

CHAPTER TWELVE

Maureen had made up her mind. She was leaving the island. She understood the arguments for staying, but wasn't willing to risk her life further since she believed there was no worthwhile reason. They'd argued all the angles, let all their self-interests show, and there was no agreement. The group's verbal rumble echoed through the Glades as everyone tried to have their opinion heard.

"You want me to leave Lilly?" Conrad said.

"And Sheryl," Raul said. He had snapped out of his trance, and his eyes were burning red as his ride ended and he came back down to earth.

Everyone was talking at once, and Maureen tried to stay patient, but listening to the babble was just making her angry. She stared at the ground, watching a scorpion work its way toward Saura's blanket. The scorpions that inhabited southern Florida couldn't kill you, but they packed a nasty sting. Maureen hoped the scorpion didn't get much closer, because then she'd be forced to decide if the young woman got a painful bite. She was afraid of the decision she might make.

"Leave? What about the trip?" Saura said. To Maureen, it looked as if the insect doubled its pace.

"Will we get our money back?" Ping asked.

"Enough!" Maureen yelled, and the bickering ceased. "Conrad, do you have a plan? We searched most of the island." Ping started to speak, and Maureen shut him down. "You've been sitting on your ass while the rest of us have been searching. You don't get a say." Ping looked pissed for an instant, but didn't speak.

"Look some more," Conrad said. "That's my plan. To search until I find her."

"Even if she can't be found, or doesn't want to be?" said Raul.

Maureen smiled. There was sober Raul. In her mind, he was the only other rational person in the group. He'd said what Maureen had been thinking. Perhaps Lilly and Sheryl didn't want to be found, though the idea made no sense at all. What made more sense was they were dead, or being held by whoever had killed Hawk and Geoff.

"What do you mean they might not want to be found?" Conrad asked.

"We should have found them. Maureen and Tim went around the entire island, you walked across it, and Raul and I zigzagged from shore to shore. Don't see how we all could have missed them, Conrad," Wendy said.

"And all that blood," Raul said. They'd seen puddles of blood, but no body parts.

Nobody wanted to say what everyone else was thinking; Lilly and Sheryl were dead. The group's angst was clear. It was like when they lost a patient in the operating theatre. There was always a delay before the patient was pronounced dead, as if the surgeon and his team were giving the deceased person one last chance to claw back from oblivion.

What made this situation more complicated was there were facts that supported the idea that Lilly and Sheryl were still alive. If they'd been murdered, why weren't their body parts with the others? Why hadn't they found their bodies, or any signs of the women? Her nurse's brain nudged her, and said, "How do you know you haven't found signs," and Maureen realized she didn't know for sure. She had assumed those were Hawk and Geoff's limbs because of the head, but how did she know some of the limbs weren't Sheryl or Lilly's? She hadn't examined the arms closely, but she had looked at the hands, and she didn't remember any nail polish, or a missing finger, nor did she recall thinking the limbs were anything other than male body parts. Then there was the bone splinters and blood.

"So you're saying they're gone? Dead?" Conrad said.

No one answered him. Instead, the group broke up, even though no decision had been made. Saura lay back down on her blanket, and Ping flipped his burgers. Apparently ride, besides giving you a thrill and improving your mood, made you a moron. Maureen ran forward and stepped on the scorpion that was now two feet from Saura's blanket. The Asian woman jumped and looked up at Maureen with contempt.

Maureen lifted her bootie, and the crushed scorpion lay there.

Saura's expression softened. "Thank you," she said.

Raul, Wendy, and Tim followed Maureen, unsure what to do. Conrad cursed and stalked off. He stopped by a large Gumbo limbo tree, and leaned against it. He covered his face with his hands, and slide down the trunk until he sat with his back to the tree, head in his hands.

Raul lifted an eyebrow. "We can't get stuck in the kayaks after dark, and I don't recall seeing another island this big where we could stop," Raul said.

"That's probably a good thing," Wendy said. Her ride appeared to have ended as well, and she looked mostly sober.

"How so?" Tim asked.

"Because we can secure a small island, or a hardwood hammock, because we'll be able to see everything," Maureen said.

"Seems we'd be more exposed to crocs," Tim said. Maureen looked at him as if he were a dead rat.

"We have the rifle. Someone can stand guard, Bradley Cooper," Raul said.

"So we'll paddle until dusk, and then in the morning we paddle out, and get the police," Maureen said.

"I can mark Hawk's location on the map, and we'll know right where to send them," Tim said.

The four conspirators nodded agreement. Maureen watched Raul as he stared at Saura and Ping, who were still oblivious to the severity of the situation despite the fact there was a blue kayak strung in the trees containing Hawk's body. Conrad still sat with his back to the tree, his face buried in hands, whimpering. "What about them?" Maureen asked.

Raul shrugged, then said, "They're adults. We can't make them come, and I understand why Conrad doesn't want to leave."

"And it's probably best he's not alone," Wendy said.

All valid points. "Okay, then. I'll tell them what we're doing while you get packed up and ready to leave." Like a huddle breaking, they went their separate ways.

Maureen and Tim were explaining things to Ping when Raul and Wendy joined them, and informed Maureen they were ready to go. Ping and Saura didn't know what to do. They didn't want to leave Conrad, but the fact that everyone else was leaving had brought Ping back to reality. Maureen doubted Saura ever lived in the reality she did.

Conrad still sat next to the tree, and every few minutes Maureen would glance in his direction to make sure he was all right. He hadn't moved, and the sobbing had stopped. He looked to be asleep. Seeing Maureen's concern, Tim said, "I'm going to try to talk to him one more time."

"I think we should go, sweetie," Ping said, and Saura's face crinkled as she twisted her hair. "We'll check in at a nice hotel on Miami Beach, and enjoy the rest of the week, no worries." At this, Saura seemed to brighten, and she got to her feet, and pulled on her sweatpants. Ping got their stuff together.

Tim screamed, a blood-curdling wail that silenced the natural chorus, and tickled Maureen's spine.

Tim was fighting off Conrad, who was trying to bite him. Conrad's eyes filled with blood, and veins swelled where the white lines on his face had been. He bared his teeth, and half-wailed, half-yelled something unintelligible. The two men danced in a spasmodic pirouette, Tim adjusting to the jerks and pulls of Conrad.

Saura screeched, and Conrad paused as he turned to see the source of the noise. Tim lashed out with his foot, knocking him backward, and out from under the tree cover into the afternoon sun. It was Conrad's turn to shriek in pain. He grabbed his head, turned, and rushed Tim. They collided, and the two men tumbled into the shade of the forest, and this gave Conrad new life.

Maureen and the rest of the party watched as Conrad gripped Tim by the arms, and bit his shoulder. Tim wailed again, but this time it was the cry of a man who was losing his battle to survive. Maureen couldn't believe what she was seeing, but in that instant, all the pieces of the confusing puzzle dropped into place.

Conrad punched Tim in the head, a powerful roundhouse that took his legs out from under him. Tim hit the ground, his head smacking a tree root, and knocking him unconscious.

Tim swelled, his face grew purple, and blood vessels pulsed through his skin. He grunted and pounded his chest with his fists. He barely looked to be the man he'd been five minutes earlier. His boyish features were gone; his mischievous eyes, baby fat cheeks, and ever-present smile replaced with swollen orbitals, distended cheeks, and a blood-thirsty sneer.

Conrad, seeing Tim's transformation, pulled back and hid in the shade, watching. Tim straightened, and appeared dazed, as if he had just been born.

"What the hell?" Raul said.

Maureen brought up the rifle, but didn't know where to point it. The tip of the gun flicked back and forth between Tim and Conrad, until finally it stopped on Conrad. Tim yelled, and appeared to be trying to communicate with Maureen, but when she didn't respond to his guttural questions, he charged her. As he exited the shade, and was drenched by sunlight, Tim cringed, agony filling his distorted face, but he didn't stop. The pain seemed to drive him on, and he came at Maureen with a single-minded purpose.

Maureen was unfazed. Her resolve had grown, and she deftly shifted her aim, and pointed the rifle at Tim as he lurched across camp. She felt pity for her deformed husband, even as he tried to kill her. Beneath the hatred, engorged muscles, and blood was a man she'd once cared about, a man she had loved.

Tim was twenty feet away and coming on hard. No one else moved, as Tim appeared to only have eyes for Maureen. Her finger tightened around the trigger, and she felt the steel beckoning her to fire, but she couldn't. Tim staggered closer, the movements of his body disjointed and abrupt. When he was ten feet away, he let loose with a battle cry, and Maureen squeezed the trigger.

The shot hit Tim in the leg, and spun him around. He staggered, teetering on the edge of losing his balance. He sat, more than fell, and as he did so, he mutated yet again. Blood drained from his eyes, the swelling of his muscles relaxed, and the veins retreated, leaving only white lines. His lips slipped back over his teeth. He squinted, his mouth fell open, and then the pain from the gunshot wound rocked him. His face twisted, but all aggression had left him.

"Okay," Raul said. "Am I in the Twilight Zone?"

"What happened?" asked Tim. Maureen still pointed the gun at him. "You shot me?" He sounded incredulous.

Maureen pulled back the rifle's bolt, discharged the empty shell, and loaded another. The sound of metal on metal as Maureen slammed the bolt home reverberated across the island, and everything paused again. Her pocket no longer bulged with bullets, and she estimated she only had three or four left.

Conrad stood in the shadows, watching. He looked like a demon as he crouched next to a tree; eyes red and his skin swollen and tight.

"Tim, you need help," Wendy said. As she went to help, Raul thrust out his arm and stopped her. He was eyeing Tim, who minutes before was crazed, but who now appeared to be himself again.

"His wife is a nurse," Raul said. "She can handle it."

Blood seeped from the leg wound, and Tim clamped his hand over it to slow the bleeding. The bite on his shoulder bled through his shirt, but didn't appear as bad. Every few moments, he would look up at Maureen, fear and anguish filling his face. He was Tim again, but like the night he'd hit her, the landscape had dramatically changed. Whatever disease Conrad had, he'd given it to Tim when he bit him.

Maureen handed the rifle to Raul, and went to her husband. She no longer loved him, but couldn't leave him. As that thought floated through her mind, she knew that's exactly what she needed to do. Lilly and Sheryl were either transformed, or had become food for someone who had. But how? There was no disease, no malady that turned people into monsters.

The ride.

It was 6:47PM. Not much daylight left, and they had a long way to go. With Wendy helping, Maureen dressed Tim's wounds and stuffed some aspirin down his throat. He claimed he felt fine, but he didn't look fine. The deep white lines on his face and body were the most worrisome. They were signs of the infection, and she'd seen similar scars on Conrad's face when he'd reappeared at camp the first time. He'd already mutated once, but had woken somehow.

"We need to wake Conrad before we go," Maureen said.

"Are you crazy?" Wendy asked. "Just leave him be. The police will be here tomorrow and a doctor can decide what's best."

"But what's keeping him from hurting himself? Or trying to attack an animal and getting himself killed. I say we wake him, and at least give him a chance to control his own actions. If he transforms back, what has been lost? It's not like he's coming with us," Maureen said.

None of them had anything to say to that. Maureen thought about how Conrad had sat against the tree, his weariness overtaking him. "I think all he needs to do is stay awake," Maureen said, and behind her Conrad wailed.

CHAPTER THIRTEEN

Miami is a sprawling metropolis. Neighborhoods bleed into industrial areas, and major interstates cut through the city like veins, with no regard for what's around them. As Don left the relative quiet of West Miami, he saw that the crisis had escalated while he'd been fighting for his life in the burbs. The side streets leading out to County Road 953 were clogged. Cars and people packed the street. The poisoned air lie worked only if residents stayed in their houses, but all it took was one brave soul to start an avalanche of humanity.

Some wore gas masks, others had clothes tied about their noses and mouths, but most didn't even attempt to filter their air. Don sighed in frustration. As he'd expected, the day had worn on with no real news, and people became restless. The hourly information provided by the emergency broadcast system wasn't nearly enough, and it took less than a day for the citizens of Miami to realize the true nature of the quarantine.

Whatever they had on hand would have to last for the near future, and possibly longer. Everything above Alligator Alley was shut off, and that meant money was worthless for the near term. Goods were now currency, and though the military would arrive in force soon, no soldiers patrolled the streets, and only a few cops. This wasn't surprising. Wars and military actions took days to ramp up. Deployments took time. The early responders were in the sky, and most likely among the people he watched, but it would take time to get large numbers of soldiers into place along with all the support necessities that came along with them. In addition, the president would never authorize putting large numbers of troops into potentially infected areas without them having the appropriate protection from the disease.

Don stopped the car. "Stay here," he said. Lester said nothing, and Tank made no sound. Don saw no one carrying guns, so he left the guns in the car. He threaded through the crowd to the corner, and looked up and down 953. The road was totally blocked going north, and the southbound lane was impassable, as people had given up trying to go north, and turned around and headed south. Many of the cars were abandoned, and it looked as though Southern Florida was hours, if not minutes, away from total anarchy.

Babies needed formula, kids needed candy, and adults needed liquor. Lines of people trailed from all the stores along the road, and gas stations were packed with people on foot, filling all kinds of containers. Without power, water would soon become limited as the massive pumps used to move drinking water through the city and its suburbs failed to provide the lifeline that human beings can only live without for three days. All fuels would soon be gone, or stockpiled, as would medicine, food, and all the other necessities that precipitated daily life.

The crowd flowed around him, forever moving like a mass of algae on the surface of a pond. These were people used to having the things they needed, and in the days ahead, they would be forced to create a new reality, one designed around survival, not comfort.

Don went back to the car. He sat there several minutes, staring out the windshield at the people aimlessly going about their business. He felt Lester and Tank's eyes on him, and shared their angst. The truck rumbled to life, and Don turned the car around. "Lester, do you know how to get over by Chicken Key via the back roads?"

"Not really, but I'll try. Turn there," Lester said, and Don made a sharp left and headed south. "The good news is we don't need to cross any bridges." Tank looked on from the back seat, peering through the windshield as if amazed at what he was seeing.

Soon backup generators would run out of fuel, and refrigeration and life support systems would fail. The information super highway would be reduced to Route 6 on Cape Cod during holiday traffic. Hospitals, sanitation, and most other government services would cease to function, and some already had. The military would provide provisions and aid, but that would take time, and many people would initially see the government and military as the enemy. Rumors upon rumors mixed with toxic bullshit would leave no agency free from criticism. As the quarantine dragged on and things become scarcer, and the rule of law receded into the past, survival would pit man against man in a way Don didn't want to think about. As the population of sleepwalkers increased, the uninfected would find themselves alone amidst a sea of mindless enemies who saw them as threat, and as nourishment.

He'd done this. He'd made the call that morning, and been so very sure of himself. As he thought about the chaos and deprivation he'd inflicted, he felt anything but sure. With an information void, folk's imaginations were left to run wild, and that never turned out well. People would see enemies where there weren't any. The citizens of Miami were now outcasts, and even now, there were newscasters relaying to the rest of the world what was happening, and he could imagine what they were saying. There would be YouTube videos, and public suicides. Parents would murder children using God and Heaven as their justification. The elderly would take too many of their pills, and cops would put guns in their mouths as they watched their loved ones become sleepwalkers. All this would play out via a bloodthirsty media looking to cover the apocalypse live at five.

As if on cue, a white line inched across the sky. Since southern Florida's airspace was restricted, Don surmised it was a recognizance plane. They were taking pictures, evaluating the situation. If Don was in charge, he'd want boots on the ground by nightfall, but that was a tall order. Putting in too few troops invited confrontations from citizens and walkers. Don estimated he'd need 10,000 troops to do the job right, but could deploy with as little as a 1,000. He'd create a command post in the city. Take the tallest building and some surrounding territory to start, and work outward from there. But he wasn't in charge. He wasn't anything anymore. The thought of going up to a cop, or soldier, and telling him or her he was a high-ranking federal agent, but he couldn't prove it, was comical. As would be any attempt to gain access to local police installations and military fortifications. He looked and smelled like a bum, and no talk of ID codes and threats of weather stations in Antarctica would work this time.

Don still had his universal ID number etched in his brain, and he knew a way he could contact his people, but what would he tell them? He still didn't have a sample of the chimera—if that was the cause—and he didn't understand how it was being transmitted, so there was no sense taking the risks necessary to contact his people until he had something to tell them. In the end, that would be his only way out. Time was his enemy now. The more time they wasted, the worse things would become, and by dawn, the uninfected would be the minority.

Every clue so far brought him back to the drug chain, so he'd continue on this line of investigation until he found a better path, and Dempsey, the biggest local ride dealer, was his strongest lead. He also had to consider the possibility that all the ride might not be tainted, and perhaps the release of the virus had been targeted, and only certain ride was poisoned. There also may be carriers with no symptoms infecting others.

He also had no way of knowing what the researchers were up to. They might already be well on the way toward a remedy. That would make things easier. Don doubted it, however. He'd been as close to patient zero as possible, and he was on the case only fourteen hours.

The plan had been to slip from West Miami and head to the coast down by Coral Gables, but they had to detour far out of their way. Every time they would get going in the right direction, they'd have to backtrack or turn down a side street. Several communities had already taken it upon themselves to seal off their roads and limit access to their communities. This was probably a good idea, except when night fell, people would go to sleep.

This posed a unique problem. Since the disease was reversible, that meant all the infected could potentially be saved. So what would the world think when they found out the US was gunning down its own diseased citizens?

They hit an industrial area that Lester recognized. He guided Don through a series of parking lots that moved them further southeast, and they came out in another neighborhood. Several small groups of people loitered on porches and in garages, and they watched them as they passed. The faces that appraised them were haggard with fear and worry. Don could almost smell the change in the air as the scent went from shit to rose-scented money. The houses had more stone than a medieval castle, and the foyer windows were taller than a cathedral's. Not all the roads were blocked or fortified, but individual houses were. Vehicles were used as walls, and men brazenly displayed their weapons through the front windows of their living rooms. He didn't blame them.

"We're not far now," Lester said. Sweat dripped down his face and rolled off his arms.

Don turned to him like he had just realized Lester was there. "Thank you for everything. I'm afraid your help is needed again."

Tank barked, and Don and Lester looked at each another. "You too, buddy," Don said. "When we get to this place, we will infiltrate the house and take this guy Dempsey so I can question him."

Don had turned his attention to Lester, and for a few moments, he hadn't been concentrating on the road. When he focused on the lane before them, two cars blocked his way. He stood on the brake, and brought the car to a screeching halt. He glanced in the rearview mirror, and two cars blocked the road behind them.

"Shit," he said. They were in a well-off area, so these folks must be desperate. Three of the cars blocking the road were SUVs, with the fourth being a large sedan. Don thought perhaps he could go around them, but the cars could simply adjust their positions and block him.

He had two options. Ram them, or get out and try to reason with them, and possibly help them. The second option would have normally been Don's choice, but given the current situation, he felt pressing forward would be the safest and best option.

He dropped the Pathfinder into reverse and put the pedal to the floor. Tires hissed and squealed as the truck jumped backward. "Buckle up, bitches," Don yelled. Lester pulled on his seatbelt, and Tank wedged himself behind Don's seat. The two cars behind him had little time to adjust their positions. The Pathfinder crashed into both vehicles, and the SUV and sedan were pushed aside with a thunderous crunch of metal, and the wailing and ripping of rubber and plastic.

As the Pathfinder broke through the blockade, the front wheels jerked to the left and the truck's momentum almost flipped it. Don compensated, and pulled the SUV back on track. The rear of the Pathfinder was smashed, but somehow, the gas tank hadn't exploded. The hatch was gone, and pieces of broken plastic fell to the road as he braked hard and came to a stop. He opened the window, and looked back up the street. Lester handed him the M16, and Don sighted it up the road, awaiting pursuit.

There was none.

The cars didn't move, and Don thought perhaps they were unable. No one exited the vehicles. Don gave the M16 back to Lester, turned the truck around, and continued on their way. Don hadn't been alert enough, and he'd almost put himself in an atrocious position. He could assume nothing any longer. Just because people owned expensive houses, that didn't mean they wouldn't panic. He would have expected that type of attack in the poorer sections of the city, where things were most likely already frantic. This neighborhood had generators, and basement freezers stocked with filet mignon and fresh fish. The people who lived here could sustain themselves for weeks if they were mindful of rationing, but Don doubted they would be. With the proliferation of apocalyptic fictions and end-of-the-world nutballs, there was no shortage of survival products. The US government even recommended its citizens create an emergency kit, and Don knew that at that very moment, many people were cursing themselves for not having done so. Americans are a spoiled breed, and these folks were most likely aggravated with the inconveniences they'd already experienced, and were certain things would be back to normal soon. This delusion was the greatest threat to their survival.

Don knew this because he hadn't grown up rich. His parents worked hard, but they wanted for nothing essential, and even had a bit left over for luxuries like off-base housing, cheap vacations, and cars. His father had once told him it wasn't the size of your car that mattered, but the size of your dash. When he was very young, he accepted the phrase, not having a clue what his father was talking about. When he was twelve, and his father had returned after a long deployment, he asked what he meant by "the size of your dash." His father had explained the dash was a metaphor for life. On your tombstone, your date of birth is listed, with a dash, then your date of death. It was the dash that mattered.

"There," Lester said, and Don was stirred from his reverie. "Turn there. That will take us to the circle."

Don followed instructions, and soon they were passing even bigger, gaudier houses. They repulsed him. Don saw every angle of his country as he travelled from town to town. This was extreme excess, and Don felt a surge of anger rise in him. These people would most likely shun him and look down their noses at him. He was a civil servant, after all.

They hit a traffic circle, and took the outlet that led over a small land bridge that turned into Paloma Street. Don pulled the car off the road next to a large patch of mangrove trees and killed the engine.

It was 6:54PM.

CHAPTER FOURTEEN

Waking Conrad turned out to be more complicated than expected. Like approaching a cornered animal, getting close to the sleepwalker was difficult. Maureen said shooting him was a last resort, though she thought they were close to that point. Urgency gnawed at her, but she couldn't just run away like a coward. She worried for Tim, but not in the way she should. Maureen was concerned he would fall asleep or get knocked out and transform again. She *should* be worried about losing her husband, the person she loved. More than once, she'd almost suggested that Tim try to wake Conrad, since he was infected.

"Just graze his leg, Bridget Jones," Raul said. "You want me to do it?"

"What if we throw a rock at him?" Wendy said.

Maureen shook her head. She knew a rock wouldn't work, but she didn't think putting a bullet in the man was right. There was no way she was giving up the gun for any reason, so she'd have to pull the trigger. Conrad hid behind a tree, staring as the group discussed his fate. His hands shook as he gripped the thin tree, and his mouth hung open, but Maureen didn't doubt he would attack at the first sign of a threat. She thought he understood them on some level, because transformed Conrad appeared to react to certain suggestions, or if Lilly was mentioned.

"What if I punched him real hard?" Raul said.

"You think you can get close enough? Without him hurting you?" Conrad was a big man, and he wasn't himself. If he got hold of Raul, Conrad would injure him, or worse. There was the rifle, but for all she knew, Conrad would take a bullet and just keep on coming.

"For certain? I can't say, but we need to do something. We're losing daylight," Raul said.

As the minutes ticked by, Maureen's angst grew. Already the sun was starting its descent to the horizon, and soon it would be dark. She wanted to be off the island by then, even if it meant they only paddled a mile or two before they hunkered down for the night. "We can try waking him with a long stick?" Maureen said. She hated the idea and thought it was cruel and evil. It wasn't Conrad's fault he'd caught whatever disease was ravaging his body. She didn't see how they could poke the man with a stick like he was a rabid animal, but she couldn't think of another way.

Raul didn't wait for the group's approval. He retrieved a long, relatively straight branch from a nearby tree, and stripped it of all leaves and smaller branches. When he was done, he had a pole of about fifteen feet, which was an inch around. "Now what?"

No one spoke.

The Glades choose that moment to erupt with life. Two birds fought in a nearby tree, insects hummed and buzzed, and leaves rattled in the wind. Conrad felt the change in the weather as well because he craned his neck, sniffing the air. Maureen watched him, shame filling her. An egret crash-landed and scattered a flock of night herons. The herons screeched and howled as they rose into the sky, disappearing over the trees.

"While I was making this pole, I thought of a problem. Won't he run when I approach him?" Raul said.

"We'll surround him," Ping said.

Nobody moved. Now that they had come to it, no one wanted to start, so Maureen did. Holding the rifle before her, she moved into the forest, and worked her way around Conrad, who tracked her every step.

Wendy, Tim, Ping, and Saura fanned out as best they could, and created a wide circle around Conrad as he jerked his head around in a crazed attempt to see everything at once. Raul held the pole standing up at his side as he inched in, but Conrad didn't appear to be paying any extra attention to him.

The creature that had been Conrad barked and wailed as the circle around him got tighter. He clawed a tree, and whimpered. Maureen pitied him, and she wondered if Conrad was aware of what was happening, but unable to control his body? Did he understand where he was, and why they were treating him like an animal? Did he know he'd mutated or recall being Conrad? Was there any trace of the man left in the transformed monster? All she knew was when he woke, he wouldn't recall what had happened and he'd be himself again.

Raul raised his hand, and the group halted. A tense minute passed, then Raul walked toward Conrad, the tree branch held at his side. Everyone else stayed where they were. Maureen had a wild thought. What if he rushed one of them? Maureen had the gun and Raul the pole, but what did the rest have? Her worries were for naught, because Conrad's attention was focused on Raul.

Conrad stepped away from the cover of the tree and stood in the open, as if daring Raul to come for him. Veins pulsed as his muscles swelled and stretched his skin. He seemed to have grown, his arms and legs tearing what was left of his shorts and tank top.

Raul paused, eyeing Conrad as he worked himself up. Raul appeared to shrink, his confidence fleeing, and leaving him to stand alone with his stick. To Maureen, the closer Raul got to Conrad the smaller the tree branch looked. When he was fifteen feet away, Raul let the pole fall from its vertical position until he held it out before him.

Conrad didn't appear to see it at first, and continued with his aggressive bluster; jumping up and down, pounding his chest with his fists, and watching Raul with eyes that told of a hatred Maureen couldn't fathom. Saura gasped when Conrad lashed out at the pole with his fist, smacking it hard, and pulling his hand back in pain. Conrad let loose with a wail, and several birds took flight.

Raul thrust forward with the stick, but missed, as Conrad knocked the pole aside. Conrad's lips slid back revealing bloody teeth—he looked to be smiling. Raul drove the pole forward again, and missed, but this time Conrad got hold of the tree branch. He yanked on it, and Raul dug in to prevent him from getting possession of the pole. They circled each other, both men holding the stick.

The awkward dance ended when Raul used Conrad's own momentum and let go of the pole at the perfect moment. Conrad fell back and dropped the stick. Raul grabbed it, and attacked. He caught Conrad on the bridge of the nose, and pasted him to the ground, blood pouring from the wound.

The blow didn't wake Conrad. It enraged him.

He snapped to his feet. Blood dripped down his face, jaws chomping air as he staggered forward in a spastic tumble, staring at nothing as if asleep. He screamed, and ran at Raul, who stood like a knight with no armor, holding his lance with the halfhearted posture of a man who can't believe what he's seeing.

"Raul!" Wendy yelled.

Conrad sprang when he was five feet from Raul, but Wendy's wail had roused her husband, and he brought the tree branch up just in time. The impact knocked both men from their feet, as they once again wrestled with the pole between them.

Raul took a hand from the branch, and punched Conrad with everything he had, but it barely fazed him, and he didn't wake. Conrad grunted, and drove Raul back with the pole. As they wrestled, Maureen and the rest moved in, closing the circle further. Maureen held the rifle at the ready, and she kept Conrad in her sight, prepared to fire at the first sign of Raul losing.

Raul took his hand off the pole again and punched Conrad in the face three times in fast succession. Three brutal rabbit punches that snapped Conrad's head back like a target at a carnival shooting gallery.

Still, he didn't wake.

Maureen watched Conrad fight for his life, and to her it seemed as though the last rays of the setting sun were burning his skin. She remembered the white scars on his face, and how he had already woken once. Maybe once was all you got? Perhaps it was harder each time? Maybe it was best to do as Wendy had suggested, just let the doctors handle it tomorrow morning.

"Wait," Maureen yelled. "Raul, leave him be. Forget it."

Raul looked over at her as he struggled with Conrad. "What?"

"I'll explain. Just back away. Please."

Raul let go of the stick and stepped back. Conrad was stunned, and paused. Raul stepped back again, and Conrad swung the pole, just missing Raul as he dropped out of the way. Conrad snarled and moved in.

A loud guttural scream echoed from the mangrove trees along the water, and then another from across camp toward the woods. Maureen's head bounced back and forth as she searched for the source of the cries. The screams didn't sound like any animal she'd ever heard. She scanned the forest, and blocked out all sound as she concentrated. There was movement in the trees. Did she see long hair on the silhouette?

Maureen heard the warning yells of Raul and Ping, and turned to see Conrad rushing at her. He was twenty feet away, and coiling to spring. She surmised he had figured her to be the biggest threat because she had the gun, so Conrad maintained some cognitive abilities. These final thoughts floated through her mind as she brought up the rifle.

Conrad lunged at her, and she fired. The shot hit him in the face, and half his head exploded in a spray of blood, bone, and skin. Saura screamed, and Maureen dropped the rifle. The world spun, and she fell. In that instant, her humanity ran from her, and though every muscle in her body had tensed, she felt a peace she couldn't explain. A release she'd never experienced before.

Conrad's body lay next to her, and so it was that Maureen saw the man she had killed. In death, Conrad returned to his original state. The blood retreated from his remaining eye as it receded into its socket, and the white scars reappeared on his skin as the veins returned to their normal size. Blood poured from where the other half of Conrad's head had been, and white brain tissue, blood, and bone could be seen in the shattered skull. Maureen heard someone wretch, then another, and soon the entire party was dry heaving, and bent over in pain.

Maureen got to her knees, grief overtaking her. When she was eight, Maureen had announced to her father she wanted to be an actress when she grew up. Maureen recalled feeling so very sure of it. Her father had explained how that wasn't a realistic occupation, and then followed up with a dissertation on money. Maureen had decided right then that if she had to work her entire life just to survive, at least she would help people while doing it. Her entire existence had been about getting by while helping others. Now she was a killer. Self-defense and war are excuses, maybe even good ones. But the reality of mankind is there are some that can kill, accept those excuses, and move on. There are those who cannot, and Maureen was afraid to find out which one she was.

She looked up, and everyone was standing around her, their faces drawn. None of them looked her in the eye. Maureen didn't see Tim. Raul came forward and put his hand on her shoulder, and picked up the rifle.

"You did what you had to do," he said, and gave Maureen the gun.

She took the weapon with a trembling hand, but as her fingers wrapped around the metal barrel, her tension eased. She got to her feet, felt for the shells in her pocket, pulled one out, and loaded it into the rifle. Maureen dusted herself off, and brushed the tears from her eyes. Her stomach rumbled, and her throat was so dry it hurt when she swallowed.

The Everglades had resumed its constant chorus, as if nothing had happened. A gust of wind pushed across the water, and the smell of peat and rot filled the air. A flock of wood ducks flew overhead in tight formation. Somewhere, a frog bellowed, and a gator grunted. Maureen said, "Where is Tim?" No one knew. Maureen had come to terms with the fact that he couldn't leave the island, so his disappearance had solved a problem.

They searched the areas where Maureen thought the yells had emanated from, and they found possible footprints in the peat, but nothing in the mangroves. The sun dropped below the horizon, and a dull grey light bled over everything. The group looked to Maureen for guidance, their faces filled with fear, angst, and pain.

A gunshot rang out, and the ground next to Maureen erupted in a spray of peat. She dropped and rolled, pointing the rifle into the forest, but it was impossible to see anything in the half-light of dusk. In the back of her mind, she heard Tim yelling. She tried to ignore him, but the memory forced its way through. If whoever was shooting at them had Hawk's gun, they only had two bullets left.

When things had been quiet for a sixty count, Maureen said, "To the boats. We're out of here."

CHAPTER FIFTEEN

Don and crew stayed out of sight the best they could as they snuck up Paloma Street toward Dempsey's house. It hit Don then for the first time that Dempsey might not be at home. If that be the case, he'd search the place and hunker down for the night, and reevaluate.

The landscaping on the block was lush and tropical, and if Don had been sick from the excess before, now he was vomiting inside. Houses that were too big for their property lined the street, each with a nice-sized backyard that went to the canal. On the opposite side of the waterway, mangrove trees stretched as far as the eye could see. There were boats of all shapes and sizes tethered along the docks, but Don doubted the boats were useable. He guessed the second somebody fired one up and headed for the sea, they'd be met by a patrol boat. The Navy would also run sonar along the entire demarcation line, monitoring everything under water.

All the homes were clearly marked, and there weren't many of them on the thin peninsula. Don was surprised the residents hadn't blocked the short land bridge they'd crossed. That would have effectively cut the entire neighborhood off from the chaos, except for swimmers. When they reached the house before Dempsey's, they ducked into a thick patch of saw palmetto and surveyed their target.

"Tank, you go with Lester, you understand?" Don pointed to Lester. "Hide in those bushes right to the side of the front entrance. I will sneak around back, enter through the rear, and then let you guys in. If I fire two shots in fast succession, I want you to break into the house. See that garden rock?" Don's finger pointed through the foliage across Dempsey's small patch of lawn.

"Yes," Lester said. Don wondered what the man had done in life before his luck had turned. He seemed attentive and smart.

"Pick that up and sail it through the window next to the door, and then reach through and let yourself in. Ignore the alarm if there is one."

"What then?"

"Find me. If I call, that means I'm in deep doo doo."

Lester laughed for the first time since Don had met him. A thin sheen of sweat covered his brown face.

Don covered Lester and Tank as they got into position. Tank followed instructions better than a human child, and as Don crept from the palmettos, he barely saw his two friends as they hid awaiting his call.

There was a fence separating the front yard from the back, and Don vaulted over it. It wasn't without effort. He was breaking down. Though he was used to not sleeping for long periods of time, he needed to eat, and recharge the batteries. If he didn't get coffee soon, the people of Miami might have a bigger problem than the walkers.

Don hid in a tight corner where the fence met the house, and listened hard the way they had taught him in Quantico. He took slow, steady breaths, categorizing sounds and blocking out the useless ones. He tuned out the beating of his heart, and a bird pecking at a tree trunk. Pain pounded through his leg wound, and a trickle of blood ran down his leg. A gentle breeze pushed across the mangroves and brought the fresh scent of hibiscus. No sounds came from within the house, and nothing moved on the street out front.

He inched along the house into the backyard. A large deck with a spiral staircase heading to a higher deck protruded from the back of the structure. A hot tub sat in one corner, and various types of furnishings were strewn about, no pattern visible that Don could discern. There were sliding glass doors all along the rear of the house, but he couldn't see inside due to dark blinds that were pulled closed. He paused there, listening.

The blinds swayed slightly, and Don pressed against the house, making himself as small as possible. Someone, or something, had just walked past the blinds. He waited. Sweat dripped down his forehead, and he felt the griminess of his clothes and body for the first time. Don was filthy, and he was never filthy. He was never neat and clean, either. He liked to think he resided in that in-between zone where real men lived.

The blinds moved again, and whoever was moving within was heading away from him, because the swaying of the blinds cascaded away from his position. He followed along the back of the house toward the spiral staircase. If he could get up it, he might surprise Dempsey.

A board creaked, and a figure moved across the deck above. Don raised the M16, his finger grazed the trigger, and the rifle loosed six shots. He hadn't meant to fire. He cursed himself. Why not just send up a flare! He examined the ribbon of bullet holes on the decking, and as he moved, he calculated the approximate age of his weapon. Don knew this particular M16 had been retired a long time ago, because the newer versions of the weapon had a burst feature, giving you the option to fire a single round, or three in quick secession. Don recalled reading that this modification alone had saved 40% in ammo costs.

He put his back to the wall. There was an arch to his left with a path that led around the house, and a retaining wall to his right that surrounded the lower part of the spiral staircase.

"Stop!" The voice came from overhead. "I don't want to shoot you. Tell me what you want and I'll give it to you."

"My name is Don Oberbier, and I'm an investigator for the government. You are Rick Dempsey? I need to ask you a few questions."

Laughter echoed off the concrete walls. "Yeah. Sure. And I'm Batman."

Don said, "Can we talk?"

"About what? Why me?"

"You know Teapot?"

No response.

"Ride dealer from West Miami?"

"Never heard of him," said the voice from above.

"Really? You have a thing for his sister, Sherri, don't you?"

No response.

"Whatever happened before is the past. I don't care what you've done, but I need your help now. Your life depends on it."

"Is Sherri okay?" The voice was timid. It was the sound of a person who had already given up.

Don moved away from the wall, and climbed the stairs to the upper deck. He held the M16 before him, his index finger resting on the outside of the trigger guard. There was nothing to be gained by accidentally shooting the guy before he could speak to him. He'd gone up three steps when the fourth creaked loudly.

"I've got a gun! I will shoot you! How do I know you are who you say you are? And not some dope head coming after my stash?"

"You don't. But I have two others with me, and they're already in your house, with guns trained on you." Don started up the steps again. His leg ached, but he'd learned over the years you always had to keep moving forward, especially when a suspect was talking, and being rational.

Dempsey fired, but it was a poor effort. The bullet came nowhere near him. Don fired into the sky as he ran up the stairs, and burst out onto the deck.

Dempsey wasn't what Don had expected. He'd expected a young, golf club type, who made his money selling junk bonds and junk to local rich suckers, but what he found was a drug dealer. The man was short, stocky, and bald. Tattoos covered his arms, and he held an old six-shooter before him in a shaking hand. The barrel of the gun moved in small, steady circles as the guy's hand shook. There was no way he'd be able to fire the weapon straight. This was a guy who went through a lot of trouble to appear tough, but who was a coward, a person who had others do his dirty work. Why that help wasn't with him now, Don didn't know.

"Put the weapon down, and I'll put mine down," Don said.

Dempsey eyed the M16, and Don could almost hear the gears of the man's mind turning as he figured his odds. He lowered the weapon, and Don lowered his. Don strode forward, snatched the gun from Dempsey's hand before he could protest, and stuffed it in his back pocket.

"What the...?"

Don grabbed him by the shirt and dropped him into a deck chair. He racked the slide on the M16 for effect and pointed it at the man's head. All haughtiness left Dempsey. Don said, "Is there anyone else in your house? People, dogs, in between things?"

Dempsey looked startled for an instant, and then shook his head no.

"I will shoot you if you're lying." Don pressed the rifle barrel into Dempsey's cheek. "You sure?"

"Jessie is in there, but that's all."

Don sighed. "Jessie?"

"My dog."

Don forced the gun harder into the man's face. "What kind of dog?"

Dempsey pointed toward the sliding glass doors. A poodle the size of a New York rat lay behind the glass, watching them as if bored.

"Inside," Don said.

The interior of the house was extravagant, but dirty and worn. The decor definitely had a woman's touch, but by the look of the place, said woman had fled long ago. Glass doors opened into a large living room, and Don told Dempsey to take a seat. Keeping the M16 trained on the man, Don went to the front door, and let in Tank and Lester. Jessie followed, and when Tank came in, there was some sniffing and circle walking, but in the end, Jessie jumped up on a chair where she appeared content to sit this one out.

Once they were all in the living room, Don said, "First things first. We're staying the night, so there's no rush. You have coffee?"

Dempsey nodded.

"Lester, take Mr. Dempsey into the kitchen and watch him while he starts a pot of coffee. Look for dog food while you're in there. Grab yourself a drink, Rideboy. I meant what I said. No one is getting hurt. Yet." Lester rose and jerked the shotgun toward the hallway. When Dempsey was in front of Lester, he turned back to Don, who mouthed, "Searching house."

There was no one else in the house, and Tank and Don were back in the living room, relaxing on the couch, Jessie watching them, when Dempsey called in from the kitchen. "You want cream and sugar?"

"Black," Don yelled back.

Lester and Dempsey emerged from the kitchen. Lester held a bottle of beer, and Don's coffee. Dempsey held a dog dish mounded with cut-up steak and a tumbler of brown liquor. When Lester handed Don his coffee, the agent looked down at Lester's beer, and shook his head.

"You need coffee, and I need beer. What's the difference?"

Don was going to answer that one impaired you, and one didn't, but then he remembered that wasn't true. He lifted the mug to his lips and sniffed the coffee as though it were a flower. Then he took a sip, and his stress and pain eased. "Like taking that first sip of wine after you've crossed the desert."

"Scent of A Women," Dempsey said, and Don chuckled.

Dempsey put the dog dish on the ground and Tank went to it and sucked down all the meat in seconds, and then returned to his spot next to Don.

"So, you ride?" Don asked.

"Nope," Dempsey said. "No idea what's in that shit. I tell my customers that. They don't care. Drugs do sell themselves. Death at twenty milligrams."

"Why do it? Is money that hard to make?"

"Yeah, it is. My parents came here from Cuba with nothing but the clothes on their backs. I swore I'd never let my children live like I did. Not knowing where their next meal would come from."

"And it doesn't matter if you kill people in the process?" Don checked himself; he was getting off track. "Listen, I'm—"

"I don't kill anybody. I've tried to cut people off and they threaten to report me to the police. Most of my customers like a little ride, not a never-ending adventure."

"I take it Rick Dempsey isn't your real name?"

"Dad thought an American name would help us blend in. Minority benefits hadn't been an issue when he had to decide." The room fell silent for an instant, then Dempsey said, "How you doing, Lester? Sherri okay?"

"No. She's not okay. She's one of them."

Dempsey's face twisted. "How'd you let that happen?"

Neither man spoke, and then together they said, "Teapot."

The sound of static came from down the hall. "My police scanner. I have a good one so I can listen in on what the pi… cops are up to. I got it hooked up to a car battery through an inverter," Dempsey said.

"You have news from outside?" Don was excited.

"A little. Most of the military traffic is in code, and I only get sporadic commercial traffic, but it sounds as though the quarantine is holding. There are no other reported cases outside the infected zone. They're still saying to stay inside, and that troops and vaccines will be on site shortly."

"Have you heard anything about the walkers?"

Dempsey looked perplexed, and then understanding spread across his face. "Two times. That's it."

"What?" Don said.

"You can only wake someone twice, and then they're lost. At least that's what the local police are saying."

"Two second chances. Do they know loud noise scares them?" Lester asked.

"Not that I've heard."

"We'll listen later when we're done talking." Don rose. "I need a refill."

Don paused in front of the sliding glass doors. To the west the sky was a bruised purple-black. To the east was the ocean, and lights stretched across the horizon like a strand of Christmas decorations. The Navy had created a barricade a seagull couldn't pass through unseen, but there were many boats that had dropped anchor inside the blockade and were waiting things out on the sea. The last rays of the setting sun fell across the canal, and the water sparkled. Dusk fell over the backyard, the color slowly draining from the world. It would be dark soon, and he needed food and rest. He heard a faint scream far off, and a dog barking.

"Sleep tight, Miami," Don muttered, as he went to get more coffee.

CHAPTER SIXTEEN

Darkness settled like a blanket over the Everglades, and the creatures that controlled the day retreated to their sanctuaries as the animals of the night started their shift. Crocodiles, giant centipedes, cotton mice, owls, and snakes ranging in the size from simple garter snakes, to enormous pythons, searched for food amidst the decaying plants at the water's edge. Maureen recalled reading that researchers estimated there were over twenty thousand spiders per acre of land in the Glades, and arachnids were among her least favorite things.

A waning gibbous moon rose in the sky, and the stars glowed bright. Shadows lurked under every tree and plant, and the vines that hung over everything writhed and slithered in the faint breeze. Maureen snapped on her flashlight, and scanned the area around the kayaks. They were a hundred feet away at the water's edge, the bright colors standing out in the darkness. She snapped off her light, and slipped it back into her jacket.

Ping and Saura were already moving slowly toward the boats, crawling along the edge of camp, keeping as low as they could. Wendy followed them, but Raul waited with Maureen. Maureen worried about those last two bullets, if it was Hawk's gun being fired at them. She hated making assumptions, and assuming their attacker had only two bullets was a big one, yet everything she'd seen so far pointed to that conclusion.

"You want me to go first? I can cover you with the rifle?" Raul whispered.

"Nay. You go. I'll cover you." The rifle with three shots was all Maureen had. Tim was gone. All sense of order and rationality had fled, and now it was her and three bullets against whatever came her way.

Raul grunted, and dropped into an army crawl, and worked his way to the boats. Soon Maureen couldn't see any of her companions as they disappeared into the murky darkness. She felt more alone in that moment than she had ever felt in her life, and angst paralyzed her. She kept the rifle at her shoulder, but saw nothing of consequence. Minutes passed, and she heard nothing from her team. To Maureen, the day grew darker, and the night symphony grew louder. The trees and vines swayed, her mind drifting, her focus waning. Weariness and hunger were getting the best of her.

She remembered lying with her brother in the field behind their house on summer nights, watching the stars roll by. She missed Calab, and a day didn't go by that she didn't remember the good times they'd had. All the support he'd given her, all the love. He gave himself to others, as she did, and he had paid for that service with his life.

The snap of a tree branch brought Maureen back to the present. She scanned the forest, and then searched for her friends who should be close to the boats, but she couldn't see anything in the darkness. She pulled her flashlight from her jacket and held the metal cylinder in her hand. If she turned it on, she might give away everyone's position, and this rational idea fought with her rising panic. She needed to know what was happening. She refused to delay any longer, hiding in the bushes, waiting to be attacked or shot.

"Raul," said Maureen in a low, restrained voice. No response. "Raul?" No response. Now Maureen thought something was wrong. Pointing the flashlight in the direction of the kayaks, she clicked on the light.

Maureen jumped back, and dropped the flashlight. It hit the soft peat and drenched most of camp in pale white light. Ten paces away, Lilly sized up Maureen. The young beauty's blonde hair was matted with blood, and she was swollen like an engorged tick. She growled, but shied away from the light as she staggered forward. Ping, Wendy, and Saura lay prone by mangroves, about half way to the kayaks. Raul was nowhere to be seen.

Maureen raised the rifle, and to her surprise, Lilly raised a revolver, and for the first time, she saw that one of Lilly's fingers was missing on her left hand.

Then Raul was there, like a flash of light firing from the shadows. He took Lilly down with a clean tackle, and the gun flew from her hand. Lilly screamed, and bit at Raul as he fought her off. They rolled across the peat, and leaves, spiders, and decayed vegetation clung to their clothes. Lilly went for Raul's face, and they tumbled out of the flashlight beam and disappeared in the shadows.

"Up and to the boats," yelled Maureen, as she ran for the kayaks. This time it was her turn to get decked.

Sheryl hit Maureen with a tree branch as she sprinted by her hiding place within the mangroves. Maureen went down, and the air left her lungs in one painful push. She lost the rifle as she writhed on the ground in pain. Sheryl was on her, and she pulled and tore at Maureen's clothes, trying to take a bite out of her as the two struggled.

A gunshot popped in the darkness, and then another. Sheryl went limp. Blood, bone, skin, and entrails splattered the ground, and the sight of Sheryl's blood seeping into the soft peat made Maureen cry. She screamed as Sheryl's body fell lifeless before her, the old woman transforming back to herself as she took her final breaths. She'd been shot by Wendy.

Maureen dropped to her knees, trying not to look at the old woman's face, but failing. In the moonlight, Sheryl stared up at her with vacant eyes, white scars crisscrossing her liver-spotted face.

Raul was still wrestling with Lilly, and when they rolled back into the glare of the flashlight beam, Wendy rushed to his aid. Ping and Saura were at the water's edge, pushing the kayaks out into the still, dark water.

The rifle lay on the ground ten feet away, so Maureen figured Wendy had shot Sheryl with Hawk's gun, and it was now empty. She crawled toward the rifle, her muscles aching, her stomach burning. She reeked of sulfur, rot, and smoke. Her fingers sank into the damp peat as she clawed toward her gun. As near as she could tell, Sheryl hadn't bitten her, and she felt no open wounds. She reached the rifle and scooped it up as she got to her feet. She moved in a wide circle around the struggling Raul and Lilly. Wendy held the revolver out before her, trained on Lilly.

"Let him go, or you're dead," Wendy yelled. Maureen wondered if the woman knew the gun was empty.

Lilly didn't heed Wendy's command, and continued to wrestle with Raul who appeared to be losing. Answering Maureen's question, Wendy hurled the gun, and it clunked off Lilly's head.

This enraged her, and she tossed Raul aside, and came at Wendy with a battle cry that woke every creature for miles around.

Maureen fired, but missed. Wendy went down, and Lilly tore her throat out. Blood, skin, and a chunk of muscle dangled from Lilly's mouth, and she jeered at Raul.

Raul screamed, and tackled Lilly hard, pounding her into the ground as she transformed. Maureen pulled him off as Lilly became herself again. Her big blue eyes cleared, and the swelling eased. She watched Maureen and Raul like a child, confusion and pain etched on her face. She was bruised from Raul's pounding, covered in Wendy's blood, and there were several gashes on her hands and legs, but other than that, she appeared to be all right, minus one finger.

Lilly saw Conrad's body and wailed in pain, tears leaking from her eyes as she shook with grief. She ran to him, and that seemed to remind Raul of Wendy, and he went to his fallen wife who lay broken on the peat a few feet away. Wailing and crying filled the night, as Raul bent over Wendy's lifeless body, and Lilly mourned over Conrad.

"Sorry, but I wouldn't touch them," Maureen said. Sometimes being a nurse sucked. She pulled a shell from her pocket and loaded it. That left one bullet in reserve.

"Hey," yelled Ping. He and Saura were in kayaks, and they floated into the sawgrass. As always, they'd gotten as far away from danger as possible. They were paddling back to shore now that the commotion had died.

Maureen's heart raced, and her ears rang, and she bit her lip. Lilly made her nervous. Only moments before, the woman had been trying to kill her, and now she didn't know what had happened. This posed a unique ethical dilemma. Should they leave Lilly? How could they bring her? It was the same thing as Tim. Neither of them could leave the island until they were treated by a doctor, and the infection within them was killed.

The moon glared down like an accusing eye, and the animals of the glades went about their business as though nothing had happened.

***

An hour slipped away while the group pulled themselves together. When adrenaline flees, only hunger and weariness remain. Ping and Saura rested while Raul wept over his wife. Lilly sat away from everyone next to Conrad with her back to the group. She seemed to understand the sickness had made her an outsider.

Maureen gave her a wet rag to clean her face, but before she could ask the girl how she was, Lilly said, "We hadn't known each other long. This trip was his idea. He said he wanted to get to know me away from all the distractions of life. I really liked him. He was so kind." She reached out a hand and ran a finger over what was left of his scarred face. She turned to Maureen, and asked, "Does my face have scars like that?" Maureen nodded. "I'll wait here. You guys go." Lilly turned her attention back to Conrad, the issue settled.

Maureen was always amazed at the courage of women. Giving up a life for the better of the group. "What if you fall asleep? Or Tim attacks?"

She didn't answer, and Maureen didn't ask again. "I'll see you tomorrow. We'll leave you food and coffee. Stay awake."

Maureen joined Saura and Ping. Ping had Hawk's camp stove going so he could cook them a fast meal. Everyone was starving, and exhausted, but Maureen was upset with him, though she didn't know why. The threat level was low, but it seemed inappropriate to be eating given what they'd just been through. Tim was the only unknown problem, but he didn't have a gun, and he was alone, so what was she worried about? To this, her logical brain reminded her she might not have all the facts, and there was always Lilly.

The sweet smell of stew pervaded camp, and Maureen's mouth watered, and hunger took over. Raul left Wendy's side, and went straight for the cooler. He pulled out a beer, opened it, and downed it with one long pull. Then he looked back at his dead wife, tears streaming down his face, creating what looked like fresh streams running through dry dirt. "This is seven kinds of bullshit. She didn't even want to come here," he said. Raul rubbed his eyes, and lowered his head. He looked up when he smelt the food. His bloodshot eyes studied Ping as he cooked, and the ridiculous image of a cartoon character changing into a hotdog while the wolf licked his chops flashed through Maureen's mind.

"Have another beer, man. Bring me one. I have a cup of stew here for you. Do you good," Ping said. Raul's face softened and filled with sorrow.

With a look back at Wendy's body, he nodded, and grabbed a few beers to ease everyone's nerves. Saura helped Maureen get cleaned up, but no matter how hard she scrubbed, Maureen still felt dirt on her face. Lilly joined them at one point, eating some stew and drinking the stiffest cup of coffee Maureen had ever brewed. When she finished, she went back to sit beside Conrad. Maureen figured Lilly sensed the group's unease at her presence—it had been easy to see.

Several evening bats fluttered out of the tree cover and zipped across the water. Crocs huffed and croaked, and the constant buzz of insects made it hard to hear a person speaking. A fox sat in a nearby tree, watching them with glowing eyes. The ground slithered and writhed with ants, spiders, millipedes, frogs, snakes, and beetles. The Glades were constantly moving, as the water, vegetation, animals, and weather danced with a grace that made Maureen wish she hadn't had a second beer.

Her stomach gurgled. She'd packed herself with stew, and the beer and gentle breeze had lulled her toward sleep. She thought something moved in the forest, a dark shadow that looked to be hiding behind a tree, but when she turned on her flashlight, there was nothing to be seen.

"Shit!" Ping yelled.

Flames rose at the water's edge. Ping had knocked over the cooking stove, and before it had splashed into the water, it set some grass on fire. Smoke poured across camp, and the wind picked up, stoking the fire and spreading it. In the darkness, the flames glowed against the water, and they spread quickly as sawgrass tops burn like tinder. Soon the fire covered half the field, and it had spread to the mangroves, where it appeared to be slowing.

The blaze roared toward the kayaks, and if they didn't get underway soon, the boats would be lost. Flames lit the smoke-filled sky, and in minutes, chunks of the island would be on fire. As the fire reached the peat shore, which separated the forest from the shallows, it was dying out.

Maureen sprinted for the kayaks, and Ping and Saura followed. As she ran, Maureen looked over her shoulder and saw Raul standing over his dead wife in the firelight. Smoke and ash covered his face and hair as he knelt beside her.

Maureen and company jumped into kayaks and pushed off without worrying about supplies, personal effects, or food. The sleek boats slide into the water, the burning sawgrass tops fizzled and popped as they reached water and were quenched. Steam and smoke filled the air. They stroked hard. Raul jumped in a boat and pushed away from shore. Maureen smiled. In the background, illuminated by the firelight, Lilly watched them leave.

"Dig'm in! Dig!" Maureen yelled, and in a few minutes, they had moved away from the blaze, into a nearby stream that led out into the wide bay to the south of the island.

Maureen spun in her seat and watched the glow of the fire in the distance. Saura, Raul, and Ping trailed after her, their faces dirty and sullen. Something darted into the shadows. It had looked like a person in a kayak.

Tim, Maureen thought, and doubled her stroke.

CHAPTER SEVENTEEN

As the night deepened, so did Don's angst. Under the light of day, things always appeared clearer, more direct, but the darkness brought worry, apprehension, and uncertainty. They sat in Rick Dempsey's living room, each pulling on their preferred drink, and staring out the large picture window in the front of the living room, but there was nothing to see. Blackness pressed in on them, and Don's thoughts drifted to West Miami, and County Road 953, and the chaos that was surely raging there. Lester was in an armchair across from Don and Dempsey, who sat on a fine leather couch. Both dogs had a place on adjacent chairs, and neither had made a sound in some time, like they were off the clock.

"So, you're a special agent?" Dempsey asked.

"Last I checked," Don said, as he worked on his third cup of coffee.

"You sure don't look like one. How'd you end up in here?"

"Same as you. Unlucky, I guess," Don said.

The room fell silent. Tank's gaze shifted from Don to Dempsey, but Jessie was uninterested. She curled in a ball facing away from them. Two windows were open a crack, but they heard nothing except the sea breeze, and the rattling of mangrove and palmetto leaves.

"What brings you here, Don? Having a federal agent protecting me during the apocalypse is cool and all, but what could you possibly want to talk to me about?"

"When was the last time you took ride?" Don asked. The man had said he didn't do ride, but Don didn't believe him.

Dempsey's eyes shifted to the floor, he rubbed his chin, and then looked back at Don, all confidence gone. "Last night. I made a pick-up, did my runs, had a meeting or two, and then came home to chill."

"Any strange effects? Anything different than you've experienced before?"

"Nope. I had a nice clean ride, and felt good after. No worries. Why? You think ride is causing this?"

Don wasn't sure how much he should tell Dempsey. The man was a criminal, and those tendencies didn't evaporate just because there were monsters running around. This wasn't a typical investigation, however. He needed this man to cooperate, and tell the truth. So he decided to do the same. "I don't think so, unless some folks are immune. I've seen people who have the disease, but who don't use ride."

"Why me then?"

"I'd hoped you would be able to help with that. The ride chain is still my best lead, and many of the early victims were connected to the drug. Tell me about where you get your stuff. Be as specific as possible."

"I get my ride from the same dude everybody does, Drago out in the Glades," Dempsey said.

Lester laughed. "The guy knows Drago was kind of a dick and a gutless coward, right? Harry beat his ass regularly," Lester said.

Don laughed. Harry Potter had become such a large part of pop culture that even he knew something of the boy wizard, despite having never read a word of the books or seen any of the films. "Not Draco. Drago. It means dragon," Don said. Lester looked away.

"Everybody gets their ride from this guy? Does he make it?"

"He's the main guy. His stuff is the best, and he's cheap. Those two things mean more money for me. As to who makes it…"

"What's his real name?"

"No clue. Only a chosen few know how to find him. I've heard he has connections to Cuban gangs, and ties to the communist party in Cuba," Dempsey said. He took a sip of his drink. "He's a scary dude. Missing half his face from a knife fight when he was a boy. Ruthless and violent. The guy scares the piss out of me every time I see him."

"So you know how to get to his place?"

Dempsey hesitated, then said, "Screw it. Doesn't matter now anyway. Yeah, I can find him."

"Does he sell anything else? Other drugs? Weapons? Anything?"

"Not that I know of. I give him money and he gives me the stuff. We didn't even talk last time. I remember, because I was in such a hurry to leave he made me come back for my change."

"Your change?" Don asked.

"Yeah. He owed me a hundred bucks. This guy likes things to be even to the penny."

The hair on the back of Don's neck stood at attention. "Do you still have that hundred?"

"Four twenties and two tens, actually, but no. I stopped at the market on my way home, plus I needed to make change for a few customers."

Don got up and paced back and forth across the plush carpet. If it wasn't the drugs, what else do drug dealers deal in? Money. If the chimera was on the money, that would make perfect sense. The federal government had been concerned with the possibility of paper money being used as a weapon for years. They feared it provided a good host device for terrorists looking to spread a virus, and all kinds of bacteria lived and even thrived on paper money. All circulated paper money has fungus and bacteria on it.

"Have you slept since you saw Drago?" Don asked, though there were no scar lines on the man's face. If money was the disease vector, then Dempsey was most likely infected. Don didn't feel the need to inform the man just yet. If he knew he was infected, he might choose to give up.

Dempsey scratched his head. "No. I came home and partied, and I tried to sleep, but couldn't."

Now that Don had a potential how, he wanted the why. "This guy Drago a radical? He ever say anything that would lead you to believe he'd want to kill all of Miami? That wouldn't be good for business."

"Drago don't care about nobody but Drago. Story goes they took him from his mother when he was a boy because he was a big kid. They forced him to be part of a gang that robbed, murdered, and raped its way across Cuba and it made him harsh and unfeeling. He ain't all there. Some say he's here because his gang sees the US as an excellent market for their product. Others say he's here to destroy the Yumas."

"Yumas?"

"Like Gringo."

So Drago wanted to destroy America. Get in line. "Let's go see what's happening on the police scanner," Don said.

They went to a downstairs bedroom where Dempsey kept the device. The room was sparsely furnished, but it had a desk on which the scanner rested. Dempsey turned it on, and they listened to static for several minutes before voices boomed from the speaker.

"Kitten, this is cat. You copy."

A pause, then, "This is kitten. Go ahead."

"Bring home the milk," said the voice, and Dempsey turned the scanner dial in frustration.

"The military uses code, but not the cops."

They listened for a while as the police still operating within the city limits did their best to deploy dwindling resources, but it didn't sound like they were having much luck. Walkers were all over the city. Emboldened by the darkness, it sounded as though things were getting out of hand, just as Don thought they would. Any doubt he'd felt about the quarantine fell away. If it hadn't been for his quick, decisive action, they would be facing at a worldwide pandemic, and still might be.

Don went back to the living room where Lester and Tank waited. Food lay strewn about the coffee table, and Don leaned over and grabbed a handful of potato chips. Dempsey strolled back into the room and plopped down on the couch. Candles burned at the center of the table, and they cast wavering light about the room. Outside, piercing screams shattered the stillness, and Don went to the window, peered out, but saw nobody.

When he looked back at Dempsey, he had his head back, eyes closed. If he was infected, and he fell asleep, they'd need to be ready to wake him. They needed him.

"You nodding off, partner. Got me?" Lester said, and Dempsey's eyes snapped open.

"So, you are worried," Dempsey said.

"No more than we are for ourselves," Don lied.

Another scream echoed outside, and this time, its source was clear. A group of walkers came up the road, hooting and screeching.

"Kill those candles," Don said, and the room fell into darkness. "Stay out of sight. They'll go by if they don't notice us." He hoped. It was troubling to see walkers out on the street. They looked emboldened, and as Don surveyed them, his stomach went cold. Their mumbling could be heard clearly in the house as they ambled forward as if sleepwalking.

A group of fifty or so walkers came up the street, and disappeared around the bend in the road. Don and his companions waited in the dark for what seemed like hours, but was only fifteen minutes, before the walkers reappeared on the road out front. They passed by without incident, and disappeared back the way they had come. Don relit the candles and took the last pull on his coffee.

"What the hell do you make of that?" Dempsey asked. He looked pale in the candlelight.

"You've never seen one before, have you?" Lester asked.

Dempsey shook his head no.

"It's much nastier up close," Lester said.

They settled in for the night. Don and Lester had no intention of sleeping, but the dogs had no problem. Tank and Jessie slept the deep sleep of the canine, and Tank's snoring went well with Jessie's barking fits as she dreamed. Don tried to watch Dempsey without looking like he was watching him. Several times, he'd closed his eyes to nothing but the barest of slits, but Dempsey showed no signs of sleeping. Don didn't know if the man was on cocaine, or had taken caffeine, but his eyes darted about, and he sweat like a man who didn't think he'd see another dawn.

Darkness washed over Don as he dozed, and Dempsey must have also fallen asleep, because the short bald man clawed at Don as he came awake. Don kicked him off, and pain from the gunshot wound paralyzed him, but he staggered to his feet. The dogs barked, and Lester jumped up, shotgun before him.

Don searched for his M16, which was across the room standing against the wall. What was he thinking? He couldn't kill Dempsey. He needed him, and getting to the Glades with Dempsey and having to deal with a bullet wound wasn't the best way to make time.

Don jumped forward and startled the walker, hoping Lester would see the opening. He did. When Dempsey cringed against

Don's fake blow, there had been the briefest of moments when his full attention was on Don. Lester had used that instant to crack Dempsey across the face with the butt of the shotgun.

Dempsey fell back, and as he floated between consciousness and sleep, his body writhed and contorted like giant bugs crawled beneath his skin.

"Shit," Don said, as he retrieved the M16.

"What now?" Lester asked.

Don switched the M16 to single shot and fired, just grazing Dempsey's leg enough to cut it open. He doubled over in pain, but it wasn't enough. The thing that had been Dempsey hovered between panic, sleep, and hunger for flesh. When it came at Don, he fired again, and blew a bigger chunk from Dempsey's leg.

Dempsey went down in a heap, and it took several minutes for him to come back to himself. The pressure beneath his skin eased, and blood vessels receded, leaving only thin white scar lines. He sat panting and coughing as they fed him water. Dempsey didn't remember any of it.

"I was one of them?" Dempsey asked.

"Yes," Don said.

Dempsey looked like a deflated balloon, all his life energy gone. "So I guess I'm done for."

"Not necessarily," Don lied. "I'm trying to get a sample of the disease to my people on the outside. Stick with me and you have a chance."

Dempsey perked up, and looked at Don with eyes filled with fear, desperation, and hope. "You think?" Then his face sagged as questions filled his mind. "Wouldn't they already have a walker? Couldn't they figure out the disease using a captive?"

"Maybe, but most likely not fast enough. When a virus enters the human body and takes hold, the biology of the situation changes," Don said. He knew a fair amount about diseases as it was part of his job, but he was no expert.

"How can I help?" Dempsey said.

"I think you know the answer to that already."

"Drago's place," Dempsey said, and he deflated again.

"You don't need to see him. Hell, you don't even need to come the entire way. I just need you to get me there," Don said.

"Fair enough."

"Do we need a boat?" Lester asked. "If he's hiding out in the middle of nowhere, I don't see how we'll get to him without one."

"We'll go by airboat," Dempsey said. "I've got one stashed for when I make the trip. That's if it hasn't been messed with or stolen."

Don pondered this. Heading out to sea would be impossible, but he doubted the Navy kept watch on the interior waterways. The Glades were a tangle of woodlands, streams, lakes, rivers, and mangrove forests, and there were no clear paths. Given that Drago was hiding, Don assumed he'd be on an isolated interior island. "You sure? When was the last time you used it? Last night when you met with him?"

"Nah, he met me at a bar last night." Dempsey looked perplexed. "That was the first time he'd ever done that."

"You think he's abandoned his place out in the Glades?" Don asked.

"I doubt it."

"You have a car we can use to get to your boat?"

"Sure do," Dempsey said. "Come see."

CHAPTER EIGHTEEN

Paddling in the pitch black with only two small flashlights to light the way, Maureen and her party threaded their way through a series of estuaries, bays, and thick mangrove patches half-buried in water. They'd been paddling for more than an hour. Maureen's watch glowed in the darkness, and it read 3:06AM. The sun would be up in a few hours, and the nightmare would be over, though she knew it would never really be over. Tim and Lilly were still alive, but infected, and Geoff, Sheryl, Hawk, and Wendy wouldn't see another sunrise.

They'd decided not to stop and to paddle through the night hoping to make it out by early morning. Maureen did her best to lead the party east, but hardwood hammocks, small islands, and mangroves impeded their path. Raul said they'd drifted too far south. Moonlight helped them navigate, but Maureen still wasn't overseeing all the glowing eyes in the darkness. When the glow of the fire had died, Maureen had another cartoon flashback. This time of Bugs Bunny staring at a wall of eyes.

Raul whimpered behind her, and she couldn't help but shed a tear for Wendy as well. Unlike Saura and Ping, she'd thrown herself into the fray to save her husband, and the guilt Raul must be feeling made her think of Tim, and of what they had become. He'd turned into the literal monster she believed him to be, and she scolded herself again for her inability to show compassion for a man she had once loved. They were through whether Tim lived or died, but this idea brought neither happiness nor peace. The "incident" was a catalyst that revealed a much bigger problem. A problem that couldn't be fixed. There was no excuse for what he'd done, but it took two to form a shitty relationship.

Ping struggled to keep up because Saura slept in her kayak, and he towed her, the lead line of her boat tied to the rear handle on his. Every few minutes, Maureen would intentionally dip her paddle a little too deep, and remove it from the water with a splash and plop, which woke the spoiled brat every time. Ping cleared his throat and sucked mucus every few seconds, and Maureen wished she had a cough drop to give him.

They had to backtrack when they hit a dead end in a thick mangrove patch. Sawgrass and cattails filled every empty space, and Maureen was sick of seeing the stuff. After several turns, Raul informed them they were going southeast, and they needed to turn hard left if they wanted to get back on course. They paddled along the west side of a hardwood hammock, and that made heading due east impossible.

"What now, Pocahontas? Portage across?" Raul asked.

"We can't portage. It would take forever in the dark. We'd have to balance ourselves on the mangrove trees while pulling our boats behind us. Even if you and I could do it..." Maureen looked back at Ping as he towed his snoring wife.

"Yeah," Raul said. She could tell by his tone what he was thinking, because she'd been contemplating the same thing: maybe they should cut Saura and Ping loose, but that just wasn't in her, and Raul didn't press.

They paddled on and soon entered a grass-choked bay, the moonlight reflecting off the spiked, variegated leaves of the sawgrass. The grass bent and snapped as they paddled through it, and Saura woke and paddled. Every stroke she moaned, or grunted, and Maureen was about to tell her to shut her cake hole when something in blackness caught her eye.

In the distance, an orange light flickered. It looked to be a fire, and Maureen's spirits rose. She doubled her stroke and pulled away from her companions. Raul did his best to keep up, but after a few minutes, Maureen fought alone through the grass, the sound of Raul and the others struggling to keep up fading behind her.

"Maureen! Slow up, Speedy Gonzales," Raul yelled.

The light wavered for a few seconds, diminished, and went out. Maureen stopped paddling. "Way to go, Raul. You scared them." Whoever's campfire it had been, it was now out, and with no light to head for, she waited for everyone to catch up.

"What the hell was that all about?" asked Raul when he arrived.

Maureen didn't answer. She didn't have an answer. She'd seen the light and every instinct in her body told her to get to it as fast as she could. Rather than try to explain that to Raul, she said, "I saw something. A light. I thought it might be help. Then you screamed, and they must have heard you."

"So they put out their fire?" Raul said.

Ping and Saura arrived, both huffing and puffing, and Saura looked putout. Her vacation wasn't going the way she wanted. Her slick black hair, which was normally held vertical via several clips of dubious styles, now fell straight to her shoulders and was almost invisible in the blackness. "What now," she said. "Like, you trying to lose us?"

Maureen said, "No one was trying to lose you. I saw a fire."

"Where?" Ping said.

"It's out now, Jackie Chan," said Raul. "I think we should stay clear. Take another route."

"What? Why? They might help us. They're probably scared of us," Maureen said.

"I doubt it. People who spend the night in the Glades aren't exactly wallflowers. They don't want to be found, so why would we want to find them?" Raul said.

"They might know the way out," Ping said.

"Yeah," Saura said, and Maureen had to stifle a chuckle.

Maureen dug in her paddle, and her kayak lurched forward. "You all can do what you want. I'm heading over there."

She took several hard strokes and glided through the grass. At first, they didn't follow her, but after two minutes she heard the telltale sounds of snapping grass as they pursued her. What choice did they have? She knew that without her, Saura and Ping would most likely starve while trying to find their way out of the semiaquatic maze that was the Everglades. Raul wouldn't help them because Maureen felt she was the only reason he hadn't taken off. His wife's broken body lay a few miles away, and she felt guilty when she sensed herself getting warm at the thought of him staying for her.

Embers glowed through a smattering of cattails. Maureen panned her flashlight revealing the remains of a manmade fire, but no people. The others talked loudly, and Maureen didn't think that was a smart idea, and she reconsidered her choice to investigate. Raul had been right. Whoever had started the fire, and put it out, didn't want to be found. What that meant she didn't know, but she didn't see how it could be good.

"Sshhh," Maureen said. She extended her paddle out as far as she could, turned her kayak, and headed back the way she'd come, but couldn't. Her companions clogged the passage they'd forced through the grass.

A guttural yell pierced the night. "Moeeen they come." To Maureen, the voice sounded a little like Tim's.

There were splashing sounds as someone came toward them in the darkness, stomping through the shallow water and vegetation. Maureen shutoff her flashlight, and that may have saved her life. An arrow whished by her ear, and she rolled to one side, and almost flipped the kayak. Another arrow hissed through the night, and Saura shouted, and cried.

Confusion ensued, as Maureen tried to paddle forward, and Raul, Saura, and Ping strained to turn their boats around in the sawgrass-choked water. In the darkness, Maureen couldn't see where she was going, and the sound of splashing got louder and closer.

There was the twang of a bowstring, the hiss of an arrow, and then a thump. Ping wailed in pain, and Maureen turned to see him slumped atop the deck of his kayak, an arrow protruding from his back. The blood that spilled over the bright yellow kayak looked black in the moonlight.

Saura trembled and cried, and Raul tried to quiet her by reaching over and putting a hand over her mouth, but this just made the woman more crazed. She thrashed and bucked in the cockpit, lashing out at Raul as he tried to help her. Saura's kayak flipped, and she went sprawling into the water.

An arrow plunked into the front of Maureen's boat, and she figured the time had come to get out of her bright green kayak. She rolled, and slithered out of the cockpit. As she moved away from the kayak, a snake wiggled past her, and several water bugs clung to her face, but she stayed silent.

Flashlight beams lit the night, and a man wearing waist-high waders stood five feet from where she hid, searching the grass and water reeds. The flashlight beam fell on Raul, who still sat in his kayak. He froze like a child caught sneaking snacks from the fridge. Another man from Maureen's right stepped forward, pulled Raul from his boat, and tossed him like a piece of garbage. They had Saura too, and the young women wailed and cried as they dragged her toward land, away from her dead husband.

"Lookie what we have here," one of the men said.

"She's pretty," said another.

"Touch her and you're dead." Raul's voice was loud and forceful, but he paid a price for his insolence.

"That's funny," said one of the men. Maureen heard the smacking and pounding as Raul was beaten.

The man in front of Maureen moved away, and she crawled closer to the commotion. She still had her gun, but it had been submerged in the water, and she didn't know if it would fire. There was only one chance. She stood, shouldered the rifle, and fired at the dark shape holding Raul.

The gun's hammer clicked, and the weapon didn't fire.

"Oh, look at that. One for me," said one of the men. Maureen was dragged through the mangroves toward the hardwood hammock where she'd seen glowing embers. The fire blazed up again, and the entire area filled with light.

There were three men. One looked to be older than the other two, and appeared to be in charge. He sat by the fire, drinking from a bottle of whiskey, while he ordered the other two around. They all wore camo waders, and from listening to them talk, Maureen had learned that their names were Jeb, Kenny, and the leader's name was Stilts. Jeb and Kenny tied Maureen, Raul, and Saura to trees, and started stripping off their clothes when Stilts yelled, "Stop that, you barbarians. They're for the boss, and if he sees you've damaged his toys, they'll be hell to pay for you both."

"Don't you want them out of here before the kid comes? He'll see them," Jeb said.

"So what?" Stilts said. "I don't give an egret's ass about the kid. What's he gonna do, call a cop?"

"Still, you think Drago would want the kid to see them?" Kenny said.

"How would he know?"

"He might run into the kid in the city. The boss likes to hit the clubs when he gets restless," Kenny said.

Stilts grunted, but conceded the point. "All right, take them back to Drago now, and I'll wait here to do the deal." The older man got up and stripped off his waders. Stilts' legs were bones covered in sagging skin, and they looked like they might snap under his weight.

Maureen remembered little the next few hours. Hands tied, they marched across the hardwood hammock, and were put on a skiff, where they waited while Jeb and Kenny partied and relaxed. Saura was out cold when the men came looking for her, and when Maureen kicked Jeb in the nuts, they figured it was best to listen to Stilts and leave them be.

Jeb piloted the skiff in the dark, being careful not to hit anything. He'd clearly traveled this way before, and he twisted and turned through the labyrinth of small streams and ponds as if on autopilot. They beached on an island, and marched through a thin forest that brought them to the edge of a lake. At its center, a tiny island stood out in the blackness, and Maureen thought of Gollum, and his island beneath the mountains.

There was a two-person kayak on the shore, and after an elaborate series of timed calls and yells, Jeb got the okay to transport his prisoners across to the island. Kenny kept an eye on Saura and Maureen as Jeb held a gun to Raul's head as he paddled. Then it was Saura's turn, and then Maureen's.

They left Kenny behind and hiked to clearing at the center of the island where Drago's camp was. The boss's was an old green army tent, which had probably once belonged to a field officer. It was four times the size of the others, and it had a Honda 2000i generator gently humming beside it.

A man came out of the main tent and met Jeb. He was huge, and wore army fatigues, a cowboy hat, and sunglasses despite the darkness. He carried a bottle of rum. He took a pull off the bottle, and sized up Maureen and crew. The man harrumphed and took another swig. "Where'd you find these city rats?" he asked.

"We was waiting for the kid, and they stumbled into our camp, all disoriented and confused. Stilts figured the boss would want them. Especially these two." Jeb grabbed Maureen's arm with one hand, and Saura's with the other, and presented them to Mr. Sunglasses.

"Put them on ice," the man said. "Drago will see them in the morning."

The blow came from behind, and Maureen had one final thought as the sky spun, and her body shut down: *I should have gone to Disney World.*

CHAPTER NINETEEN

Like many people, Dempsey's choices when it came to automobiles reflected his personality and image, or at least the appearance he wanted to project. Don chuckled when they entered the ride dealer's garage. There were two vehicles there, and they reflected the two lives of Rick Dempsey.

An old Toyota Celica that looked like it had been through a war sat in one garage bay, and a classic VW bus restored to its former glory, and tricked out with many modern conveniences and flourishes occupied the second bay. The VW was deep purple, and narrow rectangular windows ran all around its upper half. With some fortification to the sides, they could easily hide from gunfire in the old bus.

The beat-up Celica was a red street racer with a black hood. It didn't take a federal agent to figure out which was drug dealer Dempsey's car, and which one Dempsey the father and husband drove. Don thought of Dempsey's family. He'd never asked the man about them.

"Dempsey, where are your wife and kids?" Don asked.

"Long gone, man. My girl is in California trying to be an actress, and I don't know where my boy is, or his bitch mother. The woman had no problem with what I did for a living until my income fell, then I became a drug dealer. She tried to poison my kids against me, and she was mostly successful. My daughter only talks to me because she feels guilty." Dempsey took a deep breath. "Shit, do I owe you money? That's more than I've told my shrink in months."

Honesty and humility always impressed Don, regardless of the situation. He pulled his hand from his pocket and thrust it toward Dempsey. "You with us? If you are, I promise I'll do everything I can to help you."

Dempsey took his hand hesitantly, and said, "I'm in. No choice really."

Lester asked, "So what's the plan?" As always, he was sweating profusely.

"We fortify the van against bullets, and then go to the airboat and drop in on Drago." The rest of the night was spent eating, drinking caffeine, working on the van, and studying a map of southern Florida. The Everglades are huge, and they could get lost in the maze of rivers, lakes, and forests. Lester suggested trying to get his GPS to work, but when he'd tried it earlier, it had been out of service. Even if they could get it to work, the Everglades would be little more than a green patch of nothingness. The GPS would also know nothing of blocked roads, or areas of possible ambush.

"The good news is we need to go south. Bad news is there's no way to avoid populated areas. We need to head down here," Dempsey said, as he pointed to a spot on the map marked Homestead.

"Where is the airboat?" Lester asked.

"It's by a friend's place out on the edge of town. I give him ride, and he lets me hide my boat on the back of his property."

"Isn't he worried that if you get caught he can be charged as an accessory?"

Dempsey laughed. "You don't get it, man. He's on the edge, and he has a hundred acres."

Don understood. His friend's piece of land was so large, and wide open, that one person couldn't be expected to know what was happening on every inch of it at all times. He'd buy that. "So we have a long walk?"

"Couple miles out into the Glades."

Lester grunted.

As they went about their final preparations, the end game came into focus. If he got a sample, and successfully communicated with his people, it was not out of the question he could be extracted before the clock struck midnight. Granted, many things had to happen in perfect succession with no delays or setbacks, but he had to make it happen. The longer he stayed within the contaminated zone, the harder it would be to get out, and the greater chance he would become infected.

Dempsey asked, "You ever been in shit this deep?"

"Not one with so many lives at stake." Dempsey's shoulder's sagged. "Fear not. I was a military brat and had to fight for everything since I was a kid. The academy, officer's candidate school, SEAL training, FBI instruction at Quantico; they all prepared me for something like this, but I never thought it would actually happen." If he couldn't get it done, few others could. This confidence drove his entire life, but also left him alone and adrift. With each passing year, that revelation came home to roost more often. Maybe when he got out of his current sea of shit, he would call Desiree and ask her to have dinner.

Dempsey shrugged. "Training ain't doing."

To that, Don had no response.

They removed the rear seats from the VW bus and screwed Dempsey's metal coffee tables to both interior sidewalls. With everyone locked and loaded, they secured the dogs in the rear via makeshift harnesses constructed by Lester. Don's wingman had also scavenged outdoor speakers from Dempsey's deck and mounted them atop the van. In case a nuclear option was needed, Don had made five high-end gas bombs from wine bottles and tiki candlewicks.

The grey of daybreak leaked into the garage as Dempsey lifted the large door. Don drove out and waited while Dempsey shut the door and jumped in the passenger seat. Dempsey rode shotgun because it was his town, and from here on out, they would be in his hands. Though the white scars on his face marked him as infected, Don's concerns about Dempsey had fallen away. The man wanted to save his skin, and that was a strong motivator.

"What kind of hole does this snake live in? And how is it the cops haven't found it?" Don asked. They hadn't discussed tactics beyond getting to Drago's place. No point. Don didn't understand what he was up against. He inched out of the driveway and headed for the land bridge.

"Drago moves around," Dempsey said. "He's got an elaborate series of tents and luxuries the pharaohs would have been jealous of. Generators and AC, TV, heat."

"Anything notable about where he is now?"

"Not really. He always picks a small island with many trees. You can only get to his current place by kayak. I've seen..." Dempsey stared out the window.

Several walkers hid under a stubby palm tree next to a driveway. Don yelled back to Lester, "Get the tunes going as loud as you can." He spun the wheel hard and pulled into the driveway. The walkers scattered like quail.

"When the boys hit the brew. When the boys hit the brew. When the b—"

Lester killed the music, and said, "So much for them learning to cover their ears, Don. Asshole."

Don laughed and backed out onto the road. They passed their abandoned Pathfinder, its rear smashed. He made several twists and turns as they left Dempsey's secluded neighborhood, and signs of the prior night's chaos increased as they went. Dark bloodstains, body parts, burnt-out cars, forlorn pets, and many other signs of civil unrest sullied Chicken Key. Houses and buildings had already been graffiti'd, and light poles lay across several roads. A silence lay over everything. A few cars moved about, but everyone on the streets was being careful and staying away from each other. Don thought he saw a police car down a side street, but when he backed up to look for it, there was nothing there.

They hit the first signs of trouble when they had to cross County Road 821. They backtracked several times because the intersections were blocked with abandoned cars and the remains of the prior night's pandemonium. When they finally found an open underpass south of where they needed to be, another obstacle sidetracked them.

A young woman was pinned on top of the concrete embankment beneath the bridge. A crowd of walkers surrounded her, and she fought them off with a pole. Don brought the van to a stop. Lester fired up the music and jumped from the bus. He fired the shotgun, and its loud *boom* rose above the clamor of the music and the barking dogs.

The walkers paused and looked his way. Lester ran toward them.

"Lester, wait," Don said. His partner was already halfway to the fray. Don knew he couldn't stop for every person in need or he'd never get the sample to his people, but Lester had acted without thought, and now Don had to support him.

From the bridge above dropped two dozen walkers. They looked like rag dolls as they lumbered toward Lester in a sleepy daze. They wore jackets, hats, masks, gloves, and every other imaginable piece of clothing to keep the sun off their infected skin. Don noted that several of these sleepwalkers were missing arms and bled from large wounds that hadn't been caused by the disease.

Don jumped from the vehicle. "Stay in the bus. Close all the windows," he yelled over his shoulder to Dempsey.

Don put the M16 on automatic and squeezed off six shots just above the walker's heads. They paused, but didn't back down. Apparently, they'd learned a few things during the night. Don flipped the setting back to single fire, sighted a walker, and fired. The bullet struck the sleepwalker in the leg, and it fell. The others backed away as Don advanced.

The young girl, feeling the opening just as Tank had the day before, ran through the crowd of walkers while their attention was focused on Don. As she ran past Lester, he backed down the embankment. He fired the shotgun, and was ready to fire again when he paused.

The walkers no longer had any interest in Don and his friends. The awoken one among them was now the focus of their attention. Don took a hesitant step forward, but realized it was hopeless. The walkers charged at the young man, who shrieked with pain as they piled on him like a rugby scrum. Don and Lester backed down the embankment and joined Dempsey and their new ward in the bus.

At the top of the embankment, the man Don had woken was getting mauled. Like a pack of wolves tearing apart a doe, the man's arms and legs were ripped off, and smaller groups of walkers broke off with them. The concrete embankment was covered in blood, and Don heard Lester and their new friend retching. Don dropped the van into gear and left the underpass, exiting into the bright sunlight.

"My name's Don, and this is Dempsey and Lester. Our two top dogs back there are Jessie and Tank." The young woman stroked the animals, but said nothing. "You okay? You hurt?" She shook her head no. "Okay, then," Don said. Both dogs were sniffing and inspecting her. Don and Lester exchanged glances. The girl's clothing didn't appear ripped, and there was no blood, but they needed to be certain.

"We need to check you for bites," Lester said.

The girl recoiled from the dogs. Her long brown hair was matted with sweat, and she trembled and shook. It was hard to guess her age. She was attractive, yet appeared innocent. No visible tattoos, plain clothes, white sneakers. She said, "Don't touch me, please. I'll do whatever you ask."

If he could become a shitheel, that would be an upgrade from what he felt like. Don and Lester exchanged glances again. "Do you have a bra and underwear on?" Don asked.

"Yes."

"So, like a bikini?" Don said.

"Yes."

"And you wear those in front of strangers, right?"

She nodded.

"What's your name?" Lester asked.

"Tristin. All you want me to do is strip down to my underwear for a minute?"

"That's it. We have to make sure. Then we have blankets and food for you," Lester said.

"Do you understand?" Don said.

She nodded and stripped.

"I feel like a perv," Lester said. Dempsey stared out the window. "She looks clean."

Tristin put her clothes back on and Lester put a blanket around her. "How'd you end up out here alone?"

"Not now, let her rest," Don said. He felt an overwhelming responsibility for the girl, and the pragmatic government agent that always prowled his head reminded him that's why he didn't want to stop for her.

Tristin looked relieved, and leaned her head against the window.

It took two more hours to complete the maze that led to Bubba and Annette Killington's house on the outskirts of civilization. As they left the more populated areas, signs of unrest diminished. Though the Killington's place wasn't a shack, it wasn't a palace like Dempsey's. The street seemed similar to Don. It was quiet, subdued, and showed no outward signs that there was any reason to pause there. The sun crested above. It was 10:19AM.

Don turned into a long driveway that led to Bubba and Ann's place. "They know this van?" Don asked.

"Yeah, he won't shoot us. Don't even stop. Drive around back into the trees. I think the van can go down the path a bit. Hide the bus that way, too," Dempsey said, and he cast a sidelong glance at their new passenger.

Don understood Dempsey's concern. They couldn't leave the girl alone in the van, and she couldn't come with them. Leaving Lester behind was an option, but he didn't like the idea of leaving his wingman. Don stopped the van.

"What are you doing?" Dempsey asked.

"You think Bubba would keep an eye on her for us if you gave him a pile of ride?" Don asked.

"I don't have a pile of ride," Dempsey said.

"We will if we're successful, and if we're not, she's better off with them," Don said.

Dempsey's face grew stern as he considered this. "Okay. You wait here, I'll go talk to him," he said.

"No need. Here he comes," Don said.

Bubba looked exactly as Don had imagined. He had a tight crew cut, and sported faded overalls with no shirt underneath. He wore round glasses and carried what looked to be an SS1 assault rifle. The big man put the rifle to his shoulder and trained it on Don.

Dempsey got out of the van. "Yo, Bubba, it's Ricky, man. It's cool. Heading out into the backcountry."

Bubba didn't take his eye from the sight. "Who are these assholes?"

"Just people who I'm helping out. The guy driving is a federal agent."

Bubba dropped the tip of his gun, looked at Dempsey, and started back to the house.

"Wait, man. You want some ride? Free?"

That made Bubba stop and turn. "How much? And what's the catch?"

"A hundred tabs, and all you have to do is keep an eye on her while we're gone." Dempsey opened the rear door of the bus and brought out Tristin. "We rescued her. Name's Tristin."

Bubba looked the girl up and down, shook his head, and turned. As he went back to the house, he said, "I don't need it. End is here."

"Why not ride it out in style?" Dempsey said.

Bubba stopped and looked back. "She ain't come'in in the house. Lock her in the garage and I'll keep an eye on her." Bubba strode forward until he was a foot away from Dempsey. "And if you don't bring me my shit, I'll stick this up your ass," he said, and shoved the muzzle of the rifle in Dempsey's face.

"Yeah, sure, no worries," Dempsey said, and he ushered Tristin into the Killington's garage.

The van didn't make it far down the path, and they had to travel the rest of the way on foot. They opened the van windows a crack, and left Jessie and Tank in the VW. Where they were going would be difficult traveling for dogs. Buttonwood and red mangrove trees surrounded them and the ground was covered in palmetto plants. It was quiet, and a sweet gentle breeze blew through the trees. They walked twenty minutes before they reached the airboat, which lay hidden under a thick patch of mangrove trees, barely visible. A camouflage-colored kayak was tied to its side, and there were several fishing poles lodged in pole holders around the short gunnel.

Don and Lester got on the boat as Dempsey spun its great air propeller. The engine kicked over after three turns, and the deafening sound of the air pressing the craft forward brought a new problem to mind. Drago would hear them coming a mile away. Don leaned over and yelled in Dempsey's ear as he guided the boat out into a wider waterway. "Will he hear us?"

Dempsey shook his head. "We'll leave the boat and hike the last couple of miles." Don looked up at the one-person kayak. "No worries," Dempsey said, "I have portage wheels for that. I need to get to all kinds of remote places, and there are hardwood stands everywhere."

The airboat tore through the Everglades, knocking turtles off their perches, and scattering birds. Dempsey continually referred to a hand-drawn map he'd produced from a hiding place beneath the steering column. He made many turns, and several times, they crossed areas of wetlands where there appeared to be no water for the boat to float upon, only sawgrass.

They came to a large stand of trees, and that's where they left the boat. Dempsey and Lester untied the kayak and strapped on the portage wheels. They headed into a thick grove of buttonwood trees, and Don sucked in the fresh air and closed his eyes. He could almost forget why he was out here. Almost. There were signs others had been this way. Bootprints, wheel tracks, and an empty dry bag lay forlorn amidst the palmetto trees.

They'd walked for half an hour when they came to a lake. Birds of all sizes and shapes soared above the clear water, and in the center was a tiny tree-covered island. Nothing moved on the island as they hide in a thicket of mangrove trees. There was a two-person kayak on the far shore of the lake, but there were no other signs people were on the island.

"How many guards?" asked Don.

"Three, maybe four, but they're always watching."

"I want you to paddle out there. Tell him you want ride. While they're distracted with you, I'll sneak onto the island. Lester, you wait here. Stay at the ready. We may need to leave fast." Lester gazed at the lake, and looked doubtful, but didn't protest. "I'll leave the M16 with you and take a gun off one of Drago's men when I get over there."

"At night, there'd be a signal call. No need during the daylight hours," Dempsey said.

"Take your time getting over there, and stall as much as you can so I have time to take advantage of your distraction," Don said.

Dempsey nodded, and said, "Wish me luck." He left them, and pushed the kayak out onto the lake, his hands up as he walked behind it. A yell of okay came from the island, and Don and Lester watched Dempsey from their hiding place as he glided across the still water in his sleek camouflage kayak. Many people's lives now rested on the shoulders of Jack Dempsey.

CHAPTER TWENTY

A ray of sunlight fell on Maureen's face, and she woke with a start. At first, she didn't know where she was, but as her vision cleared, the gray canvas roof of a tent came into focus. Sunlight streamed through a gap in the tent door, and a faint breeze brought the scent of smoke and earth. She wasn't tied up, or secured to her cot in any way, and Saura and Raul lay on similar cots, still fast asleep. Both looked troubled as they slept, and both had small cuts all over their faces and arms, which resulted from being dragged through sawgrass.

The events of the prior night came rushing back, and Wendy's broken and bloodied body filled her mind's eye, and then an image of an arrow sticking out of Ping's back, his black blood running over the deck of his kayak. She rubbed her temples, thinking about what to do next. The second she got off the cot, she'd be met by Drago's men. She was hungry, and exhausted. The events of the last twenty-four hours had sucked all the life from her, and she didn't think she had any more strength to fight. It was useless anyway. Drago's men had guns, and they were trapped on an island, in the middle of the nowhere, with no way of communicating with the outside world. Her phone was long gone, as was her rifle. This panicked her, and she reached into her pocket, and wrapped her fingers around the final bullet.

There were voices outside, and all it would take is a yell, or a few words to bring their guards. What would happen then, she didn't know. She had an idea, and the thought of being raped, or worse, filled her eyes with tears, though she didn't allow them to fall. She would fight until they killed her if need be, and maybe she'd take one of the bastards with her.

"You okay?" It was Raul.

"Nothing broken," Maureen said.

"Saura," called Raul. Saura didn't stir.

"Let her sleep," said Maureen. "You have any thoughts?"

"Yeah, we're screwed."

They were whispering, trying not to alert their guards, but apparently they hadn't been quiet enough. Mr. Sunglasses strode into the tent like a general, and two men in camouflage fatigues flanked him. The men reeked of smoke, and liquor and sweat. Their faces were smeared with dirt, and their eyes were red and haunted.

"You sure are," Mr. Sunglasses said. "Sit up."

Maureen and Raul complied, but Saura didn't move. Before one of the men awakened her with a boot heel, Raul reached across his cot, and poked her several times. Nothing. She snored for a second, and then went back to faint, shallow breaths. Raul poked her again, harder, and still she didn't wake.

"Go wake Sleeping Beauty," said Mr. Sunglasses, and one of his henchman stepped forward.

Raul was faster. He slid off his cot and shook Saura. Mr. Sunglasses pushed him aside, and yanked Saura to her feet. She was dazed, and looked very small. Her eyes darted around the tent, and when she saw Maureen, she tried to run to her. Mr. Sunglasses grabbed her, and tossed her back onto the cot.

"Listen up!" The man yelled so loud, Maureen jumped. "Next person who moves without permission will be shot. No one knows you're here." He paused and let the ramifications of that statement settle in their minds. "I will bury you all in a shallow grave if you so much as make a sound without being asked to do so. Do you understand?" Maureen, Saura, and Raul wagged their heads as fast as they could. "Good. My boys here will bring you food. Eat, get yourselves together, and get ready to meet the man." With that, he spun on his heel, and left the tent, followed by his men.

The tent was silent for a few moments, and then Saura cried. She'd lost her husband, and from what Maureen had seen, Ping had taken care of her like a child, and now that's what Saura was. Raul sat and put his arm around her. Maureen could tell he'd done this to comfort himself as much as her. They'd all lost someone dear to them, and neither Maureen, nor her friends, had any time to deal with the losses.

One of the men returned with food and water. The stale bread and baked beans were surprisingly good, and the water tasted like wine to their parched mouths. In minutes, they were done and waiting for a meeting they understood wasn't going to be pleasant.

"I must look like shit. Maybe they'll leave me be," Maureen said, only half-joking.

"What about me?" Saura said in a shaky voice.

"I won't let anything happen to you," said Raul. He dropped his chin to his chest. He knew the folly of his words, and the utter helplessness of their situation.

"What do you make of these guys?" Maureen asked.

"Drug dealers would be my guess. They probably bring coke and weed up by boat, then use their camp as the distribution point," Raul said. "They live in tents, and move around a lot. Stilts and crew are just watchdogs, the first line of defense on their main trade route for low-level suckers."

"Like us," Maureen said.

"How are we going to get out of here?" Saura asked.

To that, no one had an answer.

Mr. Sunglasses returned with his two men, and they all silently shuffled out of the tent. Sunlight blinded Maureen as she entered the clearing, but the warmth felt good on her face, and as her vision cleared, she saw no other people as they walked through camp. There was no fire pit, no children, or women. She searched for anything that might help them escape, but there was nothing but trees, bugs, and the smell of rot.

Mr. Sunglasses stopped at the main tent's entrance and turned to his charges. "This is not the time to be a wiseass, or ask questions. Drago's temper is short, and he needs none of you. Get my drift?" Mr. Sunglasses pulled his shades to the tip of his nose, and ogled them with bloodshot eyes.

Maureen nodded. The tent flap was pulled back, and they all stepped inside. Despite the bright day, the interior was dark and shadowy. It was setup like a king's main audience chamber, and Drago sat on his camping chair throne at the end of the tent opposite the entrance.

Drago was a huge man, clearly of Cuban decent, and his tiny black eyes shinned like opals. He wore a Lakers T-shirt, a camouflage hat, and an ammo belt. Thick gold chains hung around his neck, and he wore several rings and bracelets. Mr. Sunglasses poked Maureen in the rear, and she walked forward, and stopped before Drago. She heard Raul and Saura's ragged breathing behind her, and she felt the tension and fear rolling off them.

Drago watched them for a few minutes, and then pointed at Saura, and rolled his finger in a "come" motion. Saura whimpered, but after one of the men grabbed her ass, she jumped forward, and then continued on until she stood quivering in front of the large man.

"My name is Drago. Come close. Let me see you," he said. Saura inched closer, and Drago lifted the sunglasses from his face, revealing one good eye, and one milky-white one. Half his face was badly scared, and the thicker ones pulsed red. He got up, and circled the young Asian woman, leering the entire time. He reached out a finger and tugged on a strap of her tank top. Saura pulled back, and Maureen heard Raul grunt behind her. "You know why you're here?" he asked.

"No," said Saura, her voice frail and broken.

"Well. Maybe you can stay around and keep me company. Sit," said Drago, and he motioned for Saura to sit in a chair at his side. Then he moved on to Maureen.

She was older, and Drago found her less attractive because the inspection only took a moment. He said, "Jeremiah, this one is for you." Mr. Sunglasses smiled. Drago moved on to Raul. "You have little to offer me."

He turned and sat back on his throne, and put his sunglasses back on. His hand dropped onto Saura's leg, and the young women flinched at his touch.

Maureen looked around the tent, and in one corner, to the right of Drago, was a pile of what looked to be money, all wrapped in small packages, and stacked neatly. Drago noticed her eyeing the pile, and said, "More powerful than a nuclear bomb that is." Maureen looked away.

Drago slid his hand down Saura's thigh, and she screamed. This just encouraged the rogue. With surprising strength, he lifted Saura off her chair with one arm, and placed her on his lap. She wiggled and thrashed, trying to get free, but his hands clamped down on her arms, and he pulled her close, and licked her neck. She struggled harder, and Drago laughed as he fought with her.

Raul pulled free of his captors and dove forward to help Saura, and knock Drago from his perch. He didn't even make it halfway. Drago's men were faster, and in seconds, Raul was pinned to the floor, his eyes rolling in his head. Drago laughed, and stuck his hand up Saura's tank top. Raul fought harder, and this earned him several punches to face, but still he didn't quit. He jerked and pulled, and got one arm free. He punched one of the men, and split his lip. Blood dripped onto Raul's face as he struggled to free himself.

Maureen stood frozen, no idea what she should do. She wanted to help Raul, but she knew there was nothing she could do. If she entered the fray, things were sure to end badly for her, but if she didn't, what hope of escape did they have?

She went for it, and threw herself on top of one of the men holding down Raul, and clawed his eyes. The man wailed, and threw her off as though she weighed nothing. Maureen landed next to the pile of money, and now she saw many piles of cash wrapped in plastic.

Drago placed Saura back in her seat and got up. He went to the pile and pulled out a wrapped stack of bills. He held it in front of Maureen's face, and said, "Do you know what will happen if I open this, and rub one of these bills on your face?"

"I think I have a good idea."

Drago laughed and threw the stack back onto the pile. "Soon all the righteous of this country will pay. I will bring the world back to the Stone Age."

They had reached the point in the meeting that Maureen most feared. The banter was done, the day was getting on, and the time had come to get things going. One of Drago's men came in, and whispered in his ear. Drago smiled, and said, "Take her to my tent. These two can watch. I doubt they'll make it through the day."

Saura was yanked to her feet and escorted out of the tent. Maureen and Raul were placed to the side, and their hands bound behind their backs. Drago took a pistol out from under his chair, and placed it on his lap, and covered it with the bottom of his Lakers jersey. The echo of voices floated into the tent, and two men entered, and Maureen gasped.

Besides Jeremiah, AKA Mr. Sunglasses, was the man Dante had been talking to in the parking lot of Chubby Rain. He was short and balding, and even in the dim light, white scars were prominent on his face. The man gave Maureen an odd look, then turned his attention to Drago.

"My friend, I hope you are well," said the man. He looked nervous, and his eyes drifted to Maureen, Raul, and their guards every few moments.

"Dempsey, you ass. Why did you come here?" Drago asked. Dempsey started to answer, but Drago cut him off. "I've told you never to come to me unless I call you. Why didn't you go see Stilts?" Dempsey lowered his eyes, but to Maureen, it seemed like an act.

"I have a huge ride order. Guy needs it fast, and I don't trust Stilts to wipe Jeremiah's ass," said Dempsey

Drago looked like he would fly into a rage, but instead, he laughed, and pulled out his pistol. "Do I look stupid to you?"

Dempsey shifted on his feet, and looked over at Maureen and Raul. Finding no fellowship or help with them, he turned back to Drago. "Of course not, my friend. Why would you say such a thing?"

Drago lifted the gun and pointed it at Dempsey. Raul squeaked, and Maureen felt her stomach turn. Drago pulled back the gun's hammer, and said, "Because you are a liar. And a thief. Your face literally tells me the story. You are lost."

Drago fired, and Dempsey stood motionless for an instant, looking up at his killer as if he couldn't believe what he'd just done. He fell, his face twisting and writhing as the disease took hold. When Dempsey had taken his last breath, his body lay on the ground in the center of the tent, a thick pool of red blood spreading all around him.

CHAPTER TWENTY-ONE

Don wasted no time. As soon as Dempsey was in the kayak, he skirted the edges of the lake, being careful to stay out of sight. When he reached the section of the lake where the gap between the shore and the island was smallest, he stripped down to his underwear, and crawled on his belly through the vegetation to the water's edge.

As an ex-SEAL, Don was an excellent swimmer, and he was in superb shape, but there was no way he'd be able to swim to the island underwater without coming up for air at least twice, and the element of surprise was crucial to their plan. He looked around, as if he hoped to find a scuba mask along with a full breathing tank. What he saw were water reeds and cattails, and his mind charged back to his childhood, and the first grown-up movie he'd watched with his father, Dr. No. In it, Bond is forced to hide underwater from Dr. No's mechanical guard machine. He'd used a water reed as a snorkel.

He snapped the thickest reed he could find, broke off the greenest part, and tested it out. It worked fine, but he had concerns about the reed coming apart or breaking when submerged underwater, but he had no other choice. Dempsey was paddling slower than Don thought possible and was halfway to the island where a man waited for him on the shore.

Don crawled into the water reeds at the edge of the lake and waited. He wanted to time his arrival on the island with Dempsey's to maximize the diversion. When he deemed he'd waited long enough, he slid into the clear water, its coolness refreshing and exhilarating. He dove down, and swam as hard as he could, thrusting with his arms, and slowly letting the air out so as not to create obvious bubbles on the surface.

Pain filled his lungs and burned his chest. His vision grew blurry, but still he stroked on, pushing through water plants, and avoiding bugs, reptiles, and small fish as best he could. His heart pounded, and his lungs were on fire. When tiny fireworks of white light appeared across his vision, he pulled the water reed from his waistband and raised his snorkel. He gently blew out his last bit of air, emptying the reed of water. Then he took a deep breath and continued on.

Don's muscles ached. He hadn't slept since the plane ride the evening prior. He and Lester had been loading up on caffeine, but his eyesight was growing blurry, and every kick of his wounded leg sent jolts of pain up his spine. Over the years, he'd conditioned himself to live with little sleep, and to take it when he could, but the last twenty-four hours had taken a toll.

Ahead the lake bottom rose to meet the shoreline, and he estimated he was almost there. The water reed bent and twisted as Don swam, but it held together. He took one last drag of air off the reed, discarded it, and swam hard for the shore. His lungs burned, and his arms were cramping, when the water plants on the bottom of the lake tickled his belly. He slowed, looking up through the clear water at the island as he tried to determine if anyone had seen him and was waiting for him, but saw no one. He slithered into a patch of sawgrass, and stifled a scream as he was slashed along his stomach by a particularly large leaf.

Blood turned the water red as he crawled from the lake like a croc, scanning the island as best he could. His leg throbbed, and now he was bleeding from his midsection. He lifted his head so his ears were above the water, and all he heard was the singing of the birds and the buzz of insects. Nothing moved, and he swam toward shore. He stopped only once when he heard a splashing noise, and turned to see a croc moving toward him.

All Don had been thinking about was human watchers, and he'd forgotten all the natural protections provided by the Glades. He doubled his pace, and made it to shore before the giant lizard, and disappeared into the trees. Mangrove, palmetto, and pond apple filled the island, and saw palmetto packed the forest floor. Don rested behind a thick tree, catching his breath. The croc that had been hunting him apparently knew better than to pursue him on land, and disappeared, leaving only swirling lake water.

Moving with the instinctual patience of a cat, Don moved deeper into the woods, taking advantage of his years of experience. As he slid from tree to tree, he tuned his hearing, and listened for manmade sounds, but it wasn't a sound that tipped him off. Smoke floated on the breeze, and Don froze.

Panic paralyzed him as the faint smell of cigarettes brought back memories of when he'd been captured, tortured, and almost killed. He had small round scars all over his arms from his guards putting out their cigarettes on him. He was told after extraction and subsequent rehabilitation that he'd been held captive for almost seven months. One hundred and ninety-eight days without daylight, significant sleep, or human contact, other than his handlers who followed a strict series of protocols that treated him like a lab animal. He'd been exposed to multiple types of fear conditioning, drugs, physical torture, and a series of mind-altering situational conditioning tests that made Clockwork Orange look like a day at the park. They'd stripped away his identity, transforming him into a weapon.

Cold cement walls surrounded him. Water dripped in his toilet, and thin beams of light snuck under the cell door. Far off, someone wailed in pain, and the squeaking of rats and the scuttling of cockroaches made him shiver.

Don hadn't known his own name, where he was from, or where he'd been. He no longer had a future or past. His conditioning was so complete, so violent and effective, that Don considered everyone a mortal enemy. It had taken years of medical treatments, counseling, and re-education before Don started to become something resembling himself again.

A bird squawked, and Don shook his head. Sunlight streamed through the tree cover, and slowly his senses returned to full strength. Cigarette smoke tickled his nostrils, all his wounds pounded, and he remembered where he was. Though considered cured by the agency, Don still had panic attacks as a result of his PTSD, and it required constant vigilance to keep them secret.

He'd stopped shaking. He rolled his shoulders and shifted his position, and headed away from the source of the smoke. Don knew that if he could get behind the guard, perhaps he'd be able to take him, and his weapon.

Several minutes passed as he worked his way through thick underbrush, being careful not to make any noise. The smell of smoke faded, and then became strong again. A sneeze echoed from above. The man sat in a pond apple tree, and he peered out through thick branches at the lake. From the guard's position, he could see half the lake, and undoubtedly, there was another man watching the other side. Every few seconds, the man would take a drag on his cigarette, and he looked to be eating something. A rifle rested on a tree branch, and a pair of binoculars hung from a lanyard around the man's neck.

Something thrashed along the shoreline and the guard didn't even look up. Had he been scanning the lake with the binoculars, Don would have never made it across. Don needed a gun, but he wouldn't be able to surprise this man where he sat, so he moved on into the interior.

Soon the forms of tents became visible. At the center of the island, there was a clearing where a camp had been erected. He got close, and waited. He didn't have to wait long, however, because within minutes, two men walked by with Dempsey before them. When they arrived at the biggest tent, they paused, and Dempsey entered with one of the men, while the other stood guard outside. The man wore an old school revolver on his hip, along with a long knife.

Don inched forward until he was as close to the clearing's edge as possible, while still remaining hidden. Then he picked up a rock, and weighed it in his hand, considering. He took a few deep breaths, calming himself and focusing. He threw the rock across the clearing and darted forward.

Two things happened at once. The guard, hearing the rock cut through the bushes surrounding the camp, turned his head toward the noise and pulled his revolver from its holster. Don closed the space between them with several long strides. He grabbed the man around the head, covering his mouth, and kidney punched him twice. The man dropped his gun and wrestled to free himself. Don gripped the man's face and twisted. There was a loud crack, and the man went limp.

Don carried the body into the underbrush, and stripped off his boots, socks, and fatigues. The man was bigger than Don, but he put on the clothes, and the footwear. He tucked the long knife into his boot. There was nothing he could do about his chest wound, but the gash had stopped bleeding, so it would have to wait.

Clothed once again, Don returned to the clearing and picked up the gun.

He stood there a heartbeat, and a gunshot popped from within the tent. Don jumped, and almost rushed in. Instead, he pulled back, peering through a gap in the tent's door flap. Dempsey lay on the ground in a puddle of his own blood, and a man wearing sunglasses stood over him. At the far end, he saw a large Cuban man, who he assumed was Drago. A man and a woman he didn't recognize sat off to the side, looking on in horror. The ruffian who had ushered in Dempsey stood behind them.

Don broke open the revolver to make sure it was loaded, and found only four bullets where they should have been six. He snapped the gun closed, inched it through the tent flap, and shot the man standing over Dempsey in the head. Then he dove to his right, and bullets pierced the tent door where he'd stood. Don counted four shots, and as he moved around to the back of the tent, he noticed two men running through the woods from opposite directions toward camp, one from each side of the island.

He dropped into a crouch, and as they got closer, he fired twice. Both men went down with fatal head wounds. A woman screamed, and Don started pulling up stakes and taking apart support poles. The tent collapsed like a deflating balloon, and when half of it was down, he pulled the knife from his boot, slashed it open, and dove into the writhing mound of canvas.

Bullets whizzed in every direction as Drago emptied his gun at an unseen foe. Don swam through the canvas and the fat Cuban man struggled to hold onto the woman he'd seen. Don brought up the revolver, sighted it, fired, and missed.

Drago tossed the women aside and started fighting through the fallen tent toward Don. They clashed, and Drago put Don in a headlock as he struggled to gain purchase, and soon Don couldn't breathe, as the man's python-like arm crushed his windpipe.

Drago grunted, and Don felt the man's hold slacken. Don doubled his efforts, and struggled to break the man's grip. A loud crack, like something hard hitting bone, resounded over the chaos. Drago fell, and Don freed himself from the canvas.

Don crawled out into the sunlight, followed by the two people he'd seen. When the three of them stood face-to-face, Don said, "Thanks."

"You're welcome," the woman said. "I hit him over the head. I think a stray bullet got the other guy."

"Name's Don Oberbier. I'm a federal agent and I'm here to get—"

"A sample of the money," she said.

"Indeed," Don said. "And you are?"

"Maureen Hughs, and this is Raul."

"Are you alone?" asked Don.

"No. Our friend Saura is being held in one of these tents," Maureen said.

"Go find her while Raul and I take care of this mess," Don said, pointing toward the fallen tent. The canvas was moving, as Drago woke from his unintended sleep.

Maureen moved away, and they pulled back the fallen tent and found Dempsey's body along with Mr. Sunglasses and his friend. They tied Drago up with a cord from the fallen tent, and stood staring at the pile of money. Drago laughed when Don started toward it.

"You can't stop it. It's already out there," Drago said.

Don turned to Raul. "Do you know what's happening in the world?"

"No," Raul said.

As Don filled him in, Maureen returned with Saura, and the two women listened to most of what Don said. Drago sat back and listened also, smiling at the chaos he'd caused.

"So you came for a sample of the money? You didn't even know about us?" Saura said.

"Had no idea. You're just lucky, I guess," Don said, and they all chuckled. It was a welcome sound after so much misery and pain, but the moment of peace didn't last long.

"You. Where did you get the stuff? Who created it?" Drago only stared at Don with a blank face, a slight smirk at the edges of his lips.

When Don stepped forward to hit Drago, the man laughed at him. "I'm not telling you anything. You will all burn." Don hit him, and the man's head snapped back, and blood dribbled through his lips. Drago smiled, his teeth dark with blood.

"So that's it? You want to destroy the US? Bullshit. You're a thug and a thief. What's really in it for you? I know you aren't a genius, but you're not stupid enough to kill all your customers."

He laughed. "You still don't get it. It's already over. Everything you care about has already been taken from you and you don't even know it."

Don said nothing. Drago was a psychopath, and it wasn't his job to figure out why.

Maureen and Raul had collected two additional knives, a basic first aid kit, some other supplies and food, and three usable guns. One gun was a sawed-off double-barrel shotgun, with sixteen shells. The other was Drago's Sig Saur 1911, which he'd emptied, and they'd only found two useable bullets in the fallen tent. The two men who'd run in from the lookout posts had empty rifles, but Maureen had a 7mm shell that fit one of the guns. Don kept the shotgun and a knife, and gave Maureen the one-shot rifle and a knife, Raul the Sig Saur, and Saura a knife. He got himself better boots, a jacket, and pulled Drago's camouflage hat off his head and put it on his own. "So, you have anything else to say?"

Drago smiled, but said nothing.

"Okay." Don went to the pile of money, and using a piece of canvas he'd cut from the tent, he enfolded two plastic-wrapped packets of money, tied it off with twine, and put it in his jacket pocket.

They'd found cigars while searching camp, and food and drink. With the immediate threat handled, they drank some water, and prepared for their journey back to what was left of civilization. As they rested, Don learned more of his companions as they told him their story.

Don offered cigars to everyone, and Saura was the only one to decline. To Don's surprise, the other woman, Maureen, accepted one. He flicked the lighter, and ignited all their stogies, and went over to the pile of money. He flicked the lighter again, and lit some of the plastic wrapped currency on fire. Black smoke poured off the pile, and Don threw the lighter at Drago, and it bounced off his forehead.

"And this for Dempsey. Good luck in the next world, asshole," Don said, as he cracked Drago across the back of the head, and the man fell unconscious.

The pile of money blazed, and had caught the tent canvas, which was smoking. It had also spread to a nearby tree and was inching into the forest. "Let's go," Don said, and nobody gave Drago a second glance.

CHAPTER TWENTY-TWO

Maureen felt nothing for Drago, but as she and her friends followed James-Bond-Don through the saw palmetto, she couldn't help but feel remorseful. She figured federal agents were used to hurting and killing people, but she wasn't. She tried to save people. They'd just left Dempsey's body to burn, and that didn't sit right with her. Then she scolded herself as she watched the back of Don's head. Drago had planned to rape Saura, and Jeremiah wanted to rape her. Then they would've killed Raul for sport, maybe set him free in the woods and played The Most Dangerous Game. So her pity for the dead men, and for Drago, didn't last long. She had questions and concerns, but Maureen knew it wasn't the right time to ask Don about them.

Two kayaks sat beached on the shoreline: the two-person Jeb had used to transport them, and Dempsey's camo model. Two more single kayaks sat stacked within the cover of a mangrove tree, and they were the large touring kind. There was also a small barge like Hawk's. Don dug one of the singles out, and punched a large hole in the other with his knife, then did the same to the barge. Saura and Raul loaded into the double, and Don and Maureen took the singles. They only had two paddles, so Don towed Maureen, and Raul paddled the double. When they'd gone about halfway across, Don made a sharp turn, and headed for a section of lakeshore tangled with trees.

Maureen looked back and tendrils of smoke rose from the center of the island. She caught a whiff of burning plastic and smoldering peat. Soon the entire island would be ablaze, leaving only a black charred scar. Maureen also knew the fire would bring new life and that in less than a year, it would be hard to tell there'd been a fire there.

They paddled into the thick vegetation, and Don called out to Lester, the man Don had told them about. Maureen looked forward to meeting Tank and Jessie as well, and she wondered how the smaller dog would handle her owner not being with them. When they heard Lester's faint return call, they moved toward his voice.

Lester waited, M16 at the ready. Don made introductions, and Maureen found that she liked Lester. He had soft, kind eyes, but she could tell there was great pain hidden behind them. Maureen gave Lester some of the food they'd found, and before long, they were dragging the kayaks through the forest. Don had argued that they still might need them if the airboat was gone, or broke.

Saura was having trouble keeping up. Don set a grueling pace, and Maureen understood why. At the same time, he had to see she was breaking down, though she didn't appear to be giving it much of an effort. Maureen slowed and stayed behind Saura. Lester wasn't doing too much better. Don didn't seem to care.

"Hey. Special agent man," Maureen said. "You out of here now that you have your sample?"

Don stopped, and Raul almost walked into him. "I'm not so sure anymore."

"Why?" Maureen asked.

"No white scars," Raul said. "On Drago's face or any of his men. Right, Reacher?"

"Right," Don said. Who the hell was Reacher?

"So how could they handle the money and not be infected?" Maureen said.

"That's the question of our lives," Don said.

"None of the packets of cash on the pile were opened. Maybe the money went out to the next link in the chain sealed, and spread via the next level of dealers. That the stacks were sealed is proof Drago didn't want to touch the stuff, I would think. Maybe he used the tainted money to buy his supply, and let others distribute the virus," Raul said.

"All possible," Don said.

"And Drago threatened Maureen by saying he'd open a package, like that was something he wouldn't normally do," Raul said.

"Maybe they wore gloves or protective hand cream," Maureen said.

"Okay. What?" Don said.

"They make cream to protect you from poison ivy and things like that. I use it when I garden. It feels like a coating of plastic on your hands. The stuff doesn't last long, though," Maureen said.

"The gloves are a possibility. Nobody would question gloves on a guy like Drago," Don said. "The cream is a stretch. Though, they knew what the virus did, so I'd think they'd be careful."

"And the cream isn't much of a stretch," Saura said. They all looked at her, but she didn't back down. "I saw that stuff in Drago's private tent. I've seen it before. Ping uses... used it."

"Raul, didn't you search in there?" Don said.

"Yes, and now that I think of it, she's right. It was in Drago's tent with his colognes and stuff. Sorry. I had no reason to mention it. He wears Brute, if that's relevant."

Don chuckled. "As to your question, Maureen, no, I'm not out of here." Don gathered Saura, Raul, Lester, and Maureen around him. "From what I can see, none you are infected. Lester's been with me, and I consider you folks members of this team, if you're willing. I need your help. If I can get these samples out, we can stop this, and bring some of the infected back."

"But what does that mean?" Raul said. "Maybe we should just wait it out in the Glades."

"You're saying when the time comes, and they extract you, we'll all come with you?" Maureen asked.

"If you're uninfected and have helped me to the best of your abilities, yes." Don held his hand out to Maureen.

She didn't take it. "I have a couple questions."

They started walking again, dragging the kayaks. "What if we're wrong?" Don said, anticipating her question. "Doesn't matter. As you can see, I'm not exactly at my best, so I'm running with the money concept and contacting my people. There's not a hell of a lot more I can do with my current resources."

"That was one question," Maureen said. "Wouldn't your people have picked up a victim by now to do research on, is another question. And can't the government get a sample of the disease from one of them?"

"You're a nurse, right?" Don said. Maureen nodded. "Think about it then. When a virus infects its host it grows, it changes and adapts. We need a pure sample of whatever they created. Plus, you're missing the bigger picture. I can also now tell my people with ninety-nine percent certainty how the pathogen is being transmitted. That will allow them to take precautions all around the world."

Saura said, "So they might not get you out."

"There is that possibility, at least initially," Don said.

"Then what?" Saura said.

Don said nothing.

All that made sense to Maureen, and she said, "One last one. Why get rid of Drago? Wouldn't you want to question him further?"

"For what? He clearly didn't create the virus, and would die before he told us anything. This way is better, and much faster," Don said. Then he read her mind yet again, and continued, "And there was nothing to be done with Dempsey's body. We couldn't bury it. No rocks for a can. It would have burned no matter what we did, so why waste time?"

"Respect," Maureen said.

"We don't have time for respect. You think the disease will show respect?" Don said.

Maureen stopped pulling the kayak and held out her hand. Don took it. "Good. You?" he asked Raul. Raul and Don shook hands, and then Saura held out hers. "You have to step it up if you want to survive," Don said to Saura.

Don's perception amazed Maureen. In the short time he'd known Saura, he'd sized up her entire life, and in his polite, straightforward way, he'd just told the woman that if she wants to live, she better act like it.

"So the plan is to contact your people and get the hell out of here with the samples?" Maureen said.

"Yup," said Don.

"How?" Saura asked.

"I need to contact my people via radio on the ultra-high-frequency emergency band," Don said. "I think if I can find the right marine radio, and Lester and I modify it and add some power, I'll be able to get them."

"How will they know it's you, Agent Mulder?" Raul asked.

"I have a special passcode," said Don.

That satisfied Maureen, and it was a lot more than she'd had that morning. They started moving again, and entered a thick patch of pine trees. The kayaks floated on top of the saw palmetto, and this made it easier to drag them, except when they got caught between plants. She watched where she stepped because Don had told them this section of woods was packed with spiders and snakes. There were footprints, and it was clear Don and Lester had come this way. The rest of the pine forest looked to be untouched by man.

"Damn," Don said as he saw the tire marks from Dempsey's kayak carrier.

"Forgot our wheels," Lester said. "I thought of them a ways back."

They came to an angular aluminum airboat tied to a tree after forty minutes of walking. The boat was small, and only seated three people, and she didn't understand how everyone, along with the kayaks, would fit on the boat. Expecting her concern, Don said, "No worries. We'll tie the kayaks up behind the airboat and go real slow. We'll all fit."

As they had since she'd meet him, Don's words put Maureen at ease. She saw why he had great authority and power. He had an innate ability to lead people without trying, and she had no doubts they'd been lucky beyond count when he'd stumbled into their lives.

Raul and Lester busied themselves with tying the kayaks up to the airboat while Don got Saura and Maureen situated. Once Raul and Lester had joined them, Don pulled a folded piece of paper out from underneath the pilot's seat.

"What's that?" Saura asked. Maureen had noticed a change in the young woman's demeanor. She was attempting to understand what was happening and get involved.

"Dempsey used this map to get us in here. I will use it to get us out," Don said. He handed the map to Maureen, then turned the airboats great propeller. It took six turns before the engine caught, and the giant propeller spun. The motor roared, and the boat flattened the plants behind it.

Don eased the airboat's yoke back, and the boat inched forward through the sawgrass choked water. Maureen sat in the chair next to Don, and Saura, Raul, and Lester sat on the deck before them. A tickle in her subconscious made Maureen look over her shoulder, back at the cypress trees. She started when she thought she saw a figure darting from tree to tree, watching the boat. She looked at Don, who watched her with a smirk on his face. None of the others seemed to notice their pursuer, so she stayed quiet.

Using the hand-drawn map, Maureen did her best to guide Don through the bays, streams, mangrove thickets and stretches of swamp. Above the sun crested over the horizon, and thick black clouds came in from the east.

"That doesn't look good," Maureen yelled over the growl of the airboat's motor.

"No. It doesn't," Don yelled. "But we're almost there."

Don made one last turn and headed down a thin waterway that led into a thick tangle of mangrove trees. Don eased the boat's yoke forward, and it slowed, and he shut down the engine. "This is where Dempsey parked it," said Don, as Lester jumped from the craft, and tied the boat off on a tree. "Make sure it's secured well. Never know. We might need this baby again."

"Really?" Maureen said.

"My people may not be ready to extract us from the city. They may want me to get clear for pickup," Don said. "Especially if I have civilians with me."

Don made sense, as always, but the idea of returning to the Everglades turned her stomach. One by one, they jumped from the boat and headed up the path to Dempsey's van. Maureen grabbed the water bottles sitting on the boat seat. She couldn't carry them all, and everyone was already off the boat, so she abandoned two bottles.

Luckily for them, Dempsey had left his keys on the airboat. Jessie and Tank were excited to see them, but when Jessie realized Dempsey wasn't with the group, the small dog balled up in the back of the van. Tank was happy to see Lester and Don, and he warmed up to everyone else fast enough. Maureen gave both dogs water, and in minutes, Dempsey's hippie van was rolling back down the dirt road that led to Bubba's house.

Maureen sat in the rear of the van, stroking both Tank and Jessie. When they reached the end of the dirt road, and turned up Bubba's long driveway, Maureen thought she heard a faint wail of pain in the distance. None of her companions appeared to have heard it.

When they reached Bubba and Annette's house, Don killed the motor and told them all to sit tight. Maureen said she was going with him, and Don didn't protest. Bubba's front door stood open, and his screen door flapped in the breeze. Don got out and went to the garage, the double-barrel shotgun held out before him. Maureen trailed behind holding her rifle with its single shot.

The side door into the garage was gone, and from the looks of it, the door had been broken in from the outside. Tristin was nowhere to be found. Don took two large red containers of gasoline, and when they left the garage, he put the extra gas in the back of the van, and headed for the house.

Bubba's living room was destroyed. All his furniture was ripped to shreds, and the flat screen TV had been torn from the wall and used to break the fish tank. Dead fish lay all around, and water and colorful little rocks covered the floor. Don and Maureen moved into the kitchen, and checked the entire downstairs. Everything was chewed up, and broken, but there was no sign of Bubba, his wife, or Tristin.

They went back around to the foyer, and Don called up the stairs, "Hello!" Silence. "It's okay. I won't hurt you. Hello!" A floorboard squeaked. "It's me, the man who saved you. Come on if you're here. I have to leave."

Nothing.

Don turned and opened the front door.

"Don?"

Tristin stood at the top of the steps, staring down at them petrified, but she appeared all right. "Come on then," Don said. "We have to get going." Don quickly finished searching the house, but found no useful weapons. He grabbed food and drink, but found little else of use.

When they got back to the van, Lester was in the driver's seat. "I'll take a turn. You need a little rest," he said.

Don didn't protest. "This is Tristin," Don said. The young girl got into the van, followed by Maureen, who put her arm around the girl and pulled her close.

"Where to?" Lester asked.

"Do you know of any big marinas? Or boat storage places? Like where they'd store big commercial fishing boats, ferries, or yachts?" Don asked.

"Yeah. Tony O's on the creek in Black Point," said Lester. "But it's back toward the coast."

"Go there. Fast," Don said.

CHAPTER TWENTY-THREE

Don rode shotgun, his head resting against the van window as he scanned the road and surrounding area. His eyes hurt, his mouth was dry, his throat sore, and every wound ached. They crept back toward civilization, and abandoned cars, and occasional bloodstains where a person or animal had been torn to shreds marred the landscape. To the northeast, smoke rose into the dark clouds above midtown Miami. He knew the chaos had no boundaries because it had reached Bubba's place on the edge of nowhere. In the city, where there were high concentrations of people, the disease would spread exponentially.

He needed to understand what had happened at Bubba's house, but he didn't want to upset Tristin just yet because she had gone through two difficult traumas in a short time. He needed to know if Bubba had transformed on his own—he used and bought ride after all—or if the house had been attacked by outsiders. If it was the latter, things had spread faster than Don had thought possible.

The clouds were thick overhead, and the rain came in large, sporadic drops that smacked the windshield and tapped the van's roof. Within seconds it was pouring, and the VW's old wiper blades couldn't keep up. As Lester pulled over, Tank lifted his head to take a look, then rested it on his folded paws. Don and Lester examined a map. "Are there drainage canals along this road?" Don asked.

"No. There are traditional storm drains on that one," Lester said.

"Good," Don said. "I want to be able to drive around obstacles, and roadside canals are beyond the vans capabilities." More stuff a GPS couldn't tell them. They went the long way around, and cut through a few housing developments hoping to avoid problems. Once the shower ended, the sun would shine again, but until then the walkers were free to roam. Then he remembered how the walkers had been all covered up when they'd saved Tristin.

Lester pulled the van back onto the two-lane road and started off through the open fields once again. Sugarcane and other crops grew well here, and other than a few houses, and some barns and metal warehouses, nothing but green fields stretched in every direction. Miami was nothing more than a distant stain on the horizon. The rain let up and abruptly stopped. Don cracked the windows open, and the fresh scent of water filled the vehicle.

"How are you, Tristin?" Don asked. He didn't want to upset the girl, but soon they'd be back in the thick of things.

The girl still pressed against Maureen, her arms around her new surrogate mother. When the girl didn't speak, Maureen said, "It's okay, honey. He just wants to help us get out of here. That's what you want, isn't it?"

Tristin nodded, then said, "I'm all right, I guess."

"No cuts or wounds we need to worry about?"

"No, sir," she said. "You want to check again?"

"I don't think so, and no need to call me sir. I work for a living," Don said. "You feeling up to telling me what happened at the house?"

The girl winced as if reliving the pain. "I… is it important?"

"A little. You can save your story about what happened before we rescued you, but what happened at the house could be relevant."

"Okay," she said.

More buildings appeared in the fields as the farmsteads got smaller, and mile-by-mile they got closer to the suburbs of Miami. The rain started again, abruptly stopped, and a huge rainbow hung over the road. Thick smoke still hung in the distance.

"Take your time. Be as detailed as you can," Don said, urging Tristin along.

"When you left me, I was terrified. I didn't know what was happening, and having seen my entire family killed, I wasn't myself, if you understand me."

"Of course. We understand," Maureen said.

"Go on," Don said. "What happened after we left you?"

"I found some old blankets on a shelf and laid them out on the floor and tried to sleep, but I couldn't. My head hurt, and my hands shook. I lay like that for a long time—until I heard the yelling and screaming." Here Tristin paused, her face filling with fear and anguish.

"At first, I hid under the blankets and hoped whatever was happening outside would pass me by. Then someone pounded on the garage door, and I hid behind a pile of wood," Tristin said. "The side door caved in, and I saw Bubba, but it wasn't the Bubba I'd seen in the driveway when you brought me there. He had…" She shrugged as if everyone knew the rest.

"How did you get in the house?" Don said.

"He didn't find you?" Raul asked, at the same time as Don.

"I hit him with a rake and ran passed him. A woman stood in the doorway of the house, calling me. I ran to her because she looked okay, but Bubba came after me. I hid upstairs. He never came for me."

Silence fell in the van. They all sat there for several minutes, the green fields rushing by. "Do you know what happened to his wife, Annette, the woman you saw?" Maureen asked.

Tristin shook her head. "No. But I heard her screams. She saved me, I think."

Lester made a hard right, and houses appeared along the road. Many had broken windows, and there were more bloodstains visible than Don would've liked to have seen. Cars were abandoned along the road, their doors open. In one case, the vehicle was still running, and a brief debate occurred about whether they should take the car, and split into two groups. The debate didn't last long.

Dogs ran free, and livestock jogged along the road, or feasted on lawns. The animals were unaffected by the disease, and perhaps that was what the creator of the pathogen had wanted, or maybe they'd been lucky. Either way, this was great news. Quarantining people presented many unique challenges, but birds and wildlife were impossible to contain. This had worried Don, and was valuable information for him to give his people. Mosquitoes carrying the virus was still of great concern, but they had a limited flying range, and the containment zone was surrounded by water on three sides.

"What's that?" Saura asked, as she pointed. She'd been silent since they'd left the Glades. There were dark patches beneath her eyes, and she looked haggard. She wasn't twisting her hair around her finger.

Behind one of the houses, an arbor covered a large picnic table. Atop the table stood a man and women, and they were fighting off about fifteen walkers. The women hid behind her husband, while he swung a 2" by 4" piece of wood.

"Pull in there," Maureen yelled.

Lester looked at Don, who shook his head, and Lester kept driving.

"Hey," Maureen yelled. "We need to help them!"

"Maureen, do you know the population of Miami and surrounding areas?" Don asked. She didn't answer. "It's approximately three million. How is it—?"

"But they're not right in front of your face," Maureen said.

The van slowed as Lester heard Maureen's plea. Don turned to Lester, and said, "Keep going." He turned back to Maureen. "I understand how you feel. I do, trust me. Someday, we may have a nice dinner and I'll tell you all about it. But right now you need to trust me."

"But they're people. How can you just let them die?" Maureen said.

"First, we don't know if they'll die. And second, there are another three million people in this quarantine, and I need to think about them. Even if twenty percent are currently infected, that leaves two and half million people I need to save."

Maureen huffed and sat back in her seat. Don felt that pain in his neck he only got when he recognized his logic was twisted. Maureen preserved life, at all costs, and Don's reasoning didn't compute for her. What she said made a lot of sense, but there was a reason Don had major threat authority, and the ability to clamp down southern Florida. Maureen said, "Fine, but I don't have to like it."

"You wouldn't be in this van if you did," Don said.

The people being attacked had disappeared. Only a mound of human bodies undulating like a pile of maggots could be seen beneath the arbor. Don and Maureen's eyes meet. Don looked away. She had the ethical high ground at the moment, but it bothered him how she acted like he was less than human because he had the right to decide who lives and who dies. That wasn't how Don felt at all.

They passed row upon row of houses, and signs of civil unrest were everywhere. Overturned cars blocked the streets, discarded bones littered the ground, and burnt-out buildings still smoldered in the sunlight. Blood was everywhere: splattered on houses, covering cars, dripping down curbs, and smeared on windows and broken glass. Don looked around the van, and everyone except Maureen stared at their legs.

Something hit the side of the van. Walkers threw rocks at them from under a garage overhang. Lester sped up, and easily went around the blockade that was set across the road. They were getting close, and the neighborhood had a warren of canals behind the houses. These manmade rivers snaked through the development giving each house a boat slip, and access to the Atlantic and inner bays.

Lester said, "We could go by boat the rest of the way? Park this baby in a garage, take a boat into the marina," Lester said.

Don hadn't thought of that. They'd been lucky on the road so far, but he knew it was only a matter of time before they were seriously waylaid. On the boat, they would have only one route, while on the road they had many. The boat's motor would roar in the relative stillness of the day with no power or vehicles on the move. They could be trapped much easier in the canal, and they would have to waste time finding a place to put the van, and then find a boat to use.

When Don looked up from his internal debate, everyone stared at him. "Nay. Keep going. Show me the marina, and we'll hunker down and come up with a plan." Tension filled the van as Lester maneuvered around obstacles. There were walkers, but they weren't attacked again. Most of them appeared content to stay in the shadows until dark.

They left the housing development via two arched concrete bridges that led toward the interstate. Lester made a sharp right, and they entered a maintenance area. Large trucks and boats in dry-dock filled the dirt lot, and beyond a large metal warehouse with the words "Tony O's" painted on the side in black lettering surrounded on three sides by canals. Most of the slips were filled with boats and a huge white rack sat at one end of the lot stacked with boats of all sizes.

Lester stopped the van, and looked to Don, who peered through the windshield, his mind working through all the angles, and figuring possible outcomes. "First," he said. "Only Lester and I are going." Maureen and Raul protested, and Don put up a hand. "Trust. Remember?" No response. "Lester knows how to modify the radio, and I will get him his parts. You will stand guard from there," said Don, as he pointed at an empty area with high grass around its perimeter. The spot looked like a boat had been dry-docked there until recently. "Lester will back the van in there, and he and I will sneak around back. Looks like it's pretty quiet."

"What about your people? Can't we hear what they say?" Saura asked.

"I'll fill you in," said Don. When he saw Maureen, Raul, and Saura exchange glances, he said, "What?"

"You could tell us anything," Maureen said. "No offense to Lester, but you guys are the original team. We're add-ons."

"I understand. Overruled. Beep the horn if there's a major problem."

Don packed his jacket with the extra eleven shells and checked the two in the shotgun. Lester racked the slide on the M16, and opened his door and got out, followed by Don.

The afternoon sun baked the ground, and steam rose into the air as the rainwater evaporated. Mangrove trees and bushes surrounded the parking lot, and Don and Lester crept through the tangled vegetation. A gentle breeze pushed across the marina, and the air smelled of smoke. When they were around the side of the warehouse, Don led Lester through a series of dry-docked boats. A stack of trailers was on display in front of the building, and a large window opened into an office.

They worked their way around back. Nothing moved, and there was no sound except the occasional tap of the guide wire against the flagpole. Piles of parts, discarded motors, and other marine trash sat stacked along one side of the warehouse, and provided excellent cover. Large roll-up doors covered the other side of the building.

Don and Lester ran the short distance from the cover of the boats to the side of the warehouse. They looked in a window, and nothing moved within. Boats stood in ordered rows in various states of repair, and it looked like nothing had been messed with. There were contact sensors on the window, but the power had been out for over twenty-four hours, so the backup battery would be close to dead. While Lester covered him, Don slipped his knife up under the windowpane and flipped open the clasp. No alarm sounded, and Don opened the window, and he and Lester slipped inside.

It was dark in the warehouse. Don had point, and he scanned the area as Lester followed. Tools were laid out on the benches, and there were no walkers in sight. The sound of the window lock clicking into place made Don freeze. "Shit," he said. Behind him, a man with black hair in his mid-fifties blocked the way, a six-shooter in his hand, the barrel of which floated back and forth between Lester and Don.

"Put those guns down, and put your hands up," the man said.

Lester looked to Don, who nodded. They both placed their weapons on the floor. The man looked tired, but there were no white scars on his face. "I'm Don, and this is my partner Lester. We're federal agents." Don looked over at Lester just in time to see him smile briefly.

"Tony Orfman," said the man. "Now get on the ground, hands behind your head."

CHAPTER TWENTY-FOUR

Stomach acid crept up Maureen's throat as she watched Lester and Don disappear into the mangroves at the edge of the marina's storage lot. It pained her to depend on Don so much. She usually counted on one person—herself, but she remembered this wasn't a typical day in the ER. Don had been trained most of his life to deal with tense situations, and it brought comfort knowing he watched out for her.

The sky was getting dark, and it looked like rain again soon. Nothing moved on the road beyond the dirt lot. The entrance was partly hidden by mangroves, and the turn toward the interstate dominated the road. Maureen opened the windows, and the sweet smell of hibiscus and smoke floated on the breeze. The boats docked in the marina bobbed and listed, and somewhere a bird tapped a tree. Maureen breathed in the fresh air, and for an instant felt relaxed.

"You think he'll be able to do this?" asked Raul. "Sounds like ten kinds of bullshit to me."

Maureen didn't answer. She stared at a section of mangroves that ran along the southern side of the metal building. "Shush," she said.

"You see something, Eagle Eye?" Raul said, as he followed her gaze.

The mangrove leaves rustled, and dark shapes appeared. She got her rifle ready, and Raul pulled the Sig Saur from his waistband. Saura and Tristin watched, their faces split with fear and apprehension. Time seemed to slow, and Maureen felt herself fading, her weariness beckoning her toward sleep.

Don and Lester ran toward the building and hid within a pile of junk parts. The top of Lester's head floated above the garbage pile for a few seconds and then disappeared. There were no sirens, no protests from within the building. All was spooky quiet.

"Who is that guy?" Tristin asked. "Don, I mean."

"He claims to be James Bond, but all we have is his word for it," Raul said.

"We have a bit more than that," countered Maureen. "At the beginning, I'd have agreed with you, but everything he's done since we meet him is consistent with what he says he is."

"Yeah, but do you know how many morons must be playing live Dead Rising right now? These video games warp the mind," Raul joked, but nobody laughed. "How do you know he's just not playing out a fantasy he's dreamt about all his life?"

"I just know," Maureen said.

"His story is very convenient," Saura said. "No ID, no way to prove who he is. That fits real neat with the idea that he can't approach the police or the military for help."

"Certainly is convenient," Raul said.

Maureen's teeth clamped down on her lip. "Look, I understand where you're coming from, but I tell you he isn't lying. I deal with liars of every color, creed, profession, and social status every day at the hospital. Everyone lies the same way, and Don isn't lying."

"How did you meet him?" Tristin asked.

Maureen told the entire story from first to last, and the minutes ticked on with no signs from Don. "If he hadn't found us, I don't want to think about where we might be."

"You know where we'd be. I'd be dead, and you both would be sex toys," Raul said, gesturing toward Maureen and Saura.

Tristin made a face, and Raul said, "I'm sorry. How old are you anyway, Emma Watson?"

"Fourteen," Tristin said, and Raul let a long sigh escape his lips.

"You lost your parents to the disease?" Raul asked.

"Yes. I had to run from my house to get away from them. That's how I got trapped by the underpass where Don and Lester found me," she said.

"Interesting. He wouldn't let me stop for the greater good, but he had no problem stopping himself to help you and Tank. But..." She sounded foolish. Tristin and Tank were the product of a different time and place, and she didn't understand Don's thought process at the time. She guessed that if those two people they'd seen fighting for their lives atop the picnic table were children,

Don would have reacted differently. At least she liked to believe so.

"Yeah, I suppose," Tristin said. "Lester was the one who came for me. I don't know that Don had a choice. What's that?" She pointed through the front windshield from the back seat. Maureen searched for what she was pointing at, but saw nothing.

"What?" Saura asked.

"There, by the smoke," Tristin said.

Several helicopters raced toward Miami central. They looked to be the big military copters that transported soldiers and supplies. "That's good news," Maureen said, putting her arm around Tristin. Tank got up and sat in the back seat, staring out the windshield. Jessie was shaking and curled up on the floor behind the driver's seat.

"Those are Chinooks. Definitely the military," Raul said.

As if on cue, a loud rumble built behind them. The hedge of mangrove made it impossible to see what was happening, but as the sound continued to rise, so did Maureen's angst. Tank barked.

"Quiet," Maureen said. Her gaze never left the marina's entrance where a small section of the road was visible. The noise had become deafening, and Maureen thought the ground was collapsing beneath them. She wrung her hands, and pulled Tristin to her. The girl shook, and all the normalcy they'd imparted to her fled. She was again the frightened young girl with wide eyes. This hurt Maureen in ways she hadn't believed possible. She didn't have kids, and there weren't plans to have any, but she felt more for Tristin than her protection instinct.

Maureen had an insane idea: when they got out of this mess, she'd adopt the girl and together they'd help each other put their lives back together. But that was crazy. She had no way of knowing if the girl had family that might want her, or if the girl even wanted to be with her. Judging by the way she gripped Maureen's arm, she thought it might work out. A daughter. It even sounded weird in her head.

The approaching rain announced its impending arrival with a crack of thunder that lit the gray sky. Squeaking and the popping of stones under rubber tires joined the grumble, and soon green army trucks were passing before the marina's entrance toward the interstate.

A line of vehicles made up of tanks, urban assault vehicles, jeeps, troop carriers, and supply trucks inched by the lot entrance. They were headed north, toward central Miami, and they didn't appear to notice the marina, or anything that was happening there.

"About time," Raul said.

"Yeah. Things are about to change dramatically," Maureen said.

The convoy passed without incident, and the rumble died away. With them went hope, and destruction. The rain started, first as a thin mist, and then a steady drizzle. The four companions sat in silence, watching the rain run down the windows into mud puddles. Maureen passed around the last of their food, and she checked her rifle a second time. Seeing her do this, Raul checked his Sig Saur and laid it on his lap. Three shots between them.

Maureen started to worry. An hour had slipped away since Lester and Don disappeared around the side of the building, and he had said they shouldn't be much longer than that. Every tick of the clock reminded Maureen that Don hadn't come back, and she thought about what it would mean if he didn't return.

"What's that?" asked Tristin. She sat bolt upright, her eyes the size of quarters. She stared at the marina entrance through the rain, and there appeared to be a person standing just within the mangroves, watching them. Then there were two dark shapes there, and then three.

"Oh poop," Maureen said, and Tristin giggled. The sound of her laughter was a like a tonic for the soul.

"There are more of them there," Saura said. "Look."

"Shitttttt," said Raul. "How the hell did they find us?"

"Probably following the convoy," Maureen said. "We're just in the wrong place at the wrong time."

"Story of my life," Raul said.

"Are you sure they see us?" Tristin asked.

"Hard to tell," Maureen said. "Everybody get down. Saura, grab Tank." Maureen and crew got as low as they could so they couldn't be seen through the van's windows.

Maureen lifted her head and peeked through the windshield. The rain was stopping, and a lit mist covered everything. Two walkers came toward the van. That the walkers had sent only two into the marina to investigate meant they were communicating, and capable of rational thought.

A walker looked their way, and Maureen dropped, but she didn't think she'd been fast enough. There was yelling and screaming, and the rain picked up, beating the roof of the van. Maureen stole another glance.

Two walkers yelled and pointed toward the van, and more sleepwalkers appeared all around the marina entrance. At first glance, there looked to be ten or fifteen, but as they moved toward the van, Maureen counted many more. She threw herself into the front seat and stabbed the van's horn with her fist. It wasn't loud, and sounded clownish, but it stopped the walkers advance. Maureen beeped the horn again, and again, but Don and Lester didn't come.

"Lester said they're afraid of loud noises," Raul said.

"They don't look afraid. They look mad," Maureen said. She looked toward the warehouse, hoping beyond hope that Don would appear, but he wasn't there.

The horde advanced again, and to Maureen's dismay, she saw they had a vehicle, and it was parked across the marina's entrance.

Maureen went to start the van, but the keys were gone. Anger and astonishment made her pound the steering wheel, but even if she could start the van, where would she go? The entrance was blocked, but at least she could try and run them down. Leaving Don and Lester behind wasn't a concern, not with a pack of walkers descending on them. They hooted and hollered, jumped up and down, and pounded their chests. The transformed ambled forward awkwardly, and there were at least fifty of them dressed in the torn clothes of the people they'd once been. Some carried clubs and other basic weapons like axes, hammers, and kitchen knives.

"He left us out here without the keys? WTF?" Saura yelled.

Maureen leaned on the horn again, and the sleepwalkers paused for an instant, and then kept coming. The walkers had almost reached them, and Maureen looked to the warehouse, but saw no one.

The horde of walkers advanced, and there were children among the damned. This made her cry. Throughout it all, she'd kept it together, but the children were too much.

One kid wore a blue dress, and was missing an eye. Dried blood filled the empty socket, and the girl's straw-like hair was wild. A boy of perhaps three hung on the leg of a bigger walker, the child's face purple. Then there was the blood—so much blood, and most of the sleepwalkers were covered in it.

The horde surrounded the van and rocked it back and forth. In response, Maureen and crew adjusted their positions with each push, trying to counterbalance the vehicle.

The infected swarmed over the van so thick it got dark. Tank barked, and Kristin screamed at the faces of sleepwalkers pressed against the windows. She buried herself in Maureen as the van rocked back and forth. Maureen remembered Don, and what he had said to Saura, and she thought Tristin needed that same speech. "Honey, you have to buck up a little if you want to make it out of here. I can only do so much for you."

The window by Raul shattered. Arms reached into the van, grasping for him. He tried to shield himself and move away, but rough hands seized him and yanked him halfway out the window. Raul wailed in pain as he clawed at the van in an attempt to get away. Tank bit the arm holding Raul, and he pulled his arm free. Raul tossed the Sig Saur to Tristin as the walkers got hold of his other arm and tore him through the broken window. The sound of breaking bone and ripping cartilage made Tristin retch, and she puked up the beef jerky she'd just eaten. Blood splattered the interior of the van, and Tristin screamed.

The van continued to rock, coming close to flipping. Raul's blood was hot on Maureen's face, and she thought of Tim. The rear window shattered. Walkers climbed in through the back of the van. Tank blocked the way, growling as if possessed. So it was that Maureen didn't see Raul's final moments, but as he was carried into the horde, she saw that his legs were already gone.

Maureen, Saura, and Tristin jumped into the front seat, knives out. Maureen aimed the rifle at the walker coming at her from the rear of the van and fired. The thing's head exploded, and the rest of the transformed froze. Maureen flipped the gun around, and held it by the barrel before her like a club. Three walkers replaced the one Maureen shot. Tristin fired the Sig Saur, and it almost knocked her to the floor. She'd missed wildly, but the horde had stopped coming again.

Boom! Boom!

The shotgun blasts were like music and the sleepwalkers scrambled like cockroaches. Tristin fired the Sig Saur for the last time, and hit a walker in the rear of the van, but the shot didn't kill or wake it. But it was enough, and the sleepwalkers fled the way they'd come, glass ripping and tearing at their flesh as they wiggled through the broken window.

Maureen stole a glance amidst the chaos, looking for Raul, but a bloodied lump of flesh was all that remained of her friend.

CHAPTER TWENTY-FIVE

Don and Lester did as they were told, and laid on the floor in front of Tony. The guns rested on the floor a few feet away, but they were out of reach. Don heard Lester breathing hard beside him, and felt his stare. Don said, "My name is Don Obe—"

"Shut up!" Tony said. "You think I want to hear your desperate bullshit?"

"I just wanted—"

"What? You think you're the first fools to think of getting away by boat? I've been listening to the Navy channel, and I understand some of their lingo. No way anyone is getting through their blockade."

Silence fell and Don waited. He'd tried to speak twice, and now he would wait to be asked a question. Several minutes passed, and all Tony did was stare at them. Then he said, "Go ahead. Who the hell are you? If you lie to me, you're done." Tony stuck his revolver in his waistband and picked up the shotgun and the M16. He leaned the shotgun against a workbench, but kept the M16.

"We're not trying to get away," Don said.

"Right. What are you doing then?" Tony asked.

"My name is Don Oberbier, and this is my associate Lester. I'm a federal agent working on behalf of the government. I came here because I thought you might have a marine radio we could modify so I can contact my people."

"Impossible. I've tried, and there's been no response. They ignore me," Tony said. "Sit up." Don and Lester sat up and brushed themselves off. "Don't get any stupid ideas. I will kill you."

"Of that, I have no doubts," said Don. "And it won't be impossible for me."

Tony laughed. "Even if you are who you say you are, how can they be sure it's you? Hundreds of people have tried to contact them with every story imaginable."

"I have a special code I can give them so they know it's me," Don said.

"You got any proof? You sure don't look like an agent," Tony said.

Don ran through his options and decided he had no real choice. In a steady, calm tone, Don told Tony most of the story from the moment he'd walked into the Redro house. Tony O said nothing, but his face seemed to soften when Don told of Maureen, Tristin, and Saura hiding in the car.

"Still don't see how I can trust you," Tony said.

"You don't need to. Take a look out your front window, and I'll show you the van with our friends in it. If that's not good enough, it doesn't matter. Let us do our work while you watch us at gunpoint. You'll know pretty fast if I'm lying."

Tony considered this. "I have a radio you can use," he said, and Don sighed with relief, and when he looked over at Lester, the tension had left his face, and his eyebrows were no longer knitted across his forehead.

"I need to get way up on the UHF scale to 2106.19MHz. Do you have an antenna?" asked Don.

"Yeah. A big one. I used to run a ferry service, and I used it to communicate with them. What I'm worried about is the power to get up that high."

"That's why we need a second marine battery," Lester said.

"So that really is the reason you came here?" Tony asked.

"That's it," said Don. Tony was coming around, and the longer they talked, the more confident Don felt. At that moment, the faint glow of a light at the end of the tunnel began to flicker.

Tony considered them for several minutes and said nothing. Then he opened a cabinet, placed the M16 and shotgun inside, and then locked it. He had pulled his revolver, and he kept it somewhat pointed at them as he handled the guns.

Lester looked to Don, who was watching Tony's every move. Don shook his head ever so slightly, and Lester looked at the floor. Don could take the man. The opening was there while his attention was focused on the guns, but he didn't think he needed to take the risk. If he went for Tony, there was always the possibility he'd get shot. If things went south, he'd have to take the risk, but now there was no need.

When Tony finished putting away the guns, he pulled up a stool and sat before Don and Lester. "You guys seem like the real deal, but the world has gone nuts, as you know well. The radio is in the backroom there, and the batteries are in the trickle charge room."

Don got up and dusted himself off, and Tony pointed the gun at him. "This isn't over. If you so much as fart the wrong way, I will not hesitate to take you down, like I did the others. Come with me."

Lester rose, and the three men went to the back of the warehouse where there was a series of small rooms. "Look in there," Tony said.

Don opened the door and the smell of rotting flesh assailed him. He coughed and covered his nose as he stepped into the room, but he couldn't make it through the door. Bodies were stacked on top of each other in neat piles. There were women, several men, and a child or two, all shot to death. The white scars that identified them as infected creased their faces, and the trauma of their final moments still showed in their expressions.

Don stepped back and closed the door. Tony said, "Like I said, you weren't the first ones with the idea to come here." Tony examined his shoes. It was clear to Don this man wasn't a killer, but when fighting for one's life, people did things they normally would never do.

"We've killed our share of innocents, and some we left to die. I understand," Don said.

"I just wanted you to understand I wasn't kidding," Tony said.

"Message received," said Lester. "Why'd you bring them inside? That's like stocking up on honey when you're fighting an army of ants. Got m..."

"I didn't want..." Tony's voice broke-up, and a tear slipped down his face. "Have you seen what they do to the dead?" Lester and Don nodded. "Well, there's no way I can let that happen. These were people. Some of which I knew," Tony said.

"We're losing daylight," Don said. "Can I get started?"

"One last condition," Tony said. "I get to listen in."

"Done," Don said.

Don went into the trickle charge room where many batteries were stacked on racks and connected to a machine that constantly charged the deep cycle units when the power was on. He removed the newest-looking battery and carried it to where Tony had the radio.

The radio was exactly what they needed. It was a high-end UHF with large metal brackets still attached to the top where it had been bolted to a ship. Lester went to work tinkering with the radio. Tony turned on the overhead light, and Don started.

"You've got power?" he asked.

"No. But I got plenty of batteries, and a large power inverter," said Tony. Don wagged his head.

There was a loud rumbling noise coming from outside, but no horn. "Can we go take a look out that front window while Lester does his thing? I'd like to check on our friends and see what's causing all that noise."

Tony's eyes shifted to Lester, then back to Don. He appeared to make a significant decision. He put the revolver in his waistband, and said, "Sure."

Don and Tony left Lester to finish modifying the radio. The place already stank from the soldering iron. When they got to the front office, Tony said, "Holy turd." A long line of military vehicles was passing the front entrance.

"See there," Don said, and he pointed to the VW van. "See my people there?"

"I do." Tony shifted on his feet, and looked nervous. "Shouldn't we go out there? Try to stop them? They may have a protected area they can take us to?"

"They probably do, but we can't," Don said. "You ever been in the service?" Tony shook his head no. "Well, you don't get in the way of a force that size unless you want to get rolled over. They are on their way to war, and I wouldn't get in their way at this point even if I could prove who I was and that we were uninfected."

This seemed to appease Tony, and when the convoy was done going by, and nothing happened to Maureen and crew, they headed back to see if Lester was finished.

He was. The radio crackled with static. Lester had a very hard time honing in on 2106.19MHz. When he thought he had the radio tuned as best as he could, and the static had diminished to a low buzz, Lester turned to Don. "All yours."

"The moment of truth," Don said.

He called into the radio, saying his name, and the code names of every person he knew. Nothing. This went on for several minutes, and Don was getting frustrated.

"How will they know to check that frequency?" Tony asked.

"They know I'm in here. I brought down the quarantine. They're listening. There must be something wrong with the radio," Don said.

"Nope," said Lester. "It's getting a little hot because of the extra power, but it's working fine."

Don continued to call into the silence, and the minutes passed. He was ready to give up when a female voice boomed from the radio. "Attention. This is a restricted military frequency. Please get off this channel immediately."

"This is Don Oberbier. I work for Big Bird. Please stand by for my security code."

Silence. Then, "Please wait one moment. Do not transmit," said the voice.

Several moments passed, and Lester said, "We better get on with this or we're gonna need to rig another unit. This thing is getting hot."

A deep male voice came over the radio. "Agent Oberbier, we've been waiting on you. Code please."

"2719 dash, 3385 dash, 0289," Don said.

Silence.

"Don. For shit sake, we thought we'd lost you. We found the van, but there wasn't much left and we feared the worst," said the voice over the radio.

"Massie?" Don asked.

"Yup," he said. "What've you got? You want out, I suppose?"

"Massie, tell the higher ups it's the money. The pathogen is being transmitted on money," Don said.

"Money? We thought it was this drug everyone's been getting high on, ride," Massie said.

"Me too, at first. But it's the money from the drug transactions that started it. I'm sure of it."

"10-4, Don. I'll speak with Big Bird and we can check all the cash supplies and send out an international alert to other governments."

"I heard the quarantine is holding," Don said.

"It is," Massie said.

Lester nudged Don and pointed at the radio. A thin tendril of smoke rose from the unit.

"Do you know they're afraid of loud noises, and that heat and sunlight hurts them?"

"We've got a few guys on the inside and they've told us that, but the things appear to be adapting and learning. Covering themselves up, and such. Driving cars and learning how to set traps and use weapons. The ones in custody have to be sedated, and they've provided little from a behavioral standpoint. We know sunlight and heat can kill bacteria, so we figure that has something to do with it."

"Yes, that's what we've seen as well. Also, animals don't appear to be affected at all," Don said.

"We know. The brains tell me the pathogen takes over the neocortex of its host, hence animals don't get infected because they don't have one. In humans, the neocortex plays an influential role in sleep, memory, and learning. The brains believe this is how it turns people into sleepwalkers. The physical aspect of it we're still working on, but we know the virus enflames all live tissue, and increases adrenaline output, which explains their extraordinary strength and speed. We've almost got a good test for the pathogen, and once we do, we'll be able to get people out."

Now Don asked that question that had worried him from the start. "What about mosquitoes?" The flying miniature vampires had spread plague since the beginning of time.

"We're doing what we can. We're spraying all along Alligator Alley, and northern Florida, while not under quarantine, is still locked down tight. Mosquitoes don't have much of a flying range, and they don't live long, so we're hopeful."

"Any ideas on an antidote? You know victims can be woken, yes?"

"Twice. Yes. After the second waking, the victim can't snap out of the trance the pathogen puts it under, and those people are effectively lost," Massie said.

"Last but not least, it's time to get me out," Don said. "Now. And I have several people with me under my protection. They aren't infected, and need to be extracted with me. I wouldn't have this information if it wasn't for them."

A long silence filled the void between Don and Massie. Smoke poured from the radio now, and in moments, it would short out. Massie's voice came back. "No can do. At least not now. Maybe in a couple of days when defensive positions within the city are setup and the testing protocols are worked out. I could put you in touch with the military on the ground, but they're in the thick of the shit. No way can I authorize you taking civilians into the city. Hunker down and wait."

It was Don's turn to say no can do. "I have a packet of money with the original pathogen," he said, and smiled, as if he'd played his last card.

"Hold on," Massie said. "We need to contact Big Bird."

Static filled the silence, and Don's mind ran back to the day he'd met Massie. He'd appeared like a ghost from the mist, and saved his life. Massie had approached with caution, sizing Don up as if he were an animal. Don hadn't known his name, where he was from, or where he'd been. Massie must have seen this in his eyes because all he remembered about their meeting was the look of pity that set him off. Many months later, he'd been told of how he'd attacked as Massie tried to set him free. Rehab had taken three years, and through it all, Massie stayed with him, and when it was over, Don was recruited.

There was a blast of static from the radio, and the sound of muffled speech, but then more gentle static.

Over the years, he'd asked himself what would have happened to him had he not been captured? Would he still be in the military? Probably not. Most likely he would've mustered out like all his friends, and he'd be married with two kids and walking a beat in Chicago or Miami. Instead, day by day, he'd fought to climb from the abyss, and when his second chance came, he grabbed it and didn't look back.

They waited for what felt like a long time, but was only a few minutes. The radio looked like it was going to explode, and more static filled the channel. When Massie came back on, he sounded sullen.

"We need that sample. You are hereby ordered to bring it to me. Alone."

"Piss off. My people get extracted with me or no deal."

"You're refusing a direct order?" Massie asked.

Don looked at Lester, and said, "Yes. I am."

"Very well. Since I told the bird that's what you'd say, she told me to tell you there would be consequences when this is over."

"Understood."

"Like, getting busted down to a desk. In Lincoln, Nebraska."

"Understood." Static filled the silence, and Don saw Massie's smiling face in his mind's eye.

"Okay. Did you ever hear of a site called Hole in the Donut?" Massie asked.

"You mean the H-69 missile site out in the Glades? I was there once," Don said.

"You think you can get there by midnight?" Massie asked.

Don looked to Lester, who said, "I've been there with Jerry. He heard about it while at boot camp years ago. As luck would have it, it's east of Homestead."

Don stood slack-jawed for an instant. He recalled thinking he hadn't seen the last of the Everglades as they left the airboat, and he felt odd when one of his gut feelings hit so close to the mark. "Yes, I can," said Don into the radio.

"Okay. Extraction at midnight. I'll see you for debriefing as soon as you're out. Then I've been ordered to transfer you up to the bird," Massie said. "One last time: come alone."

"No can do, and you know it."

"I do. Good luck."

"That's a 10-4. Oberbier, out." Don sifted through Massie's words, and worried that if there wasn't a viable test by midnight, they'd take the sample and leave them. The good of the many mantra was followed by his superiors also.

As Tony shut down the radio it sparked, but there was no fire.

Then they heard the VW's horn piercing the stillness, and Don turned to Lester. "Time to hit the road." When Don turned to speak with Tony, he was gone.

They found him by the cabinet where he'd locked up their guns. He handed them back their weapons, and Don said, "Thank you, Tony. We couldn't have done this without you."

"Don't thank me yet. I'm coming with you."

CHAPTER TWENTY-SIX

What remained of Raul took Maureen's breath away, and for a moment, she stood paralyzed, chomping on her lip, which was half-swollen and bleeding. They'd been through a lot, and she despaired for her survival without him. Over the last thirty-six hours, she'd been forced to accept a new reality, one in which she was hunted, and Raul had helped her. Only now, with him gone, did she realize she'd been attracted to him, and all his wiseass nicknames. Tank still barked, and the remaining walkers scrambled off the van as two more shotgun blasts rocked the day.

Don, Lester, and a man with black hair Maureen had never seen before walked across the dirt parking lot like old school gunslingers. They fired into the horde of sleepwalkers, and they went down all around the van. Smoke rose from their gun barrels, and their faces were sad and angry. Some of the walkers woke for an instant before they died, their frightened eyes staring at their attackers in confusion. Others died instantly, transforming as they fell.

Five victims were awake and lay bleeding from bullet wounds. Pity surged through her. They had no idea what had happened to them, or why they were being attacked. There was nothing she could do for them, and that's what kept her from leaping from the van. Don and crew continued to fire at the walkers, and in minutes the horde broke up and scattered. Several of the sleepwalkers retreated to their vehicle, which was still parked across the marina's entrance.

Maureen watched with growing relief as Don, Lester, and the mystery man came toward the van. She was reminded of the Glades: what would they do with the diseased awake people?

Maureen opened a van door and Tank jumped out and ran to Don. As Maureen got out, Don yelled, "Bring the first aid kit." She chuckled to herself. Don had found his heart. She grabbed the kit and stepped over several bodies as she made her way to Don.

"You okay?" he asked.

"As good as expected," Maureen said, and her gaze strayed to Raul's remains. "You have the van keys?"

"No," Don said. "Lester, did you take the van keys?"

Lester patted his pockets. "Shit, I did," Lester said. "Didn't think anything of it. I put them in my pocket like I always do. Habit."

"Having them would have been a help!" she shouted.

Don looked to the van, and when he didn't see Raul, he lowered his head. "I'm sorry, Maureen."

"Me too," she said.

"Little help here," said one of the awakened walkers.

Maureen went to help, but Don put out an arm. "You shouldn't get any of their blood on you."

"What am I supposed to do? Nothing?"

"I have rubber gloves and plastic suit and mask I wear when I'm under boats defouling their bottoms," Tony said. "Just give me a minute."

Tony rushed off, and returned two minutes later. Maureen suited up and went about the task of stopping the bleeding and bandaging the man's leg. Then she moved on to the others, and when she was done, only one person had died. Four people now looked up at Don with expectant eyes.

He had the same concerns she did. "You can't come with us," Don said as he introduced Tony to his people, and updated everyone. "Tony, can they stay in your place?"

Tony appeared skeptical, and he looked back at the warehouse as if it was a living thing, and he couldn't separate himself from it. "Guess it doesn't matter, since I'm leaving. The room I showed you in the back is locked down."

Maureen and Lester directed the survivors into the marina office, where they found cold coffee and stale donuts. They were all scared, and nervous, but there wasn't much that could be done for them. Every time Maureen thought of them as people, she saw the thin white scars on their faces and remembered they were infected.

"Stay awake. If you feel you can't, separate yourselves in the various sections of the warehouse and lock all the interior doors.

At least then you won't go at each other and you'll be somewhat protected."

"You're leaving us?" asked a young woman. Her strawberry-blonde hair was matted with blood, and she shook with fear.

"You heard Agent Oberbier. We're helping him with something very important. We'll send help as soon as it's available. They're working on an antidote as we speak," Maureen said. She did her best to sound positive, but she didn't think she was successful. The woman lowered her head, and Maureen felt a pang of guilt.

"Don says we need to roll," Lester said.

She was about to abandon four people to certain death and the nurse in her rose up. "I can't leave them here," she said.

Lester frowned, and took her by the elbow. When they were alone, he said, "They're already dead, Maureen." She moved away, and he grabbed her arm. Sweat dripped down his face, and his hands were clammy and wet. She shook him off. "I know that sucks hard. Trust me. We've all suffered, and you've lost your husband. But the only way to help them is to get that sample out. The faster we do that, the better chance they have, and we need your help."

Maureen knew he was right. This entire odyssey had been a test of her metal and ethics. She'd seen that her view of the world, while noble and righteous, wasn't how you survived in chaos. Don knew what he was doing, and by extension, so did Lester.

"Sorry, I just…"

Lester put his arm around her. "This goes against everything you stand for. I get it. But we've been thrust into the extremely important position of having to take all the people of Miami into account when making our decisions," Lester said.

"Are you sure you're not fooling yourself? Justifying our escape for our own personal safety?" asked Maureen.

Lester didn't answer and looked away.

"What?"

"We are human, Maureen," Lester said. "I'd be lying if I said some of this isn't about self-preservation."

With that settled, nothing had changed. They both went back to the victims. Everyone said their goodbyes, and good lucks, and there were more promises to send help. When the time came to leave them, Maureen couldn't help but cry.

They made their way out the front entrance and heard the door lock fall into place behind them. Don talked with Tony and Tristin. Saura, Jessie, and Tank were in the van. Walkers still loitered by the car at the marina entrance, and Maureen and Lester went to Don.

"Why not blow through them?" Tony asked.

"You remember what Massie said? That they'd learned to set traps. That," said Don, as he pointed toward the entrance, "is a trap."

Tony appeared unconvinced. When Don saw Maureen and crew, he asked, "How'd it go?"

"As best as could be expected," Lester said, with a sidelong glance at Maureen.

Picking up on Lester's unease, he asked, "Are you all right, Maureen?"

"As well as possible, I guess. What's the plan?"

Don looked at Tony. "Tony thinks we should just blow through the walkers and make a break for it. I believe there's more to it than meets the eye."

"What other choice do we have?" Tony said. "Right or wrong, I don't see another way."

"What about what Lester said before about taking a boat? There are many here to choose from. We take one to a house, find a new vehicle, and go on our way," Maureen said.

Don said, "It would be too easy to get trapped on the water, and I think we'd draw even more attention."

Maureen didn't argue further. Don would do what he thought was right. He was just pretending to debate the situation so everyone felt like they'd had their say. Then Don surprised her.

"All right. We'll do it Tony's way. I don't see a better way at the moment myself," Don said.

Maureen headed for the van, and then stopped when she saw Don listening intently. She heard it also, the distant *whomp whomp* of a helicopter approaching. The sound grew until it was a thunderous roar that ripped at the plants and trees. A helicopter tore across the sky so fast they barely saw it. The wind eased, the sound retreated, and the copter was gone. It reminded her of the copters they'd seen in the Glades. It reminded her of Tim.

"Too bad they can't pick us up," Tony said.

That wasn't as crazy as it sounded. If Don had talked to his people, why hadn't he told them where they could be picked up? Maureen shook her head, and she felt her neck scar pulse with heat. She was becoming suspicious about the color of the sky.

"Not that simple and you know it. My agency is buried deep within Washington's power base. Most people on the hill don't even know my division exists. An order to get the military to stand down wouldn't be impossible, but in the middle of an offensive, which by all accounts has just started, it would be beyond difficult and would put people unnecessarily at risk. It makes much more sense for us to get clear before they pick us up. Much less risk," Don said.

Maureen bought what Don was selling. She didn't have a choice.

They loaded into the van. There were a few other vehicles and trucks in the dirt lot, none of which came close to holding them all, and Don was adamant about everyone staying together, so they stuck with their trusty VW hippie van. Don drove now, and Lester rode shotgun. Saura, Tristin, Maureen, Tony, and the dogs sat in the back. They all buckled up as best they could, and took stock of the weapon situation. Lester had forty-seven rounds left for the M16, and Don had seven shotgun shells. They also had three knives, five fire bombs, and two six-gallon containers of gasoline.

"Fire sparingly and only when absolutely necessary," Don said. He started the van and turned to look at those in the back seat. "I will do my best to go around them and avoid a collision, but we might get banged up. Be ready to flee the vehicle on my command. If that happens, stay close. If we get separated, make sure you have a partner. I don't want anyone being alone."

"What do we do if we get separated? How will we find you?" asked Tristin.

Maureen watched Don struggle with the question. The answer was, I don't know, but Maureen gathered Don never uttered those words. She jumped in and helped him. "I'll be with you. I won't let you out of my sight no matter what."

"What time we got?" Don asked.

"It's 4:19."

"Hard to believe this all started less than forty-eight hours ago," said Lester.

"Everybody ready?" Don said.

There were no protests, and Maureen hunkered down and put her arm around Tristin. Jessie sat on Saura's lap, wagging her tail, and Tank sat between them, alert and ready, his brown eyes shifting in his head, his muscles tense.

Don slipped the van into gear and it crept over the tall grass. When he was in the center of the lot, he put the car in park, and waited. The walkers at the entrance didn't appear to notice that the van had moved.

"That's strange," Lester said.

"I don't think so. They want us to come at them," said Don. He craned his neck and looked over his shoulder, and then out the side windows. "Tony, is there anything behind those mangroves there?" He pointed to his right.

The road ran behind the ticket, but she thought there was a fence in there somewhere. Tony surveyed the spot, considering.

"There's a fence there, but the van might get through it," Tony said.

"Okay, then. Buckle up."

He pressed the gas pedal to the floor, and the engine raced, but still the sleepwalkers didn't look their way. With a squeal, and a cloud of dust, Don dropped the van in gear, and it jumped forward. Even with the van coming right at them, the walkers didn't shift their positions.

When the van was halfway to the entrance, Don spun the steering wheel, and headed for the mangrove thicket. They crashed into the hedge at thirty miles per hour, and the thin spider-like trunks snapped and twisted as they passed. All around them branches scraped and tore at the van, ripping off the side mirrors and cracking the windshield, but Don didn't slow.

"Hold on," he yelled.

The van shuddered and bucked as it struck the four-foot chain-link fence hidden within the hedge. Metal bent, glass broke, and pieces of fencing clung to the vehicle as its tires dug deeper into the soft earth, shooting dirt and sand behind them. A tall metal pole flashed by. Don had maneuvered the van between two fence posts, thus avoiding a massive collision.

The street loomed up through the tree branches. The van rocked hard when it hit a hole, and Tristin and Tank tumbled off their seats as the rear shocks bounced, and everyone got jolted upward. Maureen smacked her head on the roof, and from the sound of it, others had also. Sunlight poured through the broken windows, glinting off the broken glass. The rain clouds had dissipated, and it would be a beautiful sunset.

They burst from the foliage onto the street and it became clear what the walkers had been hiding. A row of vehicles were lined up on the road. Walkers hid within the relative comfort of the cars and trucks.

Had they come out the entrance, trucks and cars would have rammed them from both directions and frozen the van in place. Game over. Don had gotten part way out, but there were still vehicles blocking his path in all directions.

"Thank you, Massie," Don said.

Don jerked the steering wheel, and the van's tires shrieked as they jumped the curb and hit pavement. The road heading to the interstate was blocked, and Don turned again, racing onto the shoulder, but that was unpassable also.

An old Honda Civic sat parked in their path, and Don had no time to react. The van smashed into the front of the Honda, and pushed it aside with the deafening sounds of tearing metal, breaking glass, and screeching rubber. The van lurched to a stop, and stalled.

CHAPTER TWENTY-SEVEN

Don turned the van's key, and the engine choked, but didn't start. He laughed, releasing his frustration and angst. Unwanted memories gripped him, and he stared out the windshield at the car they'd just hit. Time slowed as panic paralyzed him, and his vision faded and his hands shook. Car doors opened, and there were already several walkers coming toward the van. They hollered and shouted, but to Don, they weren't there. None of his companions spoke. They'd come to trust him, even when they had no reason to.

Five seconds passed, and men and women of all colors and sizes came forward in a mindless sleep, their brains under the diseases' spell.

Memories of his captivity and the loss of his humanity came rushing back like the tide. Don remembered little about the one hundred and seventy-eight days he'd been under. He recalled the early part of his imprisonment, but there were no memories of the advanced torture training. No memories of the people he'd killed. The pieces of those days lay like an unfinished puzzle in his mind, and he constantly tried to wipe it from his consciousness.

There were triggers, and he didn't control when they came, what they were, or how hard they hit him. In this case, it was seeing the walkers, but it could've been talking to Massie, a color, or a certain sound or smell. He caressed his temples, calming himself, and pushing back what he hid from everyone. He wasn't perfect. He was human.

"Don."

A voice called his name came through the haze. Everything went black at the edges of his vision. The walkers faded. Carnival music filled his head, and he was alone again, surrounded by people he didn't know, the Ferris wheel spinning before him in slow motion. Then blood. So much blood.

He was tied to a wooden board, and hot oil dripped onto his chest. He screamed, gripping the steering wheel so hard his knuckles went white.

"Don. Don!"

That voice again.

"Wake up, soldier!"

Someone grabbed his shoulders and shook him hard. His world vibrated, and his vision went white.

The sting of Maureen's slap brought him around, and Don stared blankly at his companions. He breathed hard and sweat rolled down his back. The walkers were almost on them.

Don shook himself like a dog trying to dry off, and turned the key again. The motor sputtered, but didn't catch. He turned it again, and the engine started, but steam leaked from under the hood. He slammed the gear shifter, and the van rocked forward, rolling over several walkers. Don grimaced. He didn't like killing innocent people.

He swerved back onto the shoulder of the road, fishtailed between two cars, and jumped over the curb back onto the road. Tires screamed as the rubber caught the blacktop, and the van listed, and everyone got tossed in their seats. Don compensated and brought the van to the center of the street. Ahead the turn to the interstate beckoned, but he was heading back the way they'd come.

"What the hell was that?" asked Lester. "You okay?"

Don shot sidelong glances at his team, but didn't speak. His PTSD reared its ugly head at the worst times, but until now, he'd been able to keep it a secret. Sometimes he'd be crippled for days, but this time, he'd been lucky. Maureen's voice broke the spell. Don didn't answer, and Lester went back to staring at the map, preparing for all contingencies as the tension in the car eased.

They were rear-ended, and the van slid across the road and almost flipped. Don spun the wheel, and for an instant, the van balanced on two tires. It came down with a crash, and a flurry of sparks. In the rearview, Don saw a line of vehicles in pursuit.

"We're not out of this yet," Don said. "Tony, take the shotgun and get in the back window. Fire on my command only. I'm trying to save ammo, and I only want you to fire when absolutely necessary. Use the fire bombs if need be."

"10-4," Tony said.

"Maureen, grab the M16, and get ready to fire on either side if I need you," Don said. She lifted the M16 off the floor and held it attentively before her. "The safety is on the side there. Switch it to single shot."

Two cars, an old Mustang and a newer Honda Civic, were right on their tail. A wound-marred walker drove the Mustang, and it appeared to be concentrating on the road. So far, they hadn't fired on them, and Don saw no guns. The sleepwalkers had their car windows closed, and most likely had the AC blasting.

Then they fired at them. Don wasn't sure what it was at first, then a small hole appeared in the upper right corner of the cracked windshield. "Everybody down!" Don yelled, as he nudged the steering wheel back and forth in small arcs so as not to give them a steady target. "Tony, can you tell where the shots are coming from?" In the rearview, he saw Tony peeking through the shattered rear window. Another hole spidered the windshield as a second bullet just missed Don.

"The passenger in the Mustang fired right through their windshield," said Tony.

"Take out the Mustang." Then Don did his best Bill Lumergh impression. "And if you can tangle-up the Honda in the process, that'd be great."

Several tense seconds passed, and Tony yelled, "Slow up now."

Don slowed, and Tony lit a firebomb, popped up, and tossed it at the car. The bottle shattered, but there was no explosion and no fire. He lit another fuse and threw a second gas bomb. Nothing. Third time was the charm. As the gas bomb exploded, and blew out the rest of the Mustang's windshield, the car swerved and caught the rear bumper of the Honda. Both cars spun out of control. The Mustang disappeared into the mangrove trees and was lost from view as flames spread across the vegetation. The Honda slammed into the curb and came to a stop, clouds of black smoke pouring from under the hood.

Don stabbed the gas pedal, and the van jumped forward. The trail of smoke leaking from the engine compartment had grown, and the temperature gauge steadily climbed. They would have to change vehicles, and that was worrisome. Finding and starting a new car would take time, and while doing so, they'd be vulnerable.

"Come on, baby, hold together," Don said.

"Well aren't you the cliché factory today," Maureen said.

"What?" Saura said. She hadn't spoken since the chase began.

Tony yelled, "Star Wars and Office Space." Saura still looked confused. "Guess you haven't seen those movies," he said.

The van vibrated badly, and the steering wheel shook in his hands, but Don laughed. "We're getting chased by monsters and talking movies. I couldn't have asked for a better crew. I mean it. No matter what happens, it's been a pleasure, folks."

The van rattled, wind hissed through the broken windows, and no one spoke. He'd seen a few things as he made his way across the US; people dying horrible deaths, things that made no sense, and some pure evil. But it was the people that kept him going; the innocents, most of whom were ready to kick ass if someone just believed in them. Had he been lucky? Maybe. He preferred to believe humans exceeded expectations when their asses were on the line.

In the rearview, Don watched the next two vehicles coming to take their turn. Industrial buildings ran along one side of the road now, and thickets of hibiscus and mangrove ran along the other. Lester sat in the passenger seat, scanning the road. He looked confused, and Don asked, "You okay? Been mighty quiet."

"I'm all right," Lester said.

But he wasn't. "You been hit?"

"Just a scratch," he said. Then he turned and showed Don where a bullet had passed through his forearm. "I don't think it hit anything."

"Tie it off. You don't want any exposed wounds," Don said.

"Turn there," Lester said.

They passed over the concrete arch bridges that led to the housing development they'd been through. Don slowed a little, then yelled, "Hold on."

He stomped on the break, and the van skidded and fishtailed. The car behind them, an old Ford Taurus, crashed into the rear of the van. Don made the turn at the last instant, leaving both cars in a cloud of dust and steam.

Saura sat with Jessie on her lap, and Tank and Tristin on either side like a mother protecting her three cubs. Fear made her look like a child. Her tender features pulled tight, her eyes wide.

Don glanced at Lester, who was still pondering over the map. "What's the problem?"

"There's a long road that leads through the Everglades to the H-69 site. I can't find it on this map, and there's no way I'll be able to find the entrance," Lester said.

"Are you shitting me? You said you knew how to get there?" Don yelled. Don was regretting the decision not to find a GPS, despite the slim odds of it helping. He didn't think private government roads were available on standard GPS.

"I do, but via the Glades. Jerry and I took his skiff to a small forest, and we hiked through it and hit the road, where a buddy of his picked us up. The road runs north to south, and I remember how to get there, but to do it, we need to go by boat," said Lester.

Don relaxed a little, the tension leaving his body like a gust of wind. He had thought this might happen, and had already come to terms with the idea. Out of the dust and smoke behind them came the Honda and five new vehicles, one of which was a pickup filled with walkers. The stream of smoke and steam coming from under the hood had lessened as Don eased up on the van, but as he pressed down the gas pedal, black smoke joined the white. The temperature gauge was almost in the red, and Don didn't think the van would last much longer.

"Lester, look for a place for us to bail," Don said.

Lester nodded. Houses raced past on both sides of the road as Don pushed the van hard. A Jeep Wrangler with the top off came up behind them. A walker stood in the back holding onto the roll bar with one hand, and he had a pistol in the other. The Jeep bounced and jumped over every depression and bump in the road, and Don didn't think the walker could hit them.

The Jeep rear-ended the van, but Don was able to keep control, and stay on the road. Gunshots rang out above the screaming engines, but Don couldn't determine where the bullets had gone. They hadn't hit them. "Tony," Don yelled.

Tony was up in an instant, and the boom of the shotgun made Tristin scream. The Jeep veered to the left, jumped the curb, ran across a lawn, and smashed into a house. Flames rose from the wreckage, vast clouds of black smoke filling the air.

The Honda returned. Tony fired again, and the small car turned sharply to the right. Its tires caught, and the car flipped over, coming to rest on its roof and spinning off the road into a thicket of saw palmetto.

"All these god-dammed places look the same," Lester yelled. "We need to take a closer look."

"We're coming up on that loop section were the road goes around an island in a circle with outlets on both ends. I can drive around the block, drop a scout, and take our friends on a wild goose chase while our scout finds a house and a car to make our switch." Don's plan wasn't the best, he knew that, but it was all they had.

"I'll go," Maureen said.

Don wasn't surprised, but the gasps and sighs he heard made him he think he might be the only one. The woman was tough as nails, this was obvious. "Lester is wounded, and Tony is doing an awesome job keeping them off my ass," said Don. He swerved around turns, and tore through the neighborhood. "You'd have to get out of the vehicle and disappear without them seeing you. Investigate until you find a house we can go to that has a functional vehicle that can hold all of us."

"Then what?" Maureen said.

"Find a garbage pail and put it in the road in front of the house you select. I'll lead them away from where I drop you off, then come back in ten minutes," Don said.

"Ten minutes," Maureen said.

"That's all I got," Don said. "The van won't go any longer. I'll drop everyone and keep going. Then I'll ditch the van and work my way back. Be ready to go when I get there."

"I can hotwire a car, so no keys necessary," Tony said.

Don made a wide turn that led back the way they had just come, except on the other side of the development. "When I make the sharp turn at the corner, I'll stop. There's a fence there. Jump it and lie flat, then work your way up the street. Give Lester the M16." She complied. Don slammed the gas pedal to the floor, and the van sprang forward with everything it had. "You can do this. I know you can."

Maureen looked at him with frightened eyes. Don smiled at her. "You can do this." He turned the van hard, and brought it to a stop. "Now!"

Saura opened the side door, and Maureen jumped out, followed by Tank. "No," Maureen yelled, but it was too late. Don pulled away, and left her in a cloud of dust.

"You see her," Don asked. He stared out the front windshield, getting ready to make another hairpin turn.

"Yeah, she's gonna make it. Tank went with her," said Lester.

"That's my boy," Don said. Jessie barked incessantly, and it took both Saura and Tristin to calm the animal.

"They're on the fence, and over," Lester said.

The rearview was still empty. As Don made the right, heading west again, the first car appeared behind them. He backed off the gas and let the van coast a little. He wanted to let the walkers catch up, so they'd all follow him out of the neighborhood. Don scanned the side of the road, looking for likely spots for Maureen, but everything went by in a blur.

Instead of taking the wide turn, and heading back around the block, he turned left, went over a land bridge, and entered another section of the housing development. The houses were smaller here, and less elaborate and not all the properties had canal access.

The pickup appeared behind them, followed by four more cars. Don swerved, and the van listed with each sharp turn of the wheel. Black smoke covered the windshield, and the smell of burning plastic filled the van.

"Listen up, folks," Don said. "If this thing dies before we make it back to Maureen, I'll head for the nearest house. Make sure you stay with me. There will be no going back."

The orderly development fell away, and older, ramshackle houses appeared. Don deemed he'd gone far enough, and he looked for a place to turn around. If he could lose them, so much the better.

He turned out onto a main road, and was sorry he had. Cars, garbage, the remains of houses and stores lay scattered across the road, making it impassable. He veered right, jumped a curb, and careened down the sidewalk. The van thumped and shook badly, and Lester said, "The rear driver's side tire is out. Blew out when you jumped the curb."

Their speed dropped, and the pickup moved alongside them. A bullet whizzed through the van, but hit no one. Don stomped on the break, and the van skidded to a stop with a squeal of rubber.

The pickup passed them by, and the van behind them swerved, and just missed crushing them. Don floored the VW, and the flat tire ripped at the pavement as it spun on the rim, and sent up plumes of black toxic smoke. Soon the entire area was bathed in a noxious cloud.

Don turned the van around and headed back the way they'd come. Two of the cars were still coming on hard, and for an instant, Don played a deadly game of chicken. Knowing the brainless walkers wouldn't know to back down, Don jumped the curb at the last instant and went around them, blowing two more tires in the process. Tony took this opportunity to use his last two firebombs, and their explosion created a wall of fire between them and their pursuers.

The VW barely moved, as it loped forward with three flat tires. Nothing emerged from the black smoke, and Don pushed the van one last time. He worked his way back to Maureen, the van sliding and heaving as it went its final mile. Ahead was the corner where they'd dropped Maureen, but the van didn't make it. It died with a sputter, and a puff of smoke, and came to a stop along the curb twenty houses shy of the end of the street. "Everyone out. Follow me."

They grabbed their stuff, leapt from the van, and ran across the nearest lawn, disappearing through a gate into a backyard. Jessie whimpered at the rumble of vehicles in the distance, and Don knew they'd find the van and come after them. Don took the M16 from Lester, and said, "Let's go."

They worked their way along the canal, going from yard to yard, doing their best to stay out of sight. The sound of the approaching vehicles was loud, and Don figured the walkers would find the van any minute. They passed about ten houses, and they were close to the turn, so they went to the front of the house and looked back up the road.

The pickup parked next to the van, and the walkers spilled out onto the road. Three cars, a white Chevy Lumina, a black luxury sedan, and a blue Nissan Sentra were driving slowly up the street, searching for them.

"Back," Don said, and they hid in the backyard they'd just come through. "It should take the searchers a few minutes to get here."

An old man and young boy watched from a window. The man held a sign which read, "Please don't make me shoot you. Stay away." Don was happy to see people were staying inside, and heeding the quarantine order. He wondered how many people remained locked up in their houses with only the standard radio broadcast to inform them of what was happening. These were the people that had a chance to live.

There were gunshots out in the road, and Don snuck through a patch of hibiscus bushes to investigate. The walkers from the pickup were still coming up the street, and in minutes, they would be on them. They needed to cross the road to get to Maureen, and Don didn't see how they'd do that without the sleepwalkers seeing them. He turned to Lester, who was grimacing in pain from the bullet wound. "I'll distract them. When I'm clear, go find Maureen and get ready to go. I'll meet up with you."

Lester looked skeptical. "How long should we wait for you?"

Don pulled the packets of money wrapped in canvas from his pocket and gave it to Lester. "Here's the sample in case I don't make it. You know where to go. Give me fifteen minutes, not a second more," said Don.

Before Lester could protest, Don skirted the bushes alongside the house, and worked his way across the front yard. When he was certain the walkers could see him, he yelled, "Yo! Buttheads! Come get me!" It only took a few seconds for the sleepwalkers to notice him, and mindlessly charge toward him. With a chuckle, Don ran for his life.

CHAPTER TWENTY-EIGHT

Maureen lay in a flowerbed, staring up at the cloud-streaked sky. Tank nestled next to her like a puppy, his head resting on her arm. The air was sweet with roses and spider lilies.

"What were you thinking, you ass?" she said to the dog. Tank licked her face, and Maureen hugged him.

The sound of cars faded as the walkers chased the van. She peeked through the fence, verified they were gone, shot to her feet, and ran for the closest house, Tank jogging beside her. She had the knife she'd taken off Drago, but if she had to use it in hand-to-hand combat, she was doomed. The guns were in the van, and that was fine with her. She intended to rely on stealth, speed, and smarts.

She passed the first two houses, as there were clearly occupied. They waved from the windows, held up notes, but Maureen didn't have time. Her mental clock told her she had already used three of her ten minutes. The third house looked like a possibility until she saw the walker sitting on the steps in the foyer when Tank starting barking. The next house was locked up tight, and the windows were boarded. Its owners had clearly made a run for it.

The next house seemed promising. It looked like all the others: accented stucco with an arch leading to an entrance breezeway. The front door on this house stood open, the screen door flapping in the wind. She pulled her knife, and warily made her way up the steps to the front door. Tank waited by the driveway, watching and sniffing. Everything appeared quiet. Whatever had rolled through the house was long gone. She sheathed her knife, ran into the house, and through the kitchen to the garage. There she found a classic Corvette covered with a custom cover, and an empty parking space. Maureen opened the garage door, collected Tank, and headed up the street.

The next house was locked down, but when she knocked on the door, no one appeared in any of the windows. She figured she had three minutes left, and she'd made no progress. She kicked the door with everything she had, and it didn't budge. Tank whined as she ran down the steps, and around back. A fishing boat sat docked on the canal, and sliding glass doors ran along the back of the house.

Without breaking stride, she picked up a lawn chair and threw it through the doors, which shattered into pebbles of glass. She ran into the house and got lost for a few seconds as she searched for the garage. When she finally found it, relief filled her because she was out of time. A Chevy Tahoe sat in the garage next to a Porsche Cayenne. Jackpot.

"Wait here, Tank," Maureen said. The dog whined a little, but sat.

If there were people in the house, they didn't show themselves. Maureen figured the owners were at their other residence up north. Lucky them. They got to watch Miami burn on TV, instead of having front row seats. She backtracked out the broken sliding glass doors, and around to the side of the house where she found the garbage pails. She dragged one out to the street and found Lester hobbling along the road, followed by Saura, Tristin, and Tony. Tristin carried Jessie, but Don was nowhere to be seen.

"In there," Maureen said as she pointed. "Where's Don?"

"He'll be along. Leave the pail and come with us," Lester said. "I need you to bandage this wound while we wait."

"What happened to the plan?" Maureen said.

"Van died," said Lester, as he pushed passed her toward the house.

When they were all inside, staring out the front window, Lester said, "Tristin and Saura, take the dogs and get in the car." He tossed them the keys to the Tahoe which he'd found hanging on a hook in the pantry. They also raided the kitchen for food, though there wasn't anything except crackers and ice pops. "Tony, cover the back."

When Maureen finished bandaging Lester's wound, she said, "I'm going out to look for him."

"No. You're not," said Lester. "Wait in the car. I'll cover the front. He'll be along soon. Trust him. He'll be here."

Trust. What was it? And what did it mean in the crazy world she now navigated through? She was separated from Don again and didn't like it, and she realized in that moment her concern went beyond her own wellbeing. They'd all come to care for each other in such a short time she wondered if her feelings were real, or simply a product of the situation. Like that moment when the subway stalls and the lights go out. Suddenly everyone's together, until the lights come back on, and they aren't.

"I'll wait here with you in case you need help," Maureen said.

Lester smiled. "No man can ever be chivalrous for you, can they?"

"Let's get out of this alive and you can get me drinks poolside all day," Maureen said.

Don's fifteen minutes came, and went.

After twenty minutes, Lester said, "He said to leave without him after fifteen minutes. What should we do?"

"It's possible he's waiting for us to make a break for it to join us, but… "

Lester put his hand on Maureen's shoulder. "Look there."

Don ran up the road, legs pistoning, head thrown back. He had a crowd of walkers on his tail, and two cars came tearing around the corner, and headed up the street.

"Let's bring the car out to him," Maureen said. "Tony, let's roll."

They ran to the garage. Photographs covered the walls, and there were the telltale signs of a cat. When they arrived in the garage, Lester jumped in the Tahoe's driver's seat, while Tony jumped in the back and Maureen opened the garage door. The Chevy started right up, and Lester didn't wait for Maureen's door to close before he raced out of the garage into the late afternoon heat. Lester's face twisted with pain as he backed out of the driveway and turned the car around. He opened the driver's side door, and slide over into the passenger seat.

Then they waited.

Don still chugged up the road, sweat soaking his shirt, his face set in a scowl of determination. When he looked up, the pain left his face, and he smiled. He had about two hundred yards on his pursuers, but she could see he was slowing. The walkers staggered forward with a single purpose, their faces contorted, dark blood vessels pulsing against purple skin. One of them fired at Don and missed. He was almost to the Tahoe.

Don jumped into the truck, dropped it in gear, and the tires squealed as the Tahoe bolted forward. "Howdy, folks," said Don. "Nice job, Maureen. This thing will be much harder to stop than the VW." The horde of walkers had been replaced by the five vehicles; the pickup, the van, and the same three cars as before. The pickup led the way, and this time, Tony didn't wait on Don's command.

He fired, and the shotgun blast tore through the pickup like it was made of tin, and it slowed, and stopped. The van replaced it, the distorted faces of walkers filling the vehicle's windshield.

They wove through parking lots in an industrial park and two of the cars reappeared. They came out of nowhere, ripping around a corner and trying to ram them. With the added power of the Tahoe, Don easily pulled away. As the engine raced, Lester leaned over and looked at the Tahoe's gauges. The gas gauge pointed to E.

"That's not good," said Don.

Maureen said, "Will we make it?"

Don shrugged.

"Scary. It's almost like they were waiting for us," Tony said.

"Not possible," Lester said.

"You sure? Maybe they followed us to the marina from out here?" Tristin said.

Maureen had to admit she had a point, and she guessed everyone else agreed because nobody said anything. The large metal buildings of the industrial park gave way to houses, small stores, and the detached randomness of the burbs.

"We're getting close," said Lester. "We should be at Bubba's in less than a half hour."

The cars did their best to keep up, and Don backed off the gas a hair to save fuel. The Tahoe skidded and swerved as Don avoided the black sedan as it pulled across the road trying to block their way. He stomped the break, but the truck didn't skid or fishtail. The antilock brake system wouldn't allow the brakes to seize, so Don didn't stop as he wanted. The Tahoe caught the front fender of the sedan and spun it off the road.

Maureen bit at her lip. They drove through the open areas now, green fields stretching out in all directions. There was nowhere to hide, and she didn't see how they would lose their tail before they got to Bubba's. Having seen several cars blown off the road, the remaining vehicles stayed back, trailing after as if waiting for them to stop.

"If we need to run to the airboat, is everything ready to fly?" Tony asked.

Maureen wagged her head, and Don said, "Yup. I had an itchy feeling we'd be back this way."

Maureen remembered Tim, and the others they'd left behind. Then she recalled that the Glades were a big place, and Tim had no way of getting around, so the odds of him finding her seemed astronomical. There were ways, however, and what about Jeb, Kenny, and Stilts? She thought Drago was lost, but his henchmen could still be floating around.

In many ways, trauma was her business. She lived it every day and was constantly reminded of the frailty of humans and their failure to respect the lives they'd been given. She wasn't religious. She'd seen too much pain to believe a benevolent god would allow the useless suffering that enveloped the world. Perhaps Drago's new world order would give rise to something better. A people who would appreciate the bounty the natural world was designed to provide if only we could avoid abusing it. Killing wasn't the answer, she knew that, but her mind was exploring options she'd had never thought possible before.

Tristin had her head down, and her thin hands shook with worry and fear. She would take that fear away. No matter what happened, she would make her feel safe.

When they were almost at Bubba's, Don looked into the rearview more often, and a sense of worry grew on his face. He was calculating what it would take to get to the boat. She could almost see his brain working. All he needed was smoke coming out his ears.

When Don spoke, he sounded tired and resigned, "When we get there, Tony and I will hold them back with the guns while you guys run for the boat. Saura, you're responsible for Tristin. Maureen, I want you on the boat. Did you see me start it?" Maureen nodded. "Good. Get it going and get everyone situated, and Tony and I will retreat to you."

"What about me?" Lester asked.

"You're wounded. Stay with Maureen and help her in any way you can," Don said. "I'm gonna stop at their curve in the dirt road. Tony and I will hold them there while you guys hit the path to the boat."

Tank barked, and so did Jessie. "Tank, you're with Maureen, since that seems to be what you want," said Don. "Saura, you'll take Jessie."

"Forever," Saura said.

The final two combatants—the white Chevy Lumina and the blue Nissan Sentra—were keeping their distance. "Get down and be prepared to run," said Don. "We're almost at Bubba's and I want to lose them."

Maureen got low and the truck jumped as Don pushed the Tahoe. From where she lay, she saw the tops of trees rushing by outside the window. The truck listed and yawed as Don made sharp turns at high speeds. Several minutes passed, and her mind wandered.

Yesterday, she'd been trapped in a failed marriage, and today, she was sort-of a widower who fantasized about adopting a teenager. The horror of her situation had snapped her from a rut so deep she never wanted to be that predictable and mindless again. She planned to volunteer in other countries. Live in the jungle for a few years and try to find out who she was when she wasn't being a nurse, because if one good thing had come from her ordeal, it was the realization that being a nurse wasn't everything. It couldn't be everything.

"Okay," Don said, and Maureen sat up.

They passed Bubba's house and garage on their right. Tristin clung to Maureen, the child's eyes staring at the house where they'd found her. "Easy," Maureen said. Then the house was gone, and they raced through the Everglades. When they came to a sharp turn, Don pulled across the dirt road.

"Everyone out," yelled Don. "See you at the boat."

Maureen helped Lester, and they all ran down the road toward the mangroves. Maureen jogged as fast as she could, marveling at the idea that they'd just run up this path less than twelve hours ago. She heard everyone panting and pulling for air. They were out of water, and everyone needed a drink.

Maureen didn't notice Tank wasn't with them until they were deep into the forest. He went where he was needed most, but a pang of loss still burned in her stomach. The dog was like a security blanket, and without him, she felt more alone. They pushed through the saw palmetto and came to the airboat. It was as they'd left it, and when she climbed aboard, Maureen found the bottles of water she'd abandoned. She took a long pull on one and handed the other bottle to Lester, who drank deeply, and passed it on down the line.

There was no movement down the path, and nothing but birds and bugs could be heard on the breeze. Lester still had the money sample, and if Don didn't arrive soon, they'd been instructed to go on without him. Lester knew the way, and getting the sample to the chopper was the only thing that mattered.

Lester sat in the copilot's seat, and Saura rested on the deck holding Jessie with Tristin beside her. Maureen turned the giant propeller blade several times, but the engine didn't start. Lester got up and helped her as much as he could, but his injured shoulder made his attempt halfhearted.

Maureen sniffed the air, the smell of rotting peat and fear making her clamp down on her lip. She felt stretched, and though she considered herself tough, she hadn't been ready for the last two days. Was it possible to be prepared for what they'd gone through? She didn't think so. A bottle came back her way, and she drank the last of the water and looked back up the path for Don. All she saw were the shadows of the fading day.

CHAPTER TWENTY-NINE

Don watched Maureen and crew disappear into the mangrove trees, and his stomach twisted. Did he feel love? Deep caring and concern? Don rarely got involved with the subjects of a case, but his current situation was unlike anything he'd ever experienced.

They'd used a woman to draw him in all those years ago, and that made any romantic relationship a challenge of trust at the edge of Don's ability. Jax had been so smart; feed him like a child screaming for candy. She'd played her part so well Don let down his guard, and that almost cost him his life.

He'd been on leave in Paris, when she "tripped" into him. He remembered thinking of the old black and white movies his mother watched. Jax had looked into his eyes and smiled. From that moment forward, everything she'd said and done was a lie. He was a young FBI agent, and she wanted to go along for the ride. It had been an easy sell. Even when they'd taken him, beaten him a few kicks to the chest short of death, he didn't believe she'd betrayed him. She tortured him first.

Don and Tony positioned themselves behind the truck, guns at the ready. The M16 had barely been fired, and the magazine was full, but the extra bullets got lost in the mayhem. They only had three shotgun shells left, so their plan was for Tony to retreat when he ran out of ammo, and Don would wrap things up. As they waited, the comforting peace of a day's end on the edge of civilization gave them a brief respite as they caught their breath. Tank sat next to Don, coiled like a spring, his tongue dangling from his mouth.

"How do you want to do this?" asked Tony.

This was a difficult question. Don thought he had enough ammo to take care of the pursuing walkers, but something within him wouldn't let him take down innocent people with headshots. He didn't know how many guns they had, and while the sleepwalkers had shown no ability to aim the weapons they'd found and figured out how to fire, there was still always a grave risk when bullets were flying.

"I don't know," he said. "Wake up wounds can be worse than kill shots. They wake up and then become targets themselves, yet they don't understand what's happening."

"Listen to your own words. We need to think about the many," Tony said.

Don knew that, but that didn't mean he didn't question himself from time to time. "I know, just trying to think of a better way, but sometimes there's only one way, and there is no choice, no path less traveled." Don stared back down the dirt road. The dust of their passage settled, but it was still clear where they'd gone. "I shouldn't have ripped in here like that. Looks like I lost them, but now they'll find us because I left them a marked trail."

No sooner had those words escaped his lips when the Lumina and Sentra rolled up the dirt road. They moved slow, taking their time. Don shouldered the M16, sighted it on the lead car's front driver's side tire, and fired. The shot rang out in the stillness, and the cars stopped.

Don looked over at Tony, who shrugged.

Don calculated that Maureen and her charges had probably reached the boat, and if he and Tony ran for it, they could avoid a confrontation. They'd bought the time Maureen, Lester, and the rest needed, but if the walkers came on hard, they could catch up to Tony and Don before the road disappeared into thick saw palmetto ahead.

"Tony, head on back. I'll be right behind you. Tank, go with him," Don said.

The dog whimpered, but trailed after Tony as he ran for the boat.

The cars rolled forward again, and he heard the punctured tire thumping on the Lumina's rim. A few seconds tick by, his mind churning through the scenarios, a gentle breeze calming his nerves, and the fates of two walkers were decided. He sighted the M16, and fired two shots at the drivers of the cars. He didn't wait to see if he'd hit anything, because he turned and sprinted away.

It was quiet as he ran, his blood pumping in his ears, sweat trickling down his forehead. His leg ached, and the bottoms of his feet tingled with pain. Don imagined the steak dinner he'd have when he got out. He'd take Lester, Maureen, and the entire crew out for drinks and fun, even if it meant he had to do it inside an army quarantine tent. Don didn't have the heart to tell his companions that even when it was confirmed they were uninfected, they wouldn't simply be allowed to go on their way once they were extracted. They would be put in a loose quarantine, and questioned endlessly about what they'd seen and experienced over the last two days.

Don caught up with Tony before the road ended and entered the thick stand buttonwood and red mangrove trees. He slowed up, and ran next to Tony. "You okay?"

"Yup," Tony said. He huffed and puffed, but he didn't look like he was going down. His cheeks were flush, and his eyes glassy, but he showed no signs of quitting. Don marveled again at how lucky he'd been to come across the people he had. Lester saved his life, and he owed him, and the rest. A pang of worry ran through him again. If his people tried to renege on their deal once they had the sample, Don didn't know what he would do.

"Keep going no matter what," Don said, and stopped running, spun around, and dropped into a crouch as he brought up the rifle. He scanned the path, which was only a boot-stomped line through thick underbrush, and saw no one. He waited, breathing as they taught him at Quantico all those years ago. He sighted the rifle, and moved it in a wide arc. Nothing moved.

Don got up and ran, weaving in and out of the palmetto. Here and there, sawgrass filled in the empty spaces, and there were signs of water. In the distance, he heard the airboat motor come to life, its loud echo ringing through the forest. Don caught up to Tony again, and this time, both men stopped and searched the woods behind them.

"I don't see anything," Tony said between breaths.

"We're close. You ready for the final sprint?"

Tony nodded, and they continued on.

They had only taken a few steps when mutated Bubba burst from the foliage. He'd approached from the side, and was almost on them. Tank was a streak of gray as he darted past Don, and launched at Bubba, who threw up his arms to ward off the animal. Tank clamped down on his arm and wouldn't let go. Bubba howled, his red eyes bulging from his head. Tank shook his head back and forth, trying to tear the arm off.

Don stepped forward, grabbed Bubba by the neck, and twisted. Bubba fell to the ground and didn't move. Tank released the dead man's arm, and shuffled backward, dazed.

"Thanks, boy," Don said. The hair around Tank's mouth was drenched with blood, his eyes still glassy with adrenaline.

Bubba transformed as life left him; his face looked peaceful. Don rubbed his eyes. Another person who'd helped was dead. The body count was getting high, and Don wondered what the bigger picture looked like. They could be dealing with victims in the hundreds of thousands already. That comforted him, and reaffirmed that his decision had been right. What it meant long term scared him. If this pathogen spread worldwide, civilization as they knew it would be over, and the new world wouldn't be pretty, and would eventually kill off most of mankind.

"Let's get out of this place. I've had just about enough of the Glades already," said Tony.

They hurried through the buttonwood trees and saw palmetto, and after a few minutes, they found Maureen and the rest waiting for them on the boat. Tank jumped aboard, and Jessie hopped from the boat to greet Tony and Don as they approached. There were smiles, greetings, and congratulatory hugs.

Jessie disappeared in a flash of splashing water, green scales, and white teeth. A gator had launched from the shallows, and snatched the dog. Jessie yelped and cried as the reptile thrashed its head about.

"No," Saura yelled.

The jungle erupted as Saura pulled her knife and dove for the croc, but as fast as it appeared, the gator was gone, and Jessie squeaked and whimpered as she disappeared beneath the water. An awestruck horror fell over the Everglades, and astonishment and pain froze everyone.

Saura screamed, a blood-curdling wail that sent a shiver through Don. She knelt on the soft peat, clawing at the water where the gator had submerged. Maureen grabbed her arm.

"She's gone. There's nothing we can do," Maureen said.

Saura pulled free, and collapsed at the water's edge, staring at the bubbles popping on the service. She wailed, and shook badly. Maureen put her arm around the young woman.

"You're too close to the water," Don said. Maureen shot fire from her eyes, and Tank sat by them, his gray eyes focused on the water as if he expected Jessie to emerge.

There were sounds of pursuit on the path.

"We gotta go," Lester said.

Don inched the boat into deeper water, and there was a brief debate about what to do with the kayaks. Less weight meant more speed, which was a major consideration. As was the fact that having kayaks tied to the side made the boat cumbersome and unbalanced.

As Tony cut loose the kayaks, Don said, "Good thing Tank's an animal. That would've sucked if I had to leave him behind."

"So if I get infected, you'll leave me?" asked Tristin. Her hair was tangled, and her big brown eyes stared up at Don with all the innocence of the world.

Pain wrapped around him like a python, every muscle in his body pulling and tightening. "Yes," he said. "And it would break my heart to do it, just like my heart has been broken many times before."

Don piloted the boat out into the open water, and as he pulled away, sleepwalkers emerged from the foliage along the shore. They hooted and hollered, and a couple threw rocks that didn't come near the boat. A limpkin wailed overhead, as if telling the outsiders to get the hell off his lawn. Insects hung in clouds around the walkers, whose bodies and clothes were covered in dried blood.

"Why? At this point, we're almost out. Couldn't they quarantine us like the victims they're researching?" Tony asked.

"If it were necessary. And there was a very good reason to defy protocol. Neither would apply to any of us, I'm afraid," Don said.

"That's just cold," Maureen said.

"But necessary. If you make exceptions, the intricate weave of military efficiency breaks down," Don said. "Plus, we're one of many rough situations at the moment, I'm sure. That's another reason they wanted us clear. A copter and three soldiers can extract us. In the city or suburbs, it would take a large commitment of resources."

The walkers on the shore were yelling and grunting at them, but they didn't appear to have any guns.

"How would they know for sure if I had the disease, anyway?" asked Tristin.

"Yeah. The symptoms don't appear until the victim falls asleep," added Maureen.

"By now, my people can probably detect the disease via a simple test. I'd expect to get pricked before you're allowed to get on the copter," Don said.

The airboat moved into deeper water and Don revved the engine. The giant propeller screamed, and the boat glided forward. They cruised down a narrow stream that led to a huge sawgrass field. Don remembered the area well, and he continued across it without hesitation. Conversation ceased, as it was difficult to be heard over the roar of the engine.

"Maureen, what time we got," Don yelled over the rumble of the motor.

"7:19PM," Maureen said.

"Not much daylight left," he said to no one in particular. The stream that headed back toward where they'd left Drago was approaching fast, and Don leaned over to Lester. "Where to?"

"Keep going straight, we have to go much further south than before. There's a nice channel through those mangroves there."

South of their current position, the grass gave way to mangrove trees, and an opening could be seen like a tunnel entrance, its maw dark and shadowy. "Looks narrow," Don said.

"It is, and there are many offshoots and byways that can get us lost for days," Lester yelled.

Don inched the airboat's yoke to the right, and the boat listed and turned. Saura still sobbed as she sat on the deck, her eyes puffy and red. Tony was next to her, his eyes half-closed with sleep. Maureen hugged Tank, and they both looked like they were asleep. Don chuckled. The airboat was so loud it could probably be heard in the stillness five miles away, but exhaustion had overtaken them. Eventually, even caffeine stopped working.

Muscles cramped, old injuries nagged, and it became harder to stay awake with each passing second. Don's leg wound ached, his back hurt, and his feet were so sore from the incorrect size boots he wore that each step was an effort.

The skiff came from an offshoot of the main passage. They were speeding through the mangrove trees when the small boat crashed into the airboat, and knocked it into the mangroves. The great air propeller kept spinning, slicing tree branches as the boat spun around, and came to a stop.

Don backed down the throttle as two men he didn't recognize jumped from their skiff onto the airboat. A melee ensued as the walkers attacked. Tony ended up in the water as he reached for the shotgun. The gun went with him, and they both disappeared under the boat. Tank barked, and went after one of the men, and Don went for the other.

"It's Tim," Maureen shouted. "And one of Drago's men, Jeb."

Maureen lifted the M16, which rested on the floor in front of the pilot's seat, but there were so many people jostling for position on the boat it appeared to Don that she was afraid to fire it for fear of hitting someone she didn't want to. Water surged onto the deck of the boat, and it listed from the shifting chaos. Don slipped, and Jeb was on him, and the two men slide down the deck into the water.

Saura screamed, and joined the fray, pounding on Tim's back as he went for Maureen, who struggled to bring the M16 to bear on her husband.

Don hit the water hard, and bolts of pain ran through his body as his leg hit a tree. Jeb was on top, driving him into the shallow water. Fear gripped him as water filled his mouth and old terrors took hold. They thrashed like two fish having sex, the walker fighting with a reckless abandon that put Don on the defense. Jeb had Don by the neck, and he desperately clawed to free himself. The last rays of the setting sun lit the dark water, and the walker's row of teeth came at him like a baby shark.

CHAPTER THIRTY

Maureen's heart sank when Don disappeared under water. Her protector, the man who had saved them all, was gone again. Her movements became slow and erratic, like her limbs were filled with concrete. She tried to steady herself as vertigo filled her, and she almost collapsed.

Tank had Tim's leg and Saura beat on his back, but still her husband came for her, his eyes blood red with a single-minded purpose as he lumbered across the airboat's deck. Maureen struggled with the M16 as she tried to keep her balance. The airboat's motor sputtered, and stalled, while the skiff's small outboard screamed and continued to drive the airboat into the mangroves.

The collision had tossed Lester from the passenger seat, and his head smacked the support structure for the airboat's massive propeller. He fell with a thud, unconscious, and useless. He lay on the deck, a thin stream of blood flowing from a cut on his head. Tristin sat frozen before the pilot seat, fear paralyzing her.

Tony emerged from beneath the boat, coughing up water. He clung to the airboat like a life raft, his eyes frantic and afraid. Tim was inching forward as he fought off Tank and Saura, and Tony reached up and clamped his hand around the walker's ankle. Using Tim's weight as support, he lifted himself partly out of the water onto the deck. He lay prone on his belly, his lower body still dragging in the water.

Maureen got the rifle sighted, and when Tim saw the barrel pointed at his head, he stopped, and shook off Saura and Tony. Tank wasn't so easy. The dog crushed Tim's leg between his jaws.

Tim punched the animal in the head; swift rabbit punches that knocked Tank's head back and forth as he held tight.

With a crack that sounded as if something had broken, Tank yelped and released Tim, who came at Maureen again. Six feet separated them when Tim pulled up and stared at his wife with a fever that reinforced her resolve. He cracked his knuckles, and she gasped. This wasn't the man she'd known, but there was some of

Tim still in there. He was covered in blood, his clothes were tattered, and his skin purple. Dark lines crisscrossed his face, as blood vessels expanded and pressed against swollen muscle and skin. She no longer even recognized him, and if it weren't for his hair color, and his wedding ring, she would have questioned if he was her husband, yet it was still Tim. Not that it mattered anymore.

"I'll shoot you. I swear," she said, the rifle shaking in her hands. Could she kill him? When it came time to pull the trigger, would she be able to? She hadn't been able to prior, and doubt seeped through her, and her finger tightened around the trigger.

Tim put up his hands, but his wide smile made Maureen take a step backward. She was up against the stalled propeller and there was nowhere to go. She had to either jump into the water and hope for the best, or she needed to shoot him, but even that option had problems. If she woke him—which by all accounts thus far would require a near death shot because he'd already been woken once— what would they do then? He was infected, and then he'd be severely wounded. They only had four and a half hours to get to the extraction point, and he wouldn't be able to come with them.

Doing nothing wasn't an option. Tim stood frozen before Maureen, breathing heavily. Saura sat on the deck, crying, and Tank growled and circled behind Tim. The dog appeared to be all right. Tony climbed onto the airboat's deck, and rolled on his back.

Don and Jeb emerged from beneath the water, and Tim turned to see what was happening.

Maureen rushed him, knocking Tim backward into the pilot's seat.

Tony clamped his arm around Tim's neck, choking him. Snarls, grunts, and the sound of splashing water came from the front of the boat where Don struggled with Jeb.

Maureen punched Tim in the stomach, over and over, pounding the man with all the anger and frustration of their lives together. She stopped hitting him and wiped her hand on her shirt. She brought up the rifle and smashed its butt into his face. Once. Twice. Three times.

Still, he didn't wake. Blood leaked from the wounds on his cheek, his jawbone exposed. Terror filled his eyes as something within told him his time was short. He thrust his elbow backward, and it connected with Tony's face, and he fell away like a leaf. At this, Tank lunged in an attempt to clamp down on the Tim's leg again, but Tim kicked the animal and Tank went sliding into the water.

Tristin ran to Saura, and they moved to the end of the boat, away from the melee. Saura looked lost, and blood dripped from a cut on her head where she'd slammed it on the deck. It was comforting to see her take control of Tristin. Don rolled and struggled with Jeb, who threw wild punches, his jaws snapping.

Maureen raised the rifle, and Tim went for her.

The shot caught him in the chest, a neat red hole that expanded as she watched. His snarl disappeared, and he fell to his knees, his face mutating back to the man she'd once loved as his life slipped away.

Maureen dropped the M16 and wretched, the candy and soda she'd eaten spraying across the deck, leaving a green-brown sludge. Guilt and heartache gripped her. She was many things, but she wasn't a killer. She told herself she had to do it. He would have killed her. To that, she asked herself why she hadn't aimed for his leg.

Tim fell forward and hit the deck with a thud. Maureen pushed his body into the water as she wept, and it floated away beneath the surface. Puke leaked from her mouth as she tried to catch her breath. Tiny pinpricks of light danced in the air.

Don screamed.

Maureen surfaced from her grief-stricken haze. She picked up the rifle, and joined Tank and Tony where they stood at the bow of the airboat, watching Don wrestle with Jeb in the brackish water.

"Here, give me that," said Tony, and Maureen handed him the M16.

Tony put the weapon to his shoulder and tried to get Jeb within its sights, but they were still trashing and pulling at each other, making a solid mass of flesh and bone. Don screamed again, and that was too much for Tank who floated in the water nearby.

He growled, and speared through the water like a torpedo, jaws open.

"Shoot him!" Maureen yelled.

"I can't get a clean shot," Tony said. "They're too close."

Jeb screamed and then fell silent. Tank had the walker by the neck, and as he jerked his head back and forth, he tore open his throat, and the walker went still.

Everything stopped for a heartbeat. Jeb's body floated listlessly in the water, and as he transformed back to himself,, Maureen saw the face of the man who had given her over to Drago as though she were meat, and they were having a barbeque. The body drifted away and sank beneath the water and was lost from view.

Tank treaded water, and blood leeched into the stream around him. The dog's eyes were wide, and he still bared his teeth, looking around as if he didn't understand the fight was over.

"Easy, boy," Don said, and moved toward the animal. Tank barked at him, and bared his teeth, but when Don extended his hand, Tank whimpered, sniffed it, and went to him.

Don helped Tank onto the airboat's deck, and Maureen ran to him and threw her arms around the dog. He was dazed, dripping wet, and bloody, but the animal's tongue lashed out, and he gave Maureen a long lick across her face, and nuzzled his head into her chest.

"Little help," Don said, who was struggling to pull himself onto the boat. Tony and Maureen each grabbed an arm, and together, they pulled the agent onto the boat, where he lay panting and choking.

There was blood all over Don, and his shirt was ripped up. He had deep scratches on his face and arms, and he looked so pale Maureen worried for her friend. "You okay?"

Don sat in the pilot's seat, and put his head back, breathing hard. "I'll be fine."

Maureen roused Lester, who had a nice knot on his head, but was otherwise okay.

"Way to go, Bilbo Baggins," Don said, referring to how the unconscious hobbit had sat out most of the battle of five armies.

Lester forced out a laugh and sat up. Maureen gave him water, and he drank deeply.

Saura worked her way forward with Tristin, and they knelt and stroked Tank. No one spoke. The skiff's outboard still screamed, sending water shooting into the mangroves. Tony jumped onto the skiff, and pulled the kill switch lanyard, and the motor sputtered out. Singing birds, insects, and frogs filled in the brief stillness.

The Glades abide.

"I wonder what happened to Kenny and Stilts?" Saura asked.

"Who?" Tony said.

"Jeb's partners," Maureen said. "They're the ones who caught us and brought us to Drago."

"Judging by what we've seen, it's easy enough to guess what happened to them," Don said.

While they fought for survival, the sun completed its descent to the horizon and the Everglades were filled with the grayness of dusk. It was then they realized they only had one flashlight, and the light on the front of the airboat to light their way.

Pig frogs croaked, the guttural sound of their call explaining their name. Crickets, birds, mosquitoes, and gator calls made the night symphony a loud and distracting force, which made things even more difficult. They all sat in the front of the boat as Tony and Lester examined the propeller and engine. The flashlight beam danced around, and when a few minutes had passed, Lester and Tony had diagnosed the situation.

"The airboat is inoperable," Tony said. "The protective cage around the propeller is bent, and without tools and time, we can't get it going."

"We'll take the skiff," Lester said.

"That'll be slow going," Don said. "Time?"

"8:06PM," Maureen said.

Don looked to Lester, who said, "If we work fast here, and hustle, we can make it."

"Strip the battery and light rig off the front of the airboat," Don said.

Maureen looked around the dark water, and in her mind, she said goodbye to her husband. Now that he was gone, she felt lost, her guilt eating away any attempt to stay calm. The night sounds soothed her, and she closed her eyes. They were almost out, and soon the nightmare would be over.

CHAPTER THIRTY-ONE

The skiff trolled through the dark water, the 9.9hp outboard motor gurgling in the night. They were moving slow as visibility was bad, the channel narrow, and the boat was severely overloaded. Saura, Tristin, Maureen, Tony, and Lester sat before Don, packed-in like sardines. Tank lay at Don's feet as he held the motor's control arm and piloted the boat. Mangrove trees fleeted by on both sides, and occasionally, a branch would scratch the side of the boat. The light they'd rigged to the front of the skiff cut through the blackness, silencing part of the night symphony, and creating spider-like dancing shadows beneath the tree canopy.

Don's leg hurt, his cuts stung, and every muscle in his body was straining to stay in motion. Everyone in the boat had gotten some sleep, except him. He was going on almost two full days without sleep, and even his well-conditioned body was breaking down.

"So where does this rank on your adventure scale, Agent Oberbier?" Tristin asked.

"Hardly an adventure. Those are fun. A nightmare, maybe," Don said. When he looked at the young girl, she was staring at him. "This is far worse than any situation I've ever heard of or been involved with. It's unprecedented. First of its kind. What's happened here will change the world like 9/11."

"Why did you stay? You could have gotten out after your first encounter," Lester said.

"First, I don't ask others to put themselves in harm's way unless I'm willing to do so myself. Something the dirtbags in Washington would do well to learn. Second, there are probably people still pissed about the way I called for the quarantine. I jumped the entire chain of command. Best I'm out of sight. Easiest for the brass as well. Plus, who knew the situation on the ground better than me? I was the most qualified, at the time, to conduct an inside investigation."

"Man, how's the weather up there?" Maureen asked.

"What?" Don said.

"That's a mighty tall horse you ride," Lester said.

"Maybe. What about you guys? You two haven't exactly lacked in confidence," Don said to Lester and Maureen.

Lester started to answer and then stopped. He stared into the night as if searching for something. "There," he said, pointing across a small pond choked with grass. "See the small sandy area where the crocs hang out." Tony panned the light to the left, revealing the dark pond and the tiny beach.

"Yeah," Don said.

"Put ashore there. Don't worry about the gators. The noise and our light will send them scattering like cockroaches," Lester said.

Don looked to Saura, who'd taken the loss of Jessie hard, and was now petrified of alligators and everything that slithered and bit. She didn't appear to have heard their conversation. Her head rested on Tristin's shoulder, and she looked to be asleep. Don pushed the motor control arm to the right, and the skiff turned left into a pond across which was the sandy shore. The sound of the sawgrass scrapping against the boat created a cacophony of squeaks and squeals that would scare away any predator. Moonlight glinted off the water, and the surface slithered and moved with bugs and snakes.

The boat crunched onto shore, and Don grabbed the flashlight and the M16, their only two remaining possessions, not counting the sample, which was safely back in Don's possession. One by one, they stepped off the boat and huddled together against the night. Don tied the airboat off on a cypress tree, gave Lester the flashlight, and led them into the woods.

A path ran through a thin patch of trees and gave way to mangroves. In the dark, it was hard to see anything outside the flashlight beam. Beneath the trees, the constant cacophony subsided somewhat, and Don noticed his ears were ringing. As they walked, saw palmetto filled the forest floor, and giant slash pines and royal palm towered above. To the northeast was a ranger station and visitor's center for Everglades National Park.

Lester tripped on a root and dropped the flashlight. It hit the ground with a thud, but didn't go off. It lit the saw palmetto from below and sent an arc of light across the Glades. Birds scattered from their resting places, owls hooted, and something unseen jumped from the tree boughs and hit the undergrowth with a crash and scurried away.

"Butterfingers," Tristin said.

Lester chuckled, and picked up the light. "That's what Cammy used to call me."

"Who is Cammy?" Tristin asked.

"Cammy was my daughter," Lester said. His face could be seen in the glow of the flashlight beam, and he looked troubled.

No one spoke. *Was* his daughter.

After a few minutes, Lester said, "She was your age, Tristin. Just walking home from school, listening to her music, and a car jumped the curb, and she was hit. She died on the scene, and a piece of me, and all of my wife, died with her."

"What happened?" asked Maureen.

"Man had a heart attack while driving. They revived him, and he lives to this day as far as I know," Lester said.

"Good God," Tony said.

"God had nothing to do it. It was a random tragedy. The old man who hit her once told me he wished he'd died because he sees Cammy's face in his dreams every night, and he can no longer sleep. My wife couldn't handle it, and I found her in our bathtub with…" Lester patted Tristin on the head. "She didn't want to live anymore."

Every muscle in Don's body tightened, and his chest burned as he fought back tears. The sensation scared him. "Man, I'm sorry. And I called you…"

"Forget it. How could you have known?" Lester said.

"Doesn't matter. I should have known better," Don said. He moved so fast through life, always calculating and making plans, and all the while justifying his every action with the idea he helped the greater good. But how often did his words or actions crush people he wasn't even aware of? He gave orders without thinking about what they might mean for families, and he thought perhaps it was time for him to change his approach. A nice thought, but one he doubted he'd be able to live up to.

They came to an old, rusty, dilapidated fence. The razor wire at its top was corroded and broken, and in spots chain link sections had fallen away entirely. "This used to be maintained when there was something to guard," Lester said. They passed through a wide gap in the fence, and the trees became sparser. "The park service gives tours of the place, so it's far from a top security zone. Normally, though, if you came out here without a ranger or park personnel, you'd get caught and fined. There are cameras around the old buildings and entrances. None of that will be working now, though."

"What do they give tours of?" asked Don. "If my memory serves, there's not much there except old buildings and a lot of cracked concrete."

"They keep a decommissioned display model of a rocket battery in the old assembly building. It's an example of the type of surface-to-surface missiles that were once the focus of the H-69 site during the Cuban Missile crisis. It was a major reclamation project for the park," Lester said.

Streams and bogs sprang up out of nowhere in the darkness, and they battled through sawgrass, passed gators, and around huge spider webs. Twice, the flashlight beam had died, and they'd stood frozen in the blackness for several minutes while Lester fiddled with the light in the pitch black. The second time he had to take the batteries out, and Don marveled at his friend's concentration. Animals squawked and howled at them, but there were no real predators. Moonlight streamed through the tree canopy, and a massive field of sawgrass ran around a large hardwood hammock to their left.

"How are we getting through that?" Don asked.

"There's a path," Lester said. "I just need to find it."

They didn't have to walk much further before they found Lester's path, and they hit the road a few minutes later. Long Pine Key Road was a lonely, unlit, barely paved two lane that ran to the entrance of H-69. They had more than two miles to go.

It was 11:19PM.

CHAPTER THIRTY-TWO

Maureen walked up the road in silence. There was nothing left to say. There would be time enough for goodbyes once they were out. Her throat hurt, she was hungry, tired, and her legs and feet were so sore each step was an effort. Survival had occupied every second for the last two days, and as her mind drifted, she contemplated life without Tim. She could go anywhere she wanted. There were hospitals everywhere, and they always needed good nurses. Every time she felt positive about her future, the memories of those lost pulled her back into despair. She remembered shooting Tim. The look on his face as he transformed.

Nothing moved on the road ahead or behind. Lester shuffled along the best he could, nursing his wounds. Saura had her arm around Tristin, and Tank trotted between Tony and Don. They walked casually, as they were less than a mile from H-69. To Maureen, her companions sounded in high spirits, but perhaps it was nothing more than the sheer relief at having survived.

She listened as Tony and Lester spoke of war, and military service. Fighting. Always fighting. They sounded so content speaking about it, as if making war was as common and acceptable as baking bread, or fixing a car. What would be the fiscal effect of the quarantine of south Florida, and how would it affect the nation? Don had called it a 9/11 type event, and that nutballs would try to copy the disease. They'd be inspired by what the puppeteers of Drago had created. Then there was Miami. If an anecdote wasn't found soon, there was little hope for the people living there.

She felt that pang of guilt again, the one where her body tried to convince her mind she was putting herself above others, but this argument didn't sway her in the slightest. She had no control in this world. A world ruled by sleepwalkers that were also human beings that could be saved. Perhaps there would be an awakening, but Maureen thought it highly unlikely. From what Don had said, the key element was maintaining the quarantine. Everything else was secondary.

Mangrove trees filled the shoulder on both sides of the road, and she imagined soldiers marching up and down the lane when the base had been in full operation. She thought she heard their ghosts urging her on, helping her take those final steps.

The trees gave way to a huge open area surrounded by a fence topped with razor wire. The area looked extra-large in the darkness after the tight confines of the Glades. The earth had been sculpted in this area, and Maureen saw why they referred to the H-69 as The Hole in the Donut. It did look like the hole in the center of a green subtropical forest.

"Normally, these lights would be on," Lester said, as they passed two poles with large lights mounted atop them.

They came to a gate secured via lock and chain. In the distance, the faint rumble of a helicopter could be heard. They had run out of time. Maureen's watch read 11:57PM.

Don checked the lock to make sure it was actually locked, and wasn't simply lined up to make it appear locked. He racked the slide on the M16, and said, "Lester, shine the flashlight on the lock."

The sound of the helicopter got louder, and a small red light approached from the north. With no time left, Don shot the lock, and removed the chain. The gate swung open with a whine, and they all ran toward a group of buildings at the end of the road. They passed a large sign with the word "restricted" in huge letters on the top, followed by paragraphs of federal legal text below.

The flashlight beam wobbled in the darkness, and the *whomp whomp* of the helicopter got louder. Maureen was on Don's heals as he ran the final section of road toward the buildings. Maureen's shins throbbed with pain as they left the worn blacktop and headed across the concrete lot at the center of the dilapidated structures. Lines of dead grass crisscrossed the concrete like pathways.

They hid behind the assembly building, and Maureen took inventory as everyone arrived, and the entire crew was present and accounted for. The copter thundered above, and the crafts landing lights dropped through the darkness.

The copter touched down like a tornado, and dirt and debris rose into the air. The craft's exterior floodlights lit the area as two soldiers jumped out.

Maureen covered her eyes, the bright light blinding her after hours of walking in the dark. Don leaned the M16 against the assembly building. "Best not to spook them," he said, when he saw Maureen watching him.

"Stay here until I call you," yelled Don to the group. He stepped out from behind the building into the bright light, his arms raised.

Doubt and desperation ran through Maureen. He would betray them. He would get on the helicopter with the sample and leave her and the rest now that he didn't need them. Her angst grew until Don argued with one of the soldiers. There appeared to be a dispute, but after a few minutes of discussion, Don waved them over.

"He wouldn't give them the sample until we're on board," Lester said. He held his shoulder, and blood dripped through his fingers.

"Oh," said Maureen when she saw the blood. "I thought I locked that down for you."

"All the commotion tore the bandage," said Lester. He waited for Tristin, Tank, Saura, and Tony to get ahead of him. Then he held out his arm for Maureen. "After you."

When Maureen arrived at the helicopter, it was difficult to hear anything over the pounding of the rotors, which still spun at a slower rate. Don stood next to the soldiers, and Maureen and crew formed a rough line leading to the open maw of the copter.

Tristin stepped up first, and a soldier met her as she went to climb aboard.

"Arm, please," the soldier yelled.

Tristin held out her arm, and the soldier produced a white device that looked like the high-tech blood meters diabetics use. He put the device to Tristin's arm, and it pricked her. She pulled her arm away with a squeal, and covered the wound with her hand. The soldier stared at the device's display screen, then yelled, "Clear. You may go aboard."

Next up was Saura, and she was clear. So it went with Tony, Lester, and Tank. When it was Maureen's turn, she stepped forward, and the knot in her stomach twisted her insides so hard she threw up in her mouth. The pinch of the device stung a little, but when the soldier pronounced her clear, a tide of relief swam through her. She climbed into the helicopter, collapsed into a cargo seat, and barely noticed as a soldier strapped her in.

Don stepped forward, the wrapped sample in his hand. The soldier pricked Don, but as he went to hoist himself into the helicopter, the soldier put out his hand. "One more time," the soldier said, as he looked quizzically at the testing device.

Maureen knew the results before the soldier announced them. Part of her had always known somehow.

"I'm sorry, Agent Oberbier, but you are infected," the soldier said.

Don pulled back his tattered shirtsleeve, revealing what looked like a small shark bite. Maureen cursed Jeb, and everything that had brought her to this time and place. There was an awkward pause, as no one was sure what to do next. Then the soldiers boarded the copter, and prepared for takeoff. Don handed the soldier who had tested him the sample of tainted money, and in return, Don received a small black box that looked like a phone. Don stared at the device as he listened to the soldier's instructions, and then stepped away.

"See you guys in another life," Don shouted.

"Noooooo," Maureen yelled. She struggled to unbuckle her harness, but the copter's turbine was already accelerating, and preparing to take off. Kristin cried, and Lester's head was in his hands.

Tank barked and bolted past the soldiers sitting by the copters open side door. The dog disappeared over the edge of helicopter's deck and was gone. Maureen fought to free herself, but they held her back, and she felt the copter lift from the ground. All the exterior floodlights went out, and Don was lost in the murky darkness. The helicopter listed as it rose, and all Maureen saw was the rolling of the stars, and her tears.

CHAPTER THIRTY-THREE

Don caught Tank as he jumped from the helicopter, and they both went to the ground in a tangle of arms, legs, and paws. The animal licked Don's face as the HH-60 Pave Hawk lifted off. Wind tore at them as they lay on the concrete, dirt and garbage swirling in the surrounding air. Don watched the copter rise into the night, his worries slipping away. The craft's floodlights winked out, and Don was plunged into darkness. He didn't know where the flashlight had ended up, but it was gone, and there was nothing for it. The sound of the helicopter's rotors cutting through the air receded into the night, and soon only the red running light could be seen moving away north.

"What a stupid move, my friend," Don said to the dog. Tank still sat on Don's chest and licked his face.

As he lay on his back staring at the stars, a wave of relief washed over him. He'd spent his entire adult life worrying for others, sacrificing for the greater good. While his ending wasn't what he'd hoped for, he'd still completed his mission. He got the sample out, discovered how the pathogen was being transmitted, and got some of his crew out alive. He'd pushed forward without thinking about tomorrow, and now he didn't have one. That thought was oddly comforting, not having a tomorrow to worry about. He'd made the best of his second chance and had no regrets.

Tank slide off him, and rested his head on Don's stomach. He turned the emergency beacon over and over in his hand. If things changed, they would contact him. The device only worked one way, and he couldn't contact them. Don could barely keep his eyes open, and when they closed, the real night would fall. He lay there a long time, watching the helicopter's red running light recede into the distance until it was only a pinprick against the stars.

When it disappeared from view, he sat up, and Tank snapped to attention. The poor animal thought they were still striving toward a goal. Under a gibbous moon, Don made his way back to the assembly building and picked up the M16. He might need the weapon. Then he put it back where he'd found it and headed for the base's entrance. What good could come of him having the rifle once he became one of them?

As he walked across the base, he tossed the emergency beacon in the air. If something changed. He had to laugh to himself, yet maybe there was hope there. His people wouldn't give up on him, and Massie would never give up. He was reaching, he knew, but what else was there left to do? Being free from worry also meant the loss of control.

He looked at the transmitter, and pulled his arm back intending to hurl the device into the darkness, and be free of hope, and all its tantalizing whispers that Don knew were nothing but fantasy, and wishful thinking. If a cure was found, he would be long gone, and the logistics of bringing him back would be the same as the other million people who would be in desperate need in the next few days. His arm shot forward, but at the last moment he changed his mind, and didn't release the device. He looked at it again, shook his head, and put it in his pocket. If they didn't call him, what had he lost by holding onto the thing? Only a fool would destroy all hope, even when it was nothing more than a way of convincing himself all wasn't lost.

When he got to the main gate, he turned to Tank, and said, "Sit, boy."

Tank did as he was told.

Don stepped through the gate, and closed it behind him, using the chain to secure it. Tank watched him with growing suspicion. The dog's muscles tensed, and he shook violently. It was obvious Tank wanted to join his partner, but instead, he obeyed the last command Don gave him.

He'd always lived by the mantra "leave no man behind," but in this case, it was for the best. By hurting his friend, he was saving him. At least that's what he told himself. Tank would find food and water, even if it meant digging for bugs, and he'd escape the base's unmaintained perimeter fence. Then he'd be on his own, and fate would decide his future. A future that wouldn't include Don attacking the animal that had been as solid as any rock he could have ever hoped for.

Don sat with his back against the fence. He let his head fall into his hands, and he tried to cry. Isn't that what you did when everything was done? But tears wouldn't come, and he searched within himself, trying to sense and feel the disease that infested his body. He felt nothing but the pain in his chest, and the pounding of his heart.

Tank came to him, and sat against the fence, trying to get close to his master. Don stroked the animal, the metal of the chain-link separating them. "I know you don't understand this, but I owe you too much," Don said. This was much harder than he'd thought it would be. He got up, tugged on the chain securing the gate, and started up the road. He never looked back, because he knew that if he did he wouldn't be able to continue on.

Desiree's face filled his thoughts. She'd been the only woman other than his mom he could honestly say he loved. Why had he never told her? Would it have mattered? He didn't question his decision to forgo a normal life, but he certainly hadn't understood the price when he'd made the purchase. If Desiree felt similar, she'd never shared it with him. As he searched for other regrets, he proclaimed himself to be more clean than dirty, until he heard Tank.

The dog barked and wailed, and each sound he made killed a piece of Don, but he stumbled on, not looking back. As he walked, the echoes of Tank's barking, and the whispers of all those who'd been lost tormented Don, his mind spinning, his body finally calling a halt. He staggered and almost fell. He was out on his feet. The adrenaline was gone, and he stopped on the roadside and sat on the ground. He had no water, no food, and no light.

The sky was clear, and stars blinked down as he sat beside the mangrove trees, the night sounds soothing his nerves and pulling him toward sleep. His leg ached, the bite Jeb had given him shrieked with pain, and Don's body had nothing left. He laid down for an instant as he tried to steady himself, taking deep breathes, and he heard Tank's faint crying on the breeze.

Don's eyes fluttered closed.

THE END

CHECK OUT OTHER GREAT APOCALYPSE BOOKS

WHITE OUT
by Eric Dimbleby

An apocalyptic snowstorm sweeps the globe. Experts predict this freak storm will be "The New Ice Age." Electricity is gone, as are all forms of communication and road travel. As each member of a divided family tries to survive in their own way, they must deal with a snow-driven madness that has gripped the underlying evil in the hearts of men. In an epic struggle to get home and reunite, they will find that terror lies around every snow drift... and even in their very own backyard.

NIGHT PLAGUE
by Rowan Rook

Humankind will soon be extinct. A mysterious pandemic cut through two-thirds of the population in just four short years, and within another four, it will decimate everything – and everyone – left.

The last days are ticking by, relentless and ruthless, and the reclusive Mason Mild finds himself torn between a peaceful end and a brutal immortality. Between his hopeless, but comfortable days with his family, and something new...something violent and wild.

Have the fang marks above his heel dealt him an early demise or a second birth?

CHECK OUT OTHER GREAT APOCALYPSE BOOKS

THE DEAD FAMILIAR
by J.D. McKenna

In the twilight hours of a failing world, one man seeks to bring his loved ones to safety. Jack Hightower: Marine, barkeep, and doomsday prepper. He knows of the coming calamity, and on the final night of an old world he seeks a new beginning.
This is the story of that night, the tale of how Jack and his survivor's colony in the north came to be.

DOMINION
by Doug Goodman

Dominion has been taken from man. Now, six friends must cross an apocalyptic wasteland dominated by a hell's menagerie of mega-fauna. Their middle-class suburban skills are no longer applicable to the world they live in. To find a safe haven in this world they will need to develop a new set of survival skills and fight the mutated denizens of the animal kingdom for every step of their terrifying journey.

CHECK OUT OTHER GREAT
APOCALYPSE BOOKS

XY
by D.S. Lillico

An iron fortress protected by automated gun turrets is the only world Elsie has ever known.

When tragedy strikes, Elsie is forced to leave the sanctuary of her home and out into a brutal new world. A post-apocalyptic wasteland filled with savage mutants.

Hunted and alone Elsie stumbles into the care of a giant named Punch, but the world is now full of worse things than giants. Cannibals are starving, bandits are roaming and war is coming.

Elsie's arrival plunges the new-world further into darkness... and is there really something hidden inside of her?

SANCTUARY
by Ian Page

Deeta Nakshband, a Connecticut physician is attacked by a local surgeon while on duty in the hospital. Her friend, Janelle Jefferson, has similar experiences in Miami. Both of them become aware of an increasingly violent world as acts of isolated brutality escalate into civil unrest. They grapple with their paranoia as family members and coworkers become dangerously unpredictable. Worldwide, military units go rogue, war begins in Korea and cities implode as people slaughter each other in the streets. Martial law is declared in an attempt to maintain order. People are arrested, detainment camps are set up and interrogations end with tragic consequences as modern civilization crumbles. Deeta and Janelle band together with family friends and coworkers to save each other and find sanctuary.